THE
VOWS
WE
BREAK

CH

Also by Briana Cole

The Unconditional Series

The Wives We Play

Published by Kensington Publishing Corp.

THE
VOWS
WE
BREAK

An Unconditional Novel

Briana Cole

Dafina
Books

KENSINGTON PUBLISHING CORP.
www.kensingtonbooks.com

DAFINA BOOKS are published by

Kensington Publishing Corp.
119 West 40th Street
New York, NY 10018

All Kensington titles, imprints, and distributed lines are available at special quantity discounts for bulk purchases for sales promotion, premiums, fund-raising, and educational or institutional use.

Special book excerpts or customized printings can also be created to fit specific needs. For details, write or phone the office of the Kensington Sales Manager: Kensington Publishing Corp., 119 West 40th Street, New York, NY 10018. Attn. Sales Department. Phone: 1-800-221-2647.

Dafina and the Dafina logo Reg. U.S. Pat. & TM Off.

ISBN-13: 978-1-4967-2197-6
ISBN-10: 1-4967-2197-7
First Kensington Trade Paperback Printing: August 2019

ISBN-13: 978-1-4967-2200-3 (ebook)
ISBN-10: 1-4967-2200-0 (ebook)
First Kensington Electronic Edition: August 2019

10 9 8 7 6 5 4 3 2 1

Printed in the United States of America

I dedicate this book to my wonderful literary agent, N'Tyse. Without you, there wouldn't have been a sequel. Thank you for seeing the vision and, most important, sharing it with the world.

Acknowledgments

As much as I love to write (and talk), it is difficult to find me at a loss for words. But when it comes to these acknowledgments, I find myself circling the airport and never landing. It's not that I don't have people to thank. But the amount of love and appreciation I have for my family, friends, and supporters—there are really no words to completely express my gratitude.

How do you put words on the amount of tears shed, the overwhelming support, the calls and text messages, the listening ears while I ranted and raved and shouted my frustration with these characters? The ones steering me back on track, the cheerleaders and boosters, the honest opinions that I hated but needed to hear. The helping hands and encouraging smiles I witnessed through bloodshot eyes. Motivating words I heard on many a sleepless night. (Forgive me. I know my poet is showing right now.) I believe what I am trying to say is this: I hope my actions and the motivation I have to keep going down this journey with you all by my side show just how much of an impact your support has on my heart. Hell, my life. I won't go down the list individually because there are so many of you that have inspired me in one way or another. But you all know who you are. So to all of my family and friends, thank you, thank you, thank you!

I want to send a special thank you to my love, Ben. Babe, you have inspired me in more ways than you will ever know. Thank you for being my support, my backbone, my rock, my listening ear, and helping me step into my full potential. I love you with everything in me and I'm ready for us to take over the world.

Of course, another huge thank you to my literary agent, N'Tyse. From day one, you have kicked me into high gear, and I absolutely love it! I am so thrilled at the many, many success stories we have and will continue to share.

Also to my publishing team at Kensington, I sincerely appreciate you. Especially my editor, Selena, who is bomb.com. Thank you all who continue to get behind my books and my career. I couldn't imagine a better publishing house for me to learn, grow, and thrive.

Last, but not least, I have to thank all of my readers and supporters! When I was too tired to write, I thought of you. When I didn't know what the hell to write about, I thought of you. You deserved a quality story, and I pushed myself because I was determined to give you nothing less than a certified best-seller. So for every text, post, inbox, tweet, like, comment, share, discussion, and review (every ounce of support big or small), thank you from the bottom of my heart.

All my love,
Briana Cole

"For every promise, there is a price to pay."

—*Jim Rohn,* Leading an Inspired Life

Prologue

"*We should just kill her.*"

Those words broke through my subconscious and sent a startling chill up my spine.

The pain, at first excruciating, had long since subsided into a dull ache and whether it was the handcuffs binding my wrists or the minimal rations of stale food and lukewarm water I'd been having to live on for the past few days, my body was now numb. Like a shell. But despite my snatches of blurred vision as I toggled in and out of consciousness, this man's face was crystal clear. What I didn't understand was why was he here? Why wasn't he helping me?

I struggled to lift my lids and through tears that blurred my vision, I stared into the eyes of a dead man.

"My love." His accent was deepened by the emotion clogging his voice. Pity. Apologetic. But he didn't move any closer, even though I'm sure I looked like the death I was slowly succumbing to.

I tried to replay everything that had happened in the past few months. Clues I had missed. Then, footsteps brought the other person into view and I remembered. My mind suddenly settled on the missing pieces that had been hidden in plain sight. How could I not have known? More importantly, what were they going to do with me now that I did?

Chapter 1

I knew I was wrong, even as I hiked up the bustle of chiffon and tulle that adorned my dress and quickened my pace toward the bathroom, my retreat causing the muffled noises of the wedding reception to fade against my back. At this point, I would just have to apologize later. For now, I needed peace. If only for a moment.

I swung into the restroom and quickly stooped to peer underneath the three stall doors. Empty. Grateful, I locked the door and walked to the porcelain countertop.

I almost didn't recognize myself. Sure, I was still Kimmy; same dramatic pixie cut, sharp cheekbones, and almond-shaped eyes. Physically, for sure, not much had changed. But what *had* changed, those mental and emotional scars sure as hell couldn't be hidden under makeup or a distracting smile. Those still waters ran deep.

I shut my eyes against my reflection, inhaling sharply through my nose before letting a heavy sigh escape my parted lips. For the first time all day, hell, weeks if I wanted to be honest with myself, I felt like I could breathe.

Of course I should have been happy. It was a wedding that I had long since given up hope would ever happen. But from the time I woke up that morning, it felt like both my brain and body were stuck on a déjà vu repeat. Everything was perfect, just like we had planned it. From the coral décor to the arrival of the vendors, right down to the gorgeous weather that hung appreciatively at seventy-four degrees despite the forecast of rain. Decorations had adorned the sanctuary, a collection of neosoul ballads had wafted through the speakers, and guests had arrived and arranged themselves in the pews with bottles of bubbles (because Daddy wasn't having rice thrown in his church) and tissues ready for the tears that were sure to come. Pictures were snapped, both from smart phones as well as by the professional photographer who crouched and maneuvered around to capture moments from every angle possible.

And I knew, even as I clutched my bouquet with sweaty palms and started my own descent down the sheer aisle runner, I knew exactly why it was taking all of my strength to feign the same excitement that was clearly evident among everyone else. And for that, I felt terrible.

Tears stung the corners of my eyes, and now that the ceremony was over, I finally let them spill over, trailing makeup streaks down my cheeks. I hadn't meant to spend the entire time comparing everything. They were two entirely different circumstances.

Last year, I had signed a contract to be a "love partner" or wife to the rich Leo Owusu. I would be just another along with the two women he already had. It had been nothing more than a business arrangement in my eyes, and I had treated it as such. But for Leo, I was his wife number three in every sense of the word. I couldn't help but shake my head at the memory of the lavish wedding from months ago, a wedding I neither wanted nor cared for. Nothing but an elaborate showcase of the extent of his money. So I stood at the altar with his other wives right up there by my side, like they too weren't wearing wedding rings vowing their lives and hearts to the same man. The entire event was fit for a queen, with all its bells and whistles and fake glory.

I grimaced at the thought, then turned my memories to the ceremony that had just taken place only moments before. I could not have foreseen I would be here again so soon. But sure enough, I was, listening to my dad's proud voice as he officiated. *Genuine.* That was the main word that came to mind as I reflected on the emotions that hung thick in the air. Vows and rings were exchanged, tears were shed, and every moment that ticked past I wanted to hold longer in my heart because it was so damn strong and authentic. This was how it was supposed to be. A constant reminder that was enough to heighten my own regret for selling myself so short before.

The door pushed against its lock as someone apparently tried to come in. I sniffed and wiped my hand against my face, smearing my makeup even more. *Pathetic*, I scolded myself as I snatched paper towels from the dispenser and blotted my cheeks. Turning, I flipped the lock and pulled open the door.

"Girl, I was looking for you." Adria breezed in with a laugh. She glanced at my face and immediately engulfed me in a hug. "Aw, I love you so much, sis. I can finally say that now."

I returned the hug with a small smile, swallowing my own pangs of jealousy. I was sure I was officially kicked out of the best friends club for being so damn selfish. While I was wallowing in my own self-pity and regret, I couldn't even be happy for my own best friend at her wedding.

Adria released me and turned to eye herself in the mirror. She had lost a few pounds, just enough to really accentuate her curves in the bead-embellished corset of her halter gown. A jewel-encrusted tiara fit neatly around her high bun and clasped an ivory veil to the back of her head, allowing it to cascade down to her mid-back. Despite the tears she had shed and the sweat that now peppered her forehead, my girl's makeup was still flawless from when I had spent two hours that morning brushing, contouring, blending, and getting it perfect. But more than anything, the pure joy that was emitted from her gaze and wide smile really made her glow with another level of beauty I hadn't seen before. Not in her, nor myself.

"I am hot as hell," Adria breathed, pulling paper towels from the dispenser and stuffing wads underneath her armpits. "Would I be too ghetto if I go back out there like this? They'll understand, right?"

I grinned, welcoming the humor. "Please don't," I said. "I don't think my brother could handle that."

Adria's lips turned up into a devious smirk as she winked. "Trust me," she said. "He can handle all of this and very, very well." She rolled her hips to exaggerate her statement, and I pursed my lips to keep from laughing out loud.

"Yeah, keep all that shit for the honeymoon."

"Honey, this honeymoon started four months ago when he proposed." Her eyes dropped to the three-carat diamond engagement ring and wedding band that glittered from her finger. I turned back to the mirror.

Her innocent gesture had tugged on another heartstring. Through the entire ceremony, I had wondered if Jahmad had been thinking about me. The man was still the love of my life, so I wondered if his imagination had taken over like mine, picturing me, instead of Adria, walking toward him in our own wedding ceremony of happily ever after. But, frankly, after everything that had happened between us, maybe that was too much wishful thinking.

"I actually came in here to talk to you about the store," Adria stated, pulling my attention back to her.

I frowned at her mention of our cosmetic store, Melanin Mystique. Thanks to the little seed money I had received from my husband's will, Adria and I had been able to rent a building and get the products for our dream business. "Girl, we are not about to talk business right now."

"I know, but I'm about to be off for a bit for the honeymoon—"

"And I can handle everything until you get back," I assured

her, tossing a comforting smile in her direction. "Between me and the new guy. What's his name?"

"Tyree."

"Yeah. He started last week, and so far, he seems to be catching on quick."

"So you'll be able to make sure everything is ready for the grand opening?"

I nodded. Come hell or high water, we were opening that store. I had made too many sacrifices not to. "I'm not saying you can't," Adria went on, circling her arm through mine. She rested her head on my shoulder. "It's just that I would feel comfortable doing this last little bit of stuff with you. I don't want you to think I'm not doing my part. And with my nephew coming home next week too, you're going to have your hands full."

The mention of my son brought an unconscious smile to my lips. I couldn't wait to bring Jamaal home from the hospital. The overwhelming joy I had for that child made me wonder why I had even considered an abortion in the first place. No way could I have lived without him. But initially, the uncertainty about my child's father, whether it was my husband, Leo, or my boyfriend, Jahmad, was enough to scare me into making an appointment and even going as far as taking the first of two medicines that would cause the abortion. But by the grace of God, I had forgotten all about my pregnancy when I got a call about Leo's car accident. Now, my son's paternity didn't even matter. As far as I and Jahmad were concerned, he was the biological father. End of story. At least I hoped.

"It's all going to work out," I said, meeting her eyes in the mirror. "I don't want you worrying about the store, the baby, nothing. Just worry about enjoying my brother and being a newlywed. Can you do that?"

Adria's expression relaxed into an appreciative smile, and I didn't feel quite as bad anymore about my little selfish jealousy.

At the end of the day, this girl was my best friend, now sister-in-law, and I loved her to pieces. Anything I was feeling was personal, and I would just have to deal with it myself. No way could I let it affect our relationship. Adria certainly didn't deserve that.

I let myself be steered back into the hallway and toward the reception hall. A collection of old-school mixes had everyone on the dance floor, moving in sync with the electric slide. I groaned, knowing no one but my dad had initiated the line dance that was a staple at every black wedding reception, family/class reunion, or cookout from coast to coast.

The venue was minimally decorated, to appeal more to comfort, with its beautiful assortment of coral flowers and floating candle centerpieces adorning each round table. Chiffon sashes draped from a stage where the wedding party sat, the remnants of the catered soul food dinner and white chocolate cake now being cleared by the waitstaff.

We hadn't even stepped all the way in the room before I was blinded by yet another flash from the photographer, and obediently I plastered another smile on my face. Adria would surely kill me if I messed up her wedding pictures.

Talking about cost efficient, Adria had certainly managed to save her coins when it came to planning this thing. Of course, my dad offered the couple his church and services free of charge, and the reception was now being held in the refurbished church basement, the sole location for numerous church events and family functions. Her aunt Pam was good friends with a caterer, and her small wedding party consisted of me and another young lady who worked at the bank with Adria. It had all worked out like it was supposed to, because Adria was set on putting as much money as possible toward their honeymoon and a house they were looking to close on in a few weeks. My sigh was wistful as her boisterous laugh rang throughout the room. Of course Adria had done everything right. Me, on the other hand, well, I was still picking up the pieces.

Speaking of pieces, my eyes scanned the crowd for Jahmad. Between this morning's argument and the chaos of the wedding operations as soon as we arrived to the church, we hadn't said much of anything to each other. Even as I had taken hold of his arm and allowed him to escort me down the aisle at the ceremony, the tension had been so thick I could taste it, and I prayed the discomfort hadn't been obvious to Adria nor to Keon. Or the photographer. Wanting to break the ice, I had given his forearm a gentle squeeze. I even tossed a smile his way, but both gestures had gone ignored.

I sighed again as I noticed him on the dance floor, his arms around one of the guests, Adria's cousin Chantel. Her face was split with a flirtatious grin and Jahmad, well, he looked more relaxed than he had in months. And that shit pissed me off.

I was weighing how to get in between them and put hands on this chick in the most discreet way when an arm draped over my shoulder. Glancing up, I met my dad's eyes and allowed my anger to subside. For now.

"Beautiful ceremony, huh," he said, and I nodded.

"It really was, Daddy."

"I'm so happy your brother finally grew up," he went on with a chuckle. "I thought I was going to have to take him to the mountain for sacrifice like Abraham and Isaac."

I laughed. "You would've sacrificed my brother?"

"I was telling God to just say the word." He winked. The humor instantly faded from his smirk as he turned somber eyes on me. "What about you, baby girl?"

"What about me?"

"You know I wanted to officiate for *both* of my kids. And, well . . ." He trailed off, and I shrugged, trying to keep from looking back over at Jahmad and failing miserably. I knew what he meant. Of course he hadn't been able to do that with me when I decided to up and tie the knot with Leo. I hadn't given him that honor. And I knew he was still hurt by that.

A slow song now had Jahmad and Chantel swaying closer, his hand on the small of her back. If I wanted to be logical, the two didn't look all that intimate. Quite platonic, actually. But I didn't give a damn about logic at that point.

My dad could obviously sense the heightened fury in my demeanor, because he took my hand and gently guided me to the dance floor, in the opposite direction.

"When are you going back to the hospital to see Jamaal?" he asked as we started to dance.

I sighed. Obviously everyone had some secret mission to keep me from wallowing in my own self-pity. Dammit.

"I went up there yesterday," I said. "He's doing really good."

"You sure you don't want him to stay with us for a few weeks? Just until you get situated in your place with the move?"

I tightened my lips. If I played my cards right, I wasn't planning on going anywhere but to Jahmad's house. In fact that's what we had been arguing about this morning when I had come over so we could ride to the church together.

The thing was, my heart still completely belonged to that man. But somewhere in these past few months, he was becoming distant. One minute it was as if we were on the same page, trying to focus on us, or so I thought. But then I would feel like I was struggling to breathe under this suffocating tension that hung between us. And I really wasn't sure how to get us back on track.

So when I suggested we move in together now that our son was coming home, I certainly hadn't expected the frown nor the subsequent questions about my motive for asking like I was up to some shit.

"What is the big deal, Jahmad?" I had asked as I paced his bedroom. "I mean I thought we agreed we would try to work on this? Us?" I pointed a wild finger first at him, then myself.

"What does that have to do with us moving in together?"

The tone of his question had a twinge of hurt piercing my heart. Here I was thinking we were taking steps forward only to realize we were actually moving backward. Why else would the idea of living together come as such a shock to him? I mean after the whole ordeal with Leo, I had moved back in with my folks because I wanted to focus on the business, which was already stressful enough. And I honestly knew, however false the hope, that it would be temporary, because Jahmad's stubborn ass would finally realize exactly where I belonged. With him. Apparently I was still in Neverland.

"Kimmy, that's doing too much." Jahmad sighed in frustration as he shrugged into his suit jacket. "The way I see it, we don't even know if there is an 'us.' And we damn sure don't need any more complications."

I sucked in a sharp breath. "Complications? Since when is being with me a complication?"

"Since when? Since I found out you were married."

And there he went again. Throwing the shit up in my face. As if I hadn't berated myself enough. As if I hadn't been laying on apology after apology so much that I was sick of hearing the words my damn self. I masked the embarrassment with anger.

"You know what my situation was about," I snapped, jabbing a finger in his direction. "And you know it wasn't real."

"That doesn't make it any better," he yelled back. "Hell, if anything that shines a negative light on you, because all the conniving and sneaky shit was for money. My love didn't mean anything to you."

"How can you stand here and say that? You know that's not true."

"Do I?" He narrowed his eyes. "How can I even trust you or anything you say?"

"Jahmad, we've had this same conversation every week for months." I threw up my arms to express my frustration. "I can't change the past. What else can I do? Or say to move past this?"

This time he was quiet so I used the opportunity to keep pushing. "There is no more marriage. No more Leo. No more lies and secrets, Jahmad. I promised you that before. Now it's just us. And our son. That is what's important to me."

I had to mentally repent even as the words left my lips. There were still a few lies between us. Among other things, whether he knew there was a question of paternity with my son. I sure as hell had to take that to my grave. And the money: Leo had given me plenty of it and since technically he had staged his death, that money was still tucked safely in my accounts. Like hell I would give that up. That would mean the whole arrangement would have been in vain.

Silence had ridden with us to the church, and we soon became so engrossed in the pre-wedding preparations we hadn't bothered, nor had time, to resume the conversation.

I tried to bring my attention back to my father as he swayed with me on the dance floor, but thoughts continued to consume me.

I glanced around, my eyes eager to catch Jahmad once more, but he had long since disappeared. I stopped my scan when I noticed a certain face appear in the crowd. I squinted through the dimness and distance, struggling to blink clarity into my vision. The face I couldn't make out but the dress, I knew that dress. And the hair was the same, too much to be a coincidence.

My dad spun me around, and I quickly angled my neck to catch another glimpse of the woman I thought I recognized. But by then, the Tina look-alike was gone.

Chapter 2

I knew Jahmad wanted to say something. It was evident in the way his jaw was clenched, the way his forehead seemed to be creased and those lips I loved remained frozen in something of a pout. Even as he kept his eyes trained on the road, his profile was stoic, and I knew whatever was on his mind rested on the tip of his tongue. But still he said nothing to me. I couldn't tell if it was worry or anger, but either way, it was awkward as hell and making me fidget uncomfortably in the passenger seat.

Funny. All during the reception I had been silently counting down until the clock signaled the party was over. I was in no mood for the ordeal, and all I wanted was to get home and snuggle up to Jahmad. The bridesmaid dress had called for the skimpiest of panties and maybe, just maybe, I could help him forget all about his little attitude as soon as we got behind closed doors. But now that the reception hall was fading in the sideview mirror, this stifling silence was making me wish we were back in the noise and laughter. Just something to fill the air besides this tension.

A familiar scene began to play in my mind, and it was one I often lingered on whenever I felt distance between us. Jamaal had just been born, granted prematurely because of Tina's crazy ass. She had tried to kill me when I'd found out she was behind the whole ordeal. Thankfully, Leo had saved me, and now, whether Tina was in jail, or dead, I didn't give a damn. Leo assured me I wouldn't have to worry about her anymore and I didn't. My only concern was my son and his survival.

But despite the labor three months early, he had been born and was doing as well as could be expected for a preemie. Jahmad and I had visited the NICU together, and as we both stared down lovingly at the baby's tiny figure in the incubator, he had slipped his arm around my waist and planted a gentle kiss on my forehead. "Thank you," he had whispered, his breath tickling my cheek. He didn't elaborate, and I didn't question his soft words. I just savored the intimacy, because right then, it felt like we, all three of us, were going to be just fine.

But that had been four months ago. My son was doing better, but I couldn't say the same for me and Jahmad. And it was tearing me up more than I cared to admit. And now this damn quiet was damn near deafening.

"I loved Adria's dress," I started. The words felt forced even as they left my lips, despite the sincerity of the statement. When Jahmad merely nodded, I sighed, struggling to mask my frustration. "You want to talk about something?"

This time, he did speak. "Yeah. Just not really right now."

"I think we need to talk about 'us,' Jahmad," I pressed. "It's so awkward between us."

"You're right. And we'll talk. Later."

"Why not now?"

"I have a lot on my mind," he stated simply, and it was evident he was ready to end the conversation.

I bit my tongue to keep from pushing the issue. Fine, he wasn't ready to talk now. I could wait until we got home if that was the case.

A phone's ring pierced the air, a welcome disturbance to the strangled silence. My phone was on vibrate, so I knew it was Jahmad's. He shifted, managing to steer the car with one hand while pulling the device from his pants pocket with the other. I tried to keep from staring as his eyes dropped to the screen, but I couldn't help but notice the little flirt of a smile at the corner of his lips as he obviously appreciated the phone call from whomever. My frown deepened, even more so when he clicked a button and lifted the phone to his ear.

"What's good?"

Now my ears were perked, trying my best to detect some sort of voice on the other end.

Jahmad listened, and so did I. Nothing.

"Glad to hear," he said, a wide smile now fully planted on his lips. Damn, I had missed that handsome face. When was the last time he had smiled at me like that?

"Sounds good. Let me call you when I get home." The caller obviously agreed because with that Jahmad was ending the call.

I waited to see if he would divulge anything about the mysterious call that had obviously lightened his mood. He didn't. As if my mind was hell-bent on making the situation worse, a sudden image of Jahmad with Adria's cousin Chantel dancing at the wedding played in my vision. Well, damn, he was back to his old ways. And here I was trying to give this man all of my heart and soul. And yet again he had me looking stupid.

It was times like this I wished I could call Adria. She would be my logic, my voice of reason. She would talk me down from this threatening anger I knew was coming only from my own assumptions. I knew I was just jumping to conclusions, but, dammit, they were rational conclusions. Jahmad hadn't always been the model one-woman man. And I would remind Adria that he had made a fool out of me before. Of course, she would be fair and put it in my face that I had done the same thing when I was with Leo. But what did I expect? My girl had always been Team Jahmad. So maybe it was best she was living and loving it up with my brother in some Buckhead hotel before their flight in the morning. Now I wouldn't have to justify my feelings. I wouldn't have to come to terms with the fact that, despite everything I had done, down to having a baby I really didn't want at first, Jahmad just didn't love me like I loved him. That shit hurt. I couldn't face that part just yet.

We pulled up to his brick townhome just as the rest of the night took over. My powder-blue Audi Q7, an upgrade from the Porsche Leo had given me, sat in his driveway encompassed in the dark with only a piece of light from the porch casting an eerie shadow on the windshield.

Jahmad cut the engine off and waited, as if he wanted me to initiate. But, hell, I didn't know what to say. I wanted to stay over, but perhaps that was too zealous.

"So, you packed some clothes," he asked as if reading my thoughts. My mood instantly lifted. I could already feel my body humming to life in anticipation.

"Who says I need clothes?" I tossed him a sideways glance.

To my disappointment, he shook his head. "Nah, we not getting all into that tonight."

"What?" Now I didn't bother hiding my anger. Had he actually told me no? "Jahmad, I know you're not serious."

As if in response, Jahmad climbed from the truck, and I quickly followed suit. Now I *knew* we needed to talk.

"Jahmad, you really not going to address me?" I asked as soon as we'd stepped inside the living room.

"I told you—"

"Yeah, I know you didn't want to talk about it." I threw up my hands in exasperation. "Well, I really don't give a damn that you don't want to talk about it. You walking around here like everything is all good between us is not fair to me."

"I'm not walking around here like we good," Jahmad said with a nonchalant shrug.

"Okay, so clearly we're not good. You know it too. So what is it?"

Jahmad stared at me, and for a brief moment, I thought he would actually speak up. Actually have this conversation. Then he sighed and rubbed his hand over his head, an outward display of his stress. Well, damn his stress. I was pissed. Not to mention horny.

"You're right," he said with a sigh. "We need to talk. And we will, Kimmy. But it's late. I'm tired. You're tired. And now is just not a good time. Not until I make some decisions."

My heart slowed as I took in his words. "Decisions?" I echoed. "About me?"

"It's late," he murmured again. "Just sleep here and head back to your parents' house in the morning."

It sounded like a pity invitation. Not at all like he wanted me to stay. I rolled my eyes at his comment. "No, I'll just leave," I snapped, snatching my keys from my clutch purse. "Wouldn't want to put more on your mind."

"Kimmy—"

"Just make sure you're at the hospital tomorrow," I said, snatching open the front door. "Wouldn't want to disappoint me *and* your son." I slammed the door on my words and stood on the porch, basking in the moonlight, the chilly air, and the heart-break. I wasn't even surprised when he didn't attempt to come outside. His silence was loud as hell.

The stark, white envelope rested on my windshield, under-neath the wiper. I glanced around the darkened street, and over my shoulder at Jahmad's house. I was alone. At least now I was. When had he come? How had he known where Jahmad stayed?

I quickly snatched the envelope from the window and got in the car. I knew what it was. Leo had been sending me a check for $6,500 every month since my son had been born. Like clockwork. He would scribble *"for child support"* on each one. No, I didn't believe Leo was Jamaal's father—I take that back. I didn't want to believe he was. But I had struggled to push that little uncertainty to the back of my mind. Because as I cashed and hid each check, I didn't feel as much like some money-hungry gold digger if I knew there was a possibility my son was actually due this money with the Owusu blood pumping through his veins. But still, the checks had always been mailed without a return address to the PO box I had for Melanin Mystique. Always mailed. Certainly never placed on my car like a hand delivery.

I glanced down both sides of the quiet street. Of course I knew Leo was alive. He had admitted to faking his death after finding out his first wife, Tina, was trying to kill him. But he had insisted he would stay away from me. I had told him that this *thing* with us was over. And he had walked away. But why, then, was he back now? Hiding in plain sight?

I flipped the envelope between my fingers and noticed for the first time the handwriting. The words were enough to send chills down my spine and shut my eyes to block out the increasing fear. *"Tell my son hello. See you both soon. Love you. —Leo"*

Chapter 3

A familiar feeling always seemed to settle on me when I walked these halls. I'm not sure if it was excitement, nervousness, fear, or, hell, a combination of all three. But each time I trekked down the glistening linoleum of the hospital, each time my steps brought me closer and closer to the NICU, a shred of panic would have me quickening my pace as if something might go wrong at any moment. I'm sure it was that lingering anxiety from when my son was born.

Jamaal had emerged at only one pound and six ounces, a micro-preemie, the nurses had called him, and with good reason. His brown body was translucent and so tiny it was a wonder he was even alive at all. What made it worse, the doctor had initially said he only had a 50 percent chance of survival. And *if*—I still cringed even now at the obscure word—*if* he survived, he would probably be disabled. Jamaal's lungs had been so underdeveloped he had to be put on life support, and his eyes were still fused shut. He had also suffered a brain hemorrhage during delivery.

Those first few weeks were delicate, and with the collection of medication, infections, surgeries, and near-death scares, Jahmad and I found ourselves damn near living at the hospital, only rotating out with Adria and my parents at their insistence that we go home, shower, and pack more clothes. I often would return and find my parents' heads dipped in prayer, gripping each other's hands so hard their knuckles were white.

"He's a fighter," my dad would murmur as worry creased my forehead and tears dampened my cheeks. "God's got him."

But each day I found myself losing faith as I would look down at my baby hidden among tubes, machines, and wires, his tiny chest lifting with the assistance of his oxygen machine.

But my dad was right. Finally, Jamaal started breathing and eating on his own, and he was taken off the heart monitor. In another week, he would be coming home. Sure, with a ton of medications and regimens, plus around-the-clock monitoring, but he was indeed coming home, and my excitement was growing for sure. Never had I considered myself the nurturing type. I was all about myself and my money. But from the moment my son came squirming into this world, it was like something changed inside of me. A good something. All that other petty shit didn't seem to matter anymore. What mattered was that I did everything in my power to make a good life for Jamaal. Whether that was with or without a father.

Speaking of which, I couldn't hide my disappointment as I rounded the corner and saw the empty waiting area. I figured even despite our argument yesterday that Jahmad would put his little bullshit attitude to the side and be here anyway. Wishful thinking.

"Good morning, Ms. Davis," the receptionist greeted as I signed in. I smiled. The staff had gotten quite familiar with me.

"Hi, Shaun. How are the twins?"

The young woman blew an exasperated breath at the casual mention of her double doses of spunky trouble, as she often referred to them. "Woke up this morning and found Mason had tried to make his own cereal and had spilled the whole gallon of milk. And Malik calls himself trying to mop it up with one of my wigs, girl." Though she rolled her eyes, the loving amusement was evident in the curl of her lips. I had to laugh, trying to picture the morning chaos.

"I don't know how you do it," I mused with a smirk.

"I quit on this mommy thing. Just take my two on home with you when you pick up Jamaal."

I dismissed the playful request with a wave of my hand. "Please. You know you would be lost without those two."

"Yeah, lost all the way to Jamaica or somewhere."

I chuckled, thinking about Shaun's typical mommyhood attitude. She once told me I would be singing that same tune one day. But I kept remembering how my son had straddled life and death too many times to count, and I knew if that happened, it would be way later than sooner.

The NICU was a secure and sterile unit, so I washed my hands using the antibacterial soap dispensers at the entrance before I was buzzed back through the doors. As soon as I stepped into the nursery, I was engulfed in the noise, the bubbling and beeping of equipment working nonstop to keep these tiny humans alive and healthy, nurses and doctors working tirelessly as they consulted in medical lingo over a baby's cry. A symphony of alarms seemed to serve as a soundtrack to each incubator and the dimmed light added to the intense mood of the nursery. I would never get used to the fast-paced activity. It was truly a scary but seemingly magical environment.

Jamaal's primary nurse greeted me, and I immediately grabbed his bottle for his feeding as she went about the task of removing him from his crib. At one point, they told me I could breastfeed, but I was apprehensive with his fragile state, so I never bothered. But the medical staff did assure me that skin-to-skin contact was beneficial. So though he wasn't latched onto my breast, I still took my shirt off so she could lay him on my chest as I popped the bottle in his mouth.

Jamaal's wide eyes stared curiously into mine as he sucked greedily. I smiled. He was looking more and more like my baby pictures as he grew into his features. I couldn't detect a hint of Jahmad, nor Leo for that matter, in him. Maybe that was a good thing.

"How you been, my baby?" I whispered, rocking him gently. "Mommy missed you so much. You ready to come home?" I paused, as if he really was answering. "Me too," I went on and lifted him slightly to brush my lips on his warm cheek. "I can't wait to get you out of this place. I promise your nursery at home is so much better than this."

Jamaal polished off the bottle, and I used my thumb to wipe away a little milk that dribbled down his chin. Then I lifted him to my shoulder and gently patted his back, coaxing a tiny burp from his lips. My heart warmed when he seemed to nuzzle closer. I kept rocking and patting, humming some tune. Not long after, his body went still with the exception of his shallow breaths, and I knew he had fallen asleep. I waited a bit longer before handing him to his nurse and watching as she settled him back into his bed. I sighed; not too much longer.

His nurse brought me up to speed. Jamaal was still progressing as expected. Still on track to come home. She gave me the layman's terms for some recent test results. All positive. I thanked her, took one last look at my perfect son, and left.

I was surprised to see Jahmad in the lobby, sitting forward on one of the hard couches resting his elbows on his knees. His head was down, and at first I couldn't tell whether he was in deep thought or deep sleep. Apparently, deep thought, I reconsidered when he lifted his face to study me as I walked closer.

"Why didn't you come in?" I asked as he rose.

"Just wanted to give you your time first."

"It's our time," I said, struggling to hide my annoyance. His half-assed answer sounded like an excuse. "You shouldn't have waited. He's asleep now."

"I'll just come back later then." He started to walk past, but I put my hand on his arm to stop him.

"Jahmad, let's please go somewhere to talk."

He sighed and, to my surprise, leaned down to kiss me. It wasn't long, or hell, even passionate, but it was welcome affection that had been absent too many days to count. My lips curved against his.

"We will talk," he said, his voice reassuring. "Soon. I have to run to the office right now, though."

I nodded. "Okay. Can I call you later?"

"You better."

My smile widened at his teasing. "Okay." I paused, then chanced it. "I love you, Jahmad."

"I love you too." Like a hallelujah chorus to my ears.

He strolled off, leaving me grinning in the waiting area. Maybe he was over whatever funk he had been in. Probably work-related. And here I was thinking it was us. But the thing about Jahmad, one of the things I hated and loved about him, when something was bothering him, he tended to close off. It was his way of dealing with it so as not to transfer his stress to others. So when he had done that, immediately I'd assumed it had something to do with our relationship. When he hadn't given me any conclusions, I'd drawn my own, however false or extreme. Had it been my own guilt-ridden conscience from past mistakes? Jahmad had obviously forgiven me. I needed to keep working on forgiving myself.

"Girl, what's got you grinning like that?"

I hadn't even noticed Shaun had walked up to stand beside me. I pursed my lips to hide the smirk, failing miserably.

"Jamaal's father," I admitted.

Now it was Shaun's turn to give a knowing smile. "Listen, I

wanted to let you know something." She shifted closer, lowering her voice. "The doctors will probably tell you too, but just so you know, some guy has been trying to get up in here to see Jamaal."

The words had a frown creasing my face. The hell?

"A guy?" I said. "What guy? Not Jahmad?"

"No. Someone not on your approved visitor list." Her eyebrows were furrowed, mirroring the concern I felt. "He always puts Jamaal's name down and insists he's Jahmad. But, clearly, we know he's not."

"'Always?'" I echoed, my concern turning to fear. "It's been more than once?"

Shaun nodded. "Several times on my shift. And the other girls said they've seen him too. They said yesterday he was so persistent to get back there and see Jamaal he had to be police-escorted off the premises." She shrugged. "I don't know if that's true, because, girl, you know how those chicks like to gossip and embellish, but still. I thought . . ." She trailed off, and I nodded my appreciation.

"Thank you for telling me, Shaun. Seriously."

"Of course."

"Hey, what does he look like?" I added, though I was sure I had a fairly good idea.

"Black guy. Dark-skinned."

"Does he have dreadlocks?"

"No, he has a haircut."

I paused then, remembering the last time I had caught Leo up here when he told me the story of how he had faked his death. He had cut his locs completely off.

"African guy?" I asked, and as I expected, she nodded. I thanked her again as she headed for the hall.

First, he was sending me child support checks to Jahmad's house, now he was adamant about seeing my child. What the hell was Leo doing? Other than pissing me off. The last thing my family and I needed was him complicating shit. Again. But this time I wasn't having it. If it was a fight he wanted, then, dammit, he had the right one.

———>•<———

The smell of pasta immediately greeted me as I walked into Jahmad's house. The stupid grin split my face and had me hurriedly putting down my keys and purse, anxious to see what he was up to.

I sure as hell didn't expect the man to be moving between pots on the stove in basketball shorts slung low on his waist. Even though he may have broken the romantic ambience with a muted basketball game playing on TV, I still couldn't have been happier. I don't know what had sparked this little change of heart, but maybe things were finally starting to look up for us. About damn time.

"Hey, handsome," I greeted, entering the kitchen. "Well, isn't this a sexy surprise." I fingered the drawstring of his shorts. "Is there dessert as well?"

Jahmad smirked. "Only if you eat all your food," he teased. He held the spoon drenched in marinara sauce in my direction, and I obediently licked it.

"Mm," I moaned my appreciation. "Smooth and savory. Just like I like my men."

"Girl, you really wanting it, huh?"

"I do," I whined. "You've been holding out on me."

"Well, you know I will take care of you." Jahmad replaced the spoon on my lips with his mouth before turning back to stir the sauce.

"Fine." I exaggerated a pout. "But after we eat, you're mine." I opened the refrigerator and took out a bottle of wine. Jahmad had already pulled out the flutes so I took the liberty of pouring us each a glass.

"Did you end up making it back to the hospital?" I asked, taking a leisurely sip. "JayJay is looking good. I'll be glad when he comes home."

"Yeah, me too. But nah, I couldn't make it back up there. I meant to, but I had to swing by Goodyear and get some new tires."

I frowned. "I thought you just got four new ones last month."

"I did. But one was completely flat when I came out the store. And, hell, the other one had a slow leak."

I watched him continue to move about casually, but his news seemed anything but casual. I usually was quick to consider things to be coincidences, but that was before. And the fact that Shaun had just mentioned the little hospital incidents with Leo didn't help ease my apprehension.

"What did they say at the tire place?" I asked, masking my investigation as sheer curiosity.

Jahmad flipped the knobs to turn the stove off and accepted the wineglass I held out to him. "Nothing much," he answered. "What were they supposed to say?"

"I don't know. Maybe there was a nail or something. Or if there was a warranty." I shrugged, trying to ignore that nagging feeling that there was more to this story.

"Nah, they didn't mention anything, but it's all good." Jahmad set his glass down and, taking mine from my hands, set it down as well. He backed me up against the counter, resting his hands on my hips. "Now." He leaned forward, nuzzling my neck. "Didn't you say something about dessert?"

"Mmm." The moan tickled my throat as his lips grazed my skin. Just that fast, all thoughts of those damn tires vanished as my body hummed to life. "I thought you said after we eat."

"Oh, I plan to eat." In one swift motion, Jahmad lifted me into his arms and wrapped my legs around his waist, the impression of his dick like steel against my thigh.

I threw my arms around his neck and pulled his face to mine, immediately assaulting his mouth. The way I figured it, we would deal with the other shit in the morning. Tonight, this was us. And, hell, my body needed it.

Chapter 4

"Girl, you should see this villa," Adria gushed, unable to contain her excitement. "He has it all decked out with rose petals, candles, chocolate-covered strawberries and shit. Who knew behind all that foolishness this boy was really a hopeless romantic."

I chuckled, repositioning the phone as I continued my trek down the walkway. "You must have brought it out of him," I said. "My brother is a lot of things, but a hopeless romantic? Hell, no."

"It must be all this good-good I've been putting on him."

"Adria. I don't need to know that."

She laughed, and I had no choice but to laugh with her. This was honestly the happiest I had seen my friend in, probably, ever. "Why are you even calling me anyway?" I asked. "You two just got to Negril. Shouldn't y'all be doing your honeymoon thing?"

"We are in a minute. I just wanted to call and let you know we got here safely. And also, I have my laptop with me so I can work on some of the financial spreadsheets for the inventory."

I groaned. Adria's dedication to this business was both a good and bad thing. "I told you I can handle it," I told her for what was the umpteenth time. "You took care of a lot before you left. The last thing I need you to be worrying about is work. Do you know the meaning of R.E.L.A.X.?"

"Yes, I plan to do plenty of that. But I told you I wasn't about to leave you hanging. The grand opening is next month."

I could only smile as the store came into view. Our sign, *Melanin Mystique,* was done up in elaborate cursive with both words sharing the first letter M. It was still surreal that this had been a dream only a few years ago, and now, here it was in all its glory and splendor. And sure enough, at Atlantic Station, one of the first locations I had envisioned for this store. All 2,890 square feet belonged to me and my best friend, all the way down to every lipstick, foundation, and eyebrow pencil that graced each glass shelf inside. Each makeup artist had been selected with the same care and precision I would expect of myself. I was proud, and I could not imagine pursuing this new venture on my own, which was why I had insisted Adria and I enter as partners despite me putting up all the money. Seeing the full-fledged benefit of my business arrangement seemed to make the whole ordeal worth it.

"I just want to make sure I'm doing my part," Adria said, bringing me back to the conversation. "You know it still feels weird for me since you paid for everything but you made me partner."

"Adria, stop it," I said, dismissing the comment. "I told you, we are in this together. All of it. This has always been our dream, so stop feeling like you owe me something. That makes me feel bad."

"I know, but—"

"Plus," I added quickly, "you are not leaving me hanging. You hired Cinnamon Sugar for me, remember?"

Adria laughed at the nickname I had given the temporary hire. With his warm cinnamon complexion and the way he twisted around the store in his tight, neon-colored V-neck shirts and skinny slacks, I thought the name was more than fitting. The man was clearly sweeter than Alaga maple syrup, but he came to work on the first day with an eager attitude and fun personality. Plus, he knew numbers like nobody's business and he loved makeup, so I was satisfied. At least until Adria returned.

"Cinnamon Sugar?" She laughed again. "I really hope you're not calling that man that to his face, Kimmy."

"Girl, he know he's gay, and it's not like he's trying to hide it."

"Well, *Tyree*"—she made sure to emphasize his real name— "sent me some reports yesterday, so it looks like he knows what he's doing."

"Yeah, it has only been a week, but so far so good. He's no Adria, though."

"Damn right," she said. "But okay, let me go. Keep me updated on everything, please."

"No. Enjoy your honeymoon and don't worry about me. Worry about making my brother some big-head-ass babies." I disconnected the call on her amused groan. She could play all she wanted. I knew she couldn't wait to pop out Keon's children. I smiled, picturing Jamaal having a little gap-toothed cousin to play with. My parents would be in hog heaven.

I swung open the door, and immediately a blast of cool air chilled my arms. The shelves were already in place and nearly all of them stocked with the exception of a few boxes stacked across a wall. Off to one side was the front desk with three cash registers and toward the back were four mirrored stations with high pub chairs for the makeup artists' appointments. An R & B mix played softly through the speakers.

I beamed at the new posters that had just come in, floor-to-ceiling vinyl with black women in various hues of brown, all close-ups of their gorgeous features adorned in boldly flawless makeup. Eye-catching, I had decided as soon as I saw the posters. I was excited too, because Adria had even managed to get in touch with a few of the models, and they had agreed to attend the grand opening. Them bringing their own supporters would generate even more buzz.

The door chimed again, and I turned as the UPS man wheeled in four more boxes on a dolly. "Ms. Kimera Davis?" he asked, and I nodded. He held out a clipboard in my direction. Probably the new business cards, flyers, and marketing materials I ordered. I signed where he indicated, and he left, just as Cinnamon Sugar himself pranced out from the back room.

His black dress slacks hugged his slender frame and a hot pink button-up was tucked into the cinched waist. A headset was planted across his low-cut fade, and he smiled widely when he noticed me standing in the center of the room, exposing glistening white teeth I was sure he had paid good money for. "Oh, good you're here, boo," he said. "The DJ for the grand opening canceled, so I called 91.6 and got us DJ Fresh. Plus, they want to do some live coverage on the day of." His smile widened at my shocked expression. "I know. Did I come through or what?"

I nodded. "You sure did. Awesome job. What would we do without you?"

Tyree winked. "Chile, I ask myself that same question all the time." He handed me a folder. "I figured Ms. Adria wouldn't have time to get to them since she's on her honeymoon, so I went ahead and took care of the financials for the new inventory." He handed me a sticky note. "And Amber Nicole returned your phone call about the model casting call for the makeup show." The light on his headset flickered, and he held up a quick index finger in my direction as he pressed the earpiece to answer. "Melanin Mystique, Tyree speaking." As if suddenly remembering, Tyree used his finger to point up and down at my outfit and snapped his approval. *That outfit, yes, boo*, he mouthed before turning and strutting off like he was in a fashion show. I muffled a smirk as I glanced down at my designer jumpsuit. Yes, the newbie was certainly a character, but I couldn't care less, because little Mr. Sweet'N Low was about business. And that's what I needed. I don't know where Adria found him, but thank God for precious miracles.

I opened the file and studied the financial reports as I made my way to the back of the store. Other than two restrooms and a storage area, there were two identically sized offices. Adria had yet to decorate hers, and now it was pretty bare with the exception of a glass desk that Tyree now sat behind. He was still on the phone as I strolled past, and I saw he alternated between scribbling on a notepad, pecking on the keyboard of a laptop, and forking through some kind of breakfast hash brown bowl spread on the desk while he murmured responses to the caller.

My office was at the end of the hall, but I had taken the time to add some personal touches. A soft, chocolate-colored accent wall with framed quotes drew immediate attention when I pushed open my door and flipped on the light. I had chosen the same glass desk as Adria's, more so for practicality versus consistency purposes. A dual monitor desktop computer still allowed desk space for the papers and trays I had neatly arranged, and because I had room, I had gone ahead and added a small bar in the corner. On top I would make sure to keep a few bottles of wine, but the cabinets would carry my mini fridge and microwave. Three oval mirrors in different sizes hung on the wall opposite my desk, and an ivory rug really added to the homey feel.

I circled my desk and plopped into the plush swivel chair on a sigh. Everything was really coming along, and I couldn't have been happier about that. Now that the plans were being finalized, I could concentrate on other stuff, like finding myself a place to stay.

My dad had mentioned it again last night, and his words really had me thinking. Not that he didn't want me there, but the baby and I needed our own space, he said. I must admit I had been hopeful, holding out for Jahmad to ask us to move in. I mean, that would be the move that made the most sense. And even though we were talking more, I was honestly scared to bring it up for fear it would have him showing his ass again. With my baby being discharged in another week or so, it was probably best I secure something.

I had perused the internet and gone ahead and secured appointments to walk through a nearby high-rise, plus a townhome near my parents, when there was a light knock on the door. I glanced up, eyeing the large bouquet of flowers that hid Tyree's face.

"Girlfriend, who you got all in love with you," he said, entering my office and setting the vase on my desk. I grinned, fingering the beautiful assortment of white and red roses. Jahmad was really laying it on thick. And I was eating it up.

"Just a little someone special," I answered with a slight blush.

"Looks like a big someone special." He nodded to the flowers. "He dropped them off personally just now."

I rose with a disappointed frown. "He was here? Why didn't you send him back?"

"I asked if he wanted me to get you, but he said he was in a rush and wanted to drop those off real quick. Hunny, he is cute too."

"Mmhmm," I commented absently. My mind was still on why Jahmad didn't at least poke his head in to say hi. That wouldn't have taken more than a couple seconds. Had he been in that big of a rush? Oh, well. I shrugged it off, taking another appreciative look at the little surprise. He had at least thought enough of me to get the bouquet and drop it off personally. That was just sweet enough.

After Tyree mentioned something else about an order at the warehouse and that he was stepping out to the bank real quick, he left me alone.

I picked up the phone and dialed Jahmad's number, surprised when it went right to voicemail. "Hey, baby," I said. "Just wanted to say I hate I missed you but thank you so much. They're beautiful. Call me when you're free. Maybe we can do lunch. I love you." I hung up and on another sigh clicked on a new internet browser to get to work. This business wouldn't run itself.

"Hey, boo." Tyree poked his head into my office. "Let's grab some lunch."

I sat back in my chair, stretching the stiff muscles in my shoulders. I had to do a double take at the time on my computer screen.

"Damn, is it really two-thirty?"

"Time flies when you're having fun." Tyree crossed to me and, grabbing my hand, pulled me to my feet. "Come on, boo. You need to eat."

"I'm not really hungry."

"Well, then you can watch me eat," he tossed back with a wink. "I got to put some more meat on my bones. My man says I don't eat enough as it is."

I hesitated, glancing back down at the open documents on my computer screen. I hated leaving my work unfinished, but he was right. I probably did need to take a little break. The bouquet resting neatly on my desk brought another smile to my face. That would give me time to call Jahmad again. I wondered why he had yet to return to my call.

We locked up the building and started down the walkway to a nearby pizza spot. It was well after the lunch rush, so within minutes, we had ordered at the counter and sat at an empty booth with our trays and drinks.

"You talked to Ms. Adria?" Tyree asked as he dove into his first slice.

I sipped my water and nodded. "Yeah, she made it safely. But you know she's still trying to work while she's on her honeymoon."

"Tell her I can handle it."

"I did," I said with a laugh. "But you don't know my girl. Adria is all business, all the time. She doesn't know how to delegate. Just tries to do everything. Maybe she'll relax if I ignore her calls while she's gone," I teased.

Tyree chuckled. "She'll panic then," he said. "Be on the first plane out of Jamaica." He took another bite of his food. "Well, sounds like I'm working for two business-savvy women."

"We're trying. Adria has the head for business," I said lovingly. "Me, I just do the makeup."

"That's a good thing. That makes me excited about the store."

"I am too. It's just so much. I'm glad we can finally see the finish line. Adria and I certainly appreciate all you've been doing, Tyree," I added with a smile. "You have been a tremendous asset."

Red colored the cheeks of his light complexion. "Well, I'm glad you two gave me a chance. I know I don't have much work history, but I love makeup and especially working with a little bit of this black girl magic."

For a while, we ate in silence, him devouring his pizza and me picking over my salad. I didn't realize I kept glancing to my cell phone until Tyree spoke up.

"Just call him."

"Who?"

"Mr. Wonderful with the flowers," he said like it was obvious, nodding his head to my phone.

I smirked, slightly embarrassed. "I already called. I'm sure he's in a meeting or something."

"Uh huh." Tyree flashed a knowing smirk. "He must really be special."

"Why do you say that?"

He shrugged. "I mean, you got a man delivering flowers to your job. Where are the ones like that in my playing field?"

"Didn't you just say earlier you had someone?"

"Boo, please." Tyree waved off the comment. "Someone is there, if that's what you mean, but no, I don't have anyone. Not really. I think I'm more serious about him than he is about me."

My mind crossed to Jahmad, and I could only nod my understanding. Damn if I didn't know what he meant.

"Men and they problems, I swear," Tyree said with a roll of his eyes. "Well, the ones I date," he corrected, his eyes twinkling. "Mr. Wonderful with the flowers is obviously an exception. So tell me your secret."

"No secret, I guess. Just love. That unconditional love."

"Ha," Tyree snorted. "I have plenty of that, and it ain't got me nowhere but a broken heart and some lies."

We both glanced down as my phone vibrated on the table and exchanged knowing grins.

"Hey, you," I answered, easing from the table and walking away for privacy.

"Hey, just got your message," Jahmad said. "I don't think I'm understanding, though."

"The flowers, babe. I was just thanking you."

A pause. "What flowers?"

"The ones you had delivered today," I said, my frown deepening at his continued silence. "The roses."

"I didn't send flowers."

I was confused as hell, but even more so, I was cursing myself for the assumption because now Jahmad's tone was filled with nothing but suspicion.

"My mistake," I said quickly. "Maybe they're for Adria or Tyree. I guess I just assumed they were for me since they were delivered to the store, but it didn't have a card."

Another pause. "All right, let me get back to work," Jahmad said and hung up, not bothering to wait for my response.

Tyree looked up from texting on his cell phone as I sat back down in front of him. "What's wrong, boo?"

I shook my head and forced a thin smile. "Nothing. Just a little headache. You ready to head back?"

He eyed my uneaten salad. "Yeah," he said. "Yeah, we can head back. You sure everything is okay?"

It wasn't, but I lied anyway, somewhat for him. Mostly for myself.

Chapter 5

I wasn't sure if people were actually whispering about it or if it was just my imagination. Either way, as I stepped into Word of Truth Christian Center, I might as well have had a bright scarlet letter embroidered on the sleeve of my Michael Kors dress.

Pairs of eyes slid in my direction as I stepped into the foyer of the church. I had to give credit to some of the congregation. They were at least trying to pretend they weren't whispering about me. I guess the rest of them said to hell with discretion as they leaned in to each other to talk while throwing narrow looks in my direction. At this point, the ushers were attempting to wave the members into the sanctuary. Apparently, my poly relationship and arrest for the murder of my husband were more important than the service. No, it wasn't necessarily new news. Keon had already told me what to expect but still, I wasn't prepared for the harsh scrutiny.

Despite the glares and upturned lips, I planted a fake smile on my face and began maneuvering my body through the crowd. If it hadn't been for my father's insistence, I wouldn't have even been here anyway. I could have found much better use for my Sunday morning than succumbing to the judgment of these holy rollers.

Either way, I made my way into the sanctuary and let myself be escorted down the aisle to the front row. One thing I noticed, even when I was in the foyer, there were not nearly as many people here as I'd seen on previous Sundays. Whereas before I'd witnessed standing room only, now there were entirely too many gaps in seating for this to be our normal Sunday service.

I took a seat next to my mom in the pew, and she immediately leaned over and kissed my cheek. "I'm so glad you came," she said. "It really means a lot to me and your father."

"Mama, I promised I would come more. And I am. I meant it." I glanced around, noting the few heads that whipped in the other direction when I looked their way. The attention was getting embarrassing. "Though I can't really say it's welcoming in here."

My mom threw an absent glance over her shoulder before rolling her eyes. "I can say a lot of things have changed around here. That's for sure. Don't even worry about it."

I looked sideways at my mother, easily detecting the concern in her stoic profile. Something was clearly bothering her. I rested my hand on hers. "You tell me not to worry about it, but it looks like you are."

She shook her head. "No, it's not that."

"Well then, what is it?"

She brought her eyes to mine, not even bothering to deny what was so clearly evident. "Let's talk about it later," she whispered. The corners of her lips turned up, but the smile nowhere near reached her eyes. We certainly would.

The choir took the stage and started the service in true Christian fashion, a collection of praise and worship songs sending the members into an anointed frenzy with a multitude of shouts, cries, and stomps bouncing off the walls.

After announcements, prayers, and offerings, I turned my eyes to my father sitting on the stage next to a few of the deacons. To my surprise, he didn't rise for the sermon; instead, his assistant pastor, Michael Hardy, took his place at the podium. I frowned, leaning close to my mother's ear.

"What's wrong with Daddy?" I whispered.

"He's not feeling well," she answered simply and left it at that. Part of me wanted to brush that off as minor, just like my mother had. But another part of me couldn't help the anxious feeling about my parents' discussion later that day. I wasn't sure what was wrong, but it certainly wasn't like my dad to get sick. Or sick enough to the point where he couldn't preach.

As if on cue, Pastor Hardy spoke up, with a slight nod in my dad's direction. "Everyone, unfortunately Pastor Davis isn't feeling the best today so if you don't mind, I have a Word on my heart that I would like to share. Is that all right with you all?" Murmurs of approval with *go on, Pastor*s and amens lifted in the air and died down before he continued. "Pastor, we pray strength and healing over whatever ailments are threatening you at this time. We look forward to hearing the Word of God from you next Sunday." My dad's face seemed to strain against a smile, clearly trying to hide his discomfort.

After the sermon, I remained seated while everyone rose around me to shake hands and exchange pleasantries. My mom had already scurried off to do her First Lady duties before seeing about my dad, and now I just waited so I could make my exit last, without the spotlight.

"Kimmy."

I swallowed a groan at the voice. So much for no spotlight. Turning, I stood as Tonya Price made her way in my direction, taking up nearly all of the aisle with her robust frame. She dabbed a napkin at the beads of sweat pearling her brow and gave me a huge smile, her eyes nearly disappearing behind the folds of her cheeks. "I thought that was you." Tonya leaned in and enfolded me in a hug riddled with sweat. I cringed. With Tonya, everything was a production. "Lord, girl, it's been a little minute, hasn't it?

You just don't care about us little people since you done got all high and mighty, huh?"

I chuckled at the awkward question. "Nothing like that. And I haven't gotten high or mighty at all."

"Please." Tonya used the napkin to slap the air as if dismissing my comment. "Word around town is you done came into some big, big money. Some settlement for killing your husband or something, right?" I didn't bother responding, and it was clear Tonya wasn't looking for one. She just kept right on talking. "When they told me that the pastor's daughter had gotten caught up in some kind of murder–ménage à trois foolishness, I knew it couldn't be. I tried to tell everyone no. Not Kimmy Davis. That Kimmy Davis is a good girl and wouldn't be involved in the devil's work." She stood back and eyed me up and down, her eyes narrowed in consideration. "But it looks like I may have been wrong. Looks like you done came into a whole lotta foolishness and it paid off."

"Ms. Price—"

"Oh, no judgment, suga." Tonya's smile returned, and she tossed me a little wink. "The way I see it, you do what you gotta do and no one ain't got no right to say nothin' 'bout nothin', ya hear me? That's between you and the Good Lord above." She lifted her hand to the sky and nodded. "Yes, hallelujah, glory be to His Name. He's the only one who can judge us for our sins here. He's the only one you need to answer to, ya hear me? I ain't got a Heaven nor Hell to put you or anyone else in." When she took the opportunity to throw her head back and laugh as if she had made a joke, I gave her arm a slight pat.

"Ms. Price, it's always good to see you, but—"

"Oh, I know, suga, you need to go see about your daddy." Tonya's face wrinkled in apparent concern. "He's probably torn up about the sale. I sure hate that too, because that is one anointed man of God, I tell ya."

I paused, picking over the woman's words. "The sale?"

Tonya nodded, her large pin curls bobbing with the brisk movement. "I've seen this church grow over the years. Remember I was one of the first members who joined your daddy's church. Every time your daddy preached he brought the Holy Ghost power in here."

I nodded, masking my confusion. "What do you mean 'the sale,' Ms. Price?"

"Oh, the church. Your daddy's having to sell the place. Announced it last week, bless his poor soul. I hate it has come to this."

"Wait a minute." I'm sure my shock was now registering on my face. What the hell was she talking about? And why hadn't my parents told me?

Tonya must have realized she had said too much, because her eyes ballooned and she quickly covered her mouth with a pudgy hand. "I'm so sorry. That wasn't my place. I just assumed . . ." She quickly glanced side to side before stepping closer and attempting to lower her voice. "Listen. No matter what anyone around here says, none of this is your fault, ya hear me? None of it." She pecked my cheek and made a hasty retreat back up the aisle, leaving me even more confused.

<hr />

I eased my car into the driveway and shut off the engine. Once more, I picked up the real estate agent's card and glanced at the phone number. I was tempted to go ahead and call to put an offer on the table. Very tempting.

Since I figured my parents would probably be held up at the church for a while entertaining someone who couldn't stop running their mouth, I had taken the opportunity to detour to one of the townhomes I had seen for sale online. I wasn't even really sure I wanted to purchase it, but it was close to my parents and in a nice neighborhood. Plus, with just me and the baby, the 2,068 square feet, four bedrooms, three and a half baths seemed just the right size. Of course I could afford bigger. Leo's money had made certain of that. But remembering the massive mansion that had become my home, and later my prison, during our relationship was enough to have me steering clear altogether. Sure, the space was a luxury, but one I could easily live without.

I had wheeled my car around the neighborhood for a moment, taking in the new construction brick exteriors, the saltwater pool, the playground with its monkey bars and plastic tubular slides glistening in the afternoon sun. The unit for sale was in the cul-de-sac at the end of a long, winding street. That was a plus at least.

I had pulled in front of the garage and called the agent on the yard sign, and she had met me at the home within twenty minutes. And she came ready for the sale. She showed me all the bells and whistles the place had to offer, from the brand-new concrete floors, stainless steel appliances, and massive master bedroom with the adjoining sitting room and mini balcony overlooking the fenced backyard. I had even pictured Jamaal's nursery in the bedroom right across from mine. Even the owner's contemporary furniture matched my style, and I had asked could I purchase that as well. Shit, might as well make it easy on everyone.

By the time we left, I was 50 percent sold on dropping the $345,000 on the home. Well, maybe 49 percent. The other 51 percent—I had to admit it was the majority—I was wanting to know what Jahmad thought about it. Sure, things had been better between us, but his position on whether I should or should not get the house was the determining factor in our relationship. And part of me was hoping and praying he would be adamantly against it. That, at least, would let me know he was ready for me to finally move in and we could raise this baby together.

I stuffed the agent's card in my purse on a sigh. I would discuss it with him later. For now, I had to see what urgent business was going on with my parents. And, most important, get answers to all this gossip Tonya had been talking about at church.

At first glance, the pearl white Infiniti truck didn't appear out of place. Black rims and dark tint made the truck more conspicuous, sure, but it seemed just as casually parked as all of the other vehicles against the curb in this neighborhood. No, the thing that had me lifting an eyebrow was I could have sworn I had seen that same truck at the property I had just left. I stared at the truck a little longer, trying to detect if I could see a little movement through the windshield. Nothing. I was probably drawing false conclusions. Had I even seen the truck in the other neighborhood? Now I couldn't even be sure.

I found my mom in the kitchen, wrist-deep in water in the sink, pulling the leaves of collards off the stems. I slid a hip on the counter, my arms crossed over my breasts, as I watched her fingers work. When she made no move to speak first, I volunteered my own news.

"I'm looking to maybe buy this place up the street," I told her. "Nice little townhome for me and the baby. Spacious enough for us and a good price."

"I'm happy for you, sweetie," she said, though her voice clearly did not reflect her happiness. She sniffed and I frowned, now noticing the glimmer of tears trailing down her face. My mind flipped to the conversation with that loudmouth Tonya Price at church. Maybe there was some truth to the gossip.

"Is this about the church?" I prompted. Mama sighed before letting out a brief nod. My heart fell. "Why didn't you tell me?" I asked. "I mean, what is it? Money? I have—"

"No, Kimmy. This has nothing to do with money." She finally met my eyes. "And I didn't want you to worry. Or feel bad."

"What do you mean?"

My mama patted her hands on the drying towel and turning, leaned up against the counter next to me, her arm bumping up against mine. "Membership is down. It's been like that for a few months now. That mess that happened with you . . . People are just . . ." She trailed off, gauging my reaction.

It was starting to make sense. This was all about me. Me and my dumb decisions. Of course, my poly relationship had been plastered all up and down every newspaper, and then when I had been accused of Leo's murder, the story broke on every piece of local media. I still cringed at the stories: "Daughter of Prominent Pastor Accused of Killing Polygamous Husband." It was downright embarrassing enough for me, but even more so when they dragged my folks into my mess. And now, the domino effect. People were pulling out of my dad's church. They wanted to go elsewhere, without the public scandal.

Now it was my turn to sigh, letting the truth sink in and pierce my heart. If I didn't feel horrible before, I damn sure did now.

"I have to talk to Daddy."

My mom shook her head. "No, he's resting. But he definitely didn't want you to feel like any of this was your fault."

I let out a snarky chuckle, her words the exact echo of Tonya's. That was easier said than done. "So he's going to what? Step down? Just . . . sell the church and do what?"

My mom's shoulder lifted and fell. "He hasn't finalized all the details yet, but yeah, that's what it looks like."

"What are we supposed to do?"

"*We* are not going to worry about it," my mom said, her voice firm. "We are going to let go and let God. We are going to let your dad decide to do what's best, and we are going to completely support whatever he decides. I trust your father's judgment."

I nodded, the idea making the most sense but still leaving a sour taste in my mouth. "I just wish none of this shi—" I coughed, catching myself. "—stuff even mattered anymore. I thought we were past all of this."

My mom nodded. "It's behind us, Kimmy." She patted my

shoulder with comfort neither of us felt. "We are not going to let what happened haunt us. It's done. We are going to move forward. You hear me?"

I pursed my lips, thinking about the church, the child support, Leo, and his note. No, I didn't hear her. It was already haunting me. And it looked to be getting worse.

Chapter 6

The knock on my door had me looking up and grinning in relief to see my dad in the doorway. My grin fell when I saw him lean against the wall, and I quickly ran to his side and grabbed his arm.

"Daddy, you're not feeling better?"

"It's this bug," he said, groaning his discomfort as he hobbled to my bed. "Can't keep anything down. No appetite."

"You need to go to the doctor."

"It's nothing," he insisted. "I'm actually doing a lot better."

I took in his ashen complexion, his unshaven beard, his weakened posture, the plaid pajama pants and long-john shirt. The man was clearly lying, but I nodded anyway to appease him.

"You know they say men get pregnancy symptoms when their women are pregnant," I teased.

"Who's pregnant? Your mother?" He mustered enough strength to laugh at my joke. "You almost made me say something unpastorlike, baby girl."

"What are you doing out of bed anyway?" I asked, sliding a look at the clock.

He gestured toward the car seat I had resting on the bed. "Your mom told me they called you and said they can discharge the baby today."

I smiled, unable to contain my excitement. "They did." And because I was sure he was wondering, I added, "We are probably going to just take him to Jahmad's place, Daddy. I know you're not feeling well and—"

"Oh, yeah, yeah I know." He nodded his understanding. "That's actually what I was going to suggest. Because we both know when I get better that grandboy of mine is going to be by my side at all times."

I laughed. "Yes, I already know."

My dad waited while I continued tossing some items in a suitcase. No, Jahmad hadn't explicitly extended the invite, but he was crazy if he thought I was sleeping anywhere but his house now that my son would be there temporarily. I say temporarily because my own home was still on the table. I planned on bringing up that discussion when we talked later.

I debated whether I wanted to bring up my mother's news from last week. She had insisted I just leave it alone, but still . . .

"Daddy, I'm sorry," I blurted helplessly. "About the church. About everything. I really wish you wouldn't let what happened affect your ministry. That was my mistake, not yours. And it's not fair."

My dad's eyes lowered, but I caught the glimpse of sadness he tried to mask. "It's nothing to apologize for, baby girl. The last thing I want to do is bring reproach on the gospel. Or do anything to taint the Word. And if my personal life can affect bringing people closer to God, well then, I would rather remove myself from the equation. The path is already narrow. People don't need distractions."

The truth stung. Bad. As much as it made sense, I still hated what this had come to.

"May I ask a favor of you, baby girl?"

"Of course, Daddy. Anything."

"Why don't you volunteer down at the church?" He held up a hand to stop me before I could respond. "Just hear me out. This new young man approached me out the blue a few weeks ago about volunteering. Said God led him to me. And it really got me thinking about some things. Despite all the rumors, the gossip and foolishness, at the end of the day, we are still making a difference. We are still doing God's work. And however the chips fall with the church, we are still a family. A united front that won't be ripped apart with scandal. And even if it's time to transition to other ventures, we want to show people we will do it together, and none of the stories will change that. Now I know you're busy with your store and now Jamaal, but I really think—"

"Daddy. You don't have to convince me," I said with a laugh. "I sure will. Especially if you think it'll help."

"Well, even if it doesn't, I want to make sure and leave with the same impression we started with."

He was right. I remembered Keon, my mother, and I had been right by my dad's side faithfully when he first started his pastoral journey. He had said those same words then. A family. A united front under God. Somewhere along the way, I had lost sight of that. Hell, somewhere along the way I had lost myself.

———◦——

"He came back."

I was expecting Shaun's bubbly attitude as I strolled up to the NICU front desk, but her words seemed to stop me in my tracks. Her expression was one of pure concern as she glanced around before beckoning me closer.

"He came back," she repeated with a concerned frown. "The guy I was telling you about."

I nodded, my own eyes darting around the empty lobby. I half expected to see Leo there, peeking around some corner, watching me. Thank God Jahmad hadn't arrived just yet, but he had agreed to meet me here to pick up JayJay, so I knew he couldn't be too far. "When?" I asked, turning back to Shaun.

"About an hour ago."

"Did you call the police?"

"No, he didn't come in this time." Shaun nodded her head in the direction of the windows, the shades drawn open to reveal the afternoon sun shining brilliantly on the parking lot. "I saw him walking outside. I thought it was him but I wasn't a hundred percent sure. So I took my break and went to see. He was kind of far, but when he saw me looking, he turned and got in the car with somebody and they drove off. Who is he? Do I need to tell security?"

I quickly shook my head. "No. Jamaal is being discharged today so we won't worry about it. Let me just get my baby out of here."

Shaun's face still carried the worry I felt, her eyes sliding to the windows again. "Do you think you need to get some kind of restraining order?"

I actually had thought about it. But how the hell would I explain that to my parents? Jahmad? As far as anyone knew, Leo was dead, killed in the hit-and-run arranged by his first wife, Tina. No one, not even Adria, knew he had told me he'd faked his death, and certainly not that he'd been sending me money. With the scandal rocking my dad's church and the delicate relationship between Jahmad and me, the last thing I wanted to do was stir up trouble. Or suspicion.

"It's fine," I lied, feigning a smile. "Let's just keep this between us, okay? I'll handle it." I had to remember Shaun was new in town. She knew nothing about my sordid celebrity status. And it was better that way. "I know one thing." I quickly changed the subject before either one of us could dwell on the issue any further. "I'm certainly going to enjoy not having to drive up here to see my baby. I can just roll over and watch him sleep right there at the house."

Shaun relaxed at the comment. "Enjoy it, girl. Because when he turns one, you won't have another moment of peace until high school graduation."

I smiled, looking forward to that. "You still coming to the grand opening, right?"

"Of course. Wouldn't miss it." She leaned up and gave me a hug across the desk. "You sure you don't want to trade?" she teased. "I take my baby Jamaal and you get a buy-one-get-one deal with the twins."

"So tempting," I said with a wink. Shit, I knew they would find my ass in a straitjacket singing nursery rhymes to myself if I had two kids right about now.

Jamaal's nurse had him ready as soon as I walked in. I fed him first before she helped me change him into a cute onesie outfit with the phrase "Hide your daughters. I have arrived" written across the front; a gift from his aunt Adria, of course. I snuggled his hat on his head, and he had just dozed off as I wrapped him in a blanket and lifted him in my arms.

Jahmad had been sitting, waiting patiently, and he rose as I reentered the lobby. I took slow, soft steps so as not to wake Jamaal, but I wanted nothing more than to run into Jahmad's arms while he held us both. In due time.

It was as if a switch had been flipped, the way Jahmad's face filled with such tender love as his eyes rested on the bundle in my arms. "May I?" he said, holding out his arms. I smiled and carefully transferred Jamaal to him. "Hey, little man," he cooed. "We have been waiting for you, son."

I felt my phone vibrating, but I quickly ignored it. No one was about to intrude on this precious moment. "The car seat is in my car," I said, readjusting the strap on the diaper bag. "I'll bring the car around and follow you home."

"Sounds good," Jahmad murmured, not bothering to look up. He just continued to stare lovingly into his son's face. I grinned and took in the image for a moment longer. Between my parents and Jahmad, apparently I was going to have a little competition on my hands for my baby's time. Which was fine by me. Jamaal was certainly loved, and we all would have no problems expressing it.

My phone vibrated again as I started across the parking lot to my car. Somewhat annoyed at the disturbance, I pulled the device from my purse and eyed the screen, frowning at the number I didn't recognize. I swiped to decline the call, and almost immediately, it started up again. My frown deepened, the vibration notification sending a slight tremble through my fingers and up my wrist. Maybe it was Adria, calling from Jamaica. I knew that was a stretch, even as the thought entered my mind. This time, I swiped to accept the call and brought the phone to my ear.

He didn't have to say a word for me to know it was him. My breath caught in my throat as I listened to the tense silence, and I willed my heartbeat to slow down. "What do you want, Leo?" I whispered, hating myself when my words seemed labored over my trembling breath.

"Where is he?"

I stood still, my back to the hospital, the sun silhouetting my frame. I caught my panicked expression in the window of my car.

"Why are you doing this?" I asked. "You said you would leave me alone."

"I tried. But you have my son. You and he are part of me, my love. Don't you get it?"

"He's not yours." I had to believe it. For all of our sakes.

"You still look just as beautiful as I remember, my love."

I stilled at the comment, and the hairs on the back of my neck stood up straight. It wasn't just his voice now. It was his presence.

Slowly, I pulled the phone from my ear as his reflection came into focus through the car window, standing behind and just off to the side of me.

My whole body trembled, despite the fearful heat that coursed through my body. When his hand lifted to touch my shoulder, I snatched back, dropping my purse and diaper bag in the process. I pressed my back against the car door, not wanting to meet his gaze.

"You need to leave," I said, my voice pleading. If Jahmad saw . . . if he knew Leo was here . . .

"Where is he?" Leo's eyes slid to the back seat, eyed the empty car seat. He then looked behind himself to the hospital.

"Just leave, Leo. Please. I'll bring him to you another time."

"Today?"

Like hell. My mind flipped through lie after lie until it settled on the most believable. "They didn't release him today. But when they do, I'll call you."

"Put me on the list. I just want to see him."

"He's not yours, Leo. Why do you care?"

"He is mine." Why did the solitary comment seem to be so convincing? How could he possibly know for sure?

"We already tested him," I lied again, strengthening my voice for more believability. It didn't work. The doubt marred Leo's face, laced with bits of irritation. I started to push past him, but he grabbed my arm, and I was suddenly thrown back into another time, seemingly another life, one that I had already lived and learned. No matter how strong of a charming accent, how many smooth words he tossed at me, I recognized the strength behind the grip. The strength and the damage. Same old Leo Owusu.

"Bring me my son, Kimera. Or I will get him myself." He shoved me back into the car, the sideview mirror stabbing like a knife into my back. I recoiled at the pain, grateful when he just walked away and left me alone.

Quickly, I gathered my stuff from the ground where I had dropped it earlier and jumped in the car. I peered through the window, scanning the rows of cars, but I didn't see Leo. Nor could I be sure where he had gone. I just hoped and prayed he wouldn't see me drive to the front of the hospital nor see Jahmad emerge with a baby I had insisted should still be in NICU.

I wheeled the car to the front, but instead of waiting for Jahmad to bring him out, I unhooked the car seat and carried it inside. Jahmad was seated in one of the lobby chairs, and as I walked up, he glanced behind him to the windows. I paused. Had he seen what had gone down in the parking lot?

"Can you take him in your car?" I asked, fixing my voice so the request was as innocent as possible. "My 'check engine' light just came on, and I don't want to chance anything with JayJay in the car." Jahmad nodded, his face neutral. Did he believe me?

I set the car seat on a nearby chair and watched as he placed the baby gently inside. He moved slowly and precisely, his fingers careful over the snaps and buckles as he took his time securing Jamaal's tiny body.

"It's probably nothing," I murmured at his continued silence. The quiet was making me even more uneasy. "Just want to be sure first before I ride with him."

"I get it," Jahmad said as he grabbed the carrier's handle. "Want to be on the safe side. Anything can happen, right?"

I didn't know if there was a subtext in the comment or if it was my own guilt, but for some reason, I didn't like the way he said that statement.

I merely nodded and walked away first. I would have to fix my issue with Jahmad later. Right now I had to be careful, just in case Leo was somewhere watching. And as a precaution I needed to leave the hospital exactly as I wanted it to appear to be. Coincidentally that was exactly how I felt: alone.

Chapter 7

It took a few days, but I finally mustered up enough courage to approach Jahmad. Walking around the house, just remaining cordial while we both occupied our time with work and Jamaal was enough to make anyone insane. Don't get me wrong, tending to my baby was rewarding enough and it did keep me distracted from my own personal issues. But while he was sleeping, it gave me time to reflect on the awkward tension that filled the house, filled the space between us, and the void was more prevalent than ever before, especially when Jahmad didn't try to dissuade me from sleeping on the futon in Jamaal's nursery while he slept in his room alone.

I laid Jamaal down in his crib and, as usual, I stood quietly staring at him. A sliver of moonlight shone through the cracked blinds and cast a dim glow onto his angelic face. A face that looked so much like mine. His lips were parted to let in tiny breaths that had his chest rising and falling in quick succession.

I glanced at the Superman clock on the wall. A quarter until eight. Still early. While I knew I should be getting some sleep for the next four hours before Jamaal woke up for his feeding, I was even more anxious to finally talk to Jahmad. I knew I wouldn't be able to sleep if I didn't.

I belted my satin robe and left the room, leaving the door slightly ajar behind me. Murmured noises from a TV echoed from downstairs, so I made my way to the living room on the main floor.

Sure enough, Jahmad was propped up on the couch wearing only a t-shirt and sweat pants. The light from the TV show illuminated his chiseled arms, and I couldn't help but take him in for a bit. The man was still as sexy as ever. And the fact that he hadn't touched me since he made dinner for me last week was enough to stir my restrained desire.

Jahmad looked up from the phone in his hand and tossed a casual look in my direction. I smiled, hoping to appear as if I had just come in the room and hadn't been standing there staring at him like some mindless dummy.

"Hey, you," I greeted, taking a seat on the leather loveseat opposite him.

Jahmad yawned and used his head to gesture to the ceiling. "Is he okay?"

"Yeah, he's asleep for now."

For a while, only the TV and gentle snores from the baby monitor filled the silence in the room. On a sigh, I turned to Jahmad, whose attention was back to something on his cell phone.

"You feel like talking?" I asked him, dreading but needing to address the elephant in the room. Jahmad obviously knew it too, because he set his phone on the coffee table and adjusted himself to a seated position on the couch. "I found a house," I started. I kept my eyes focused on him, attempting to judge every breath, every blink in his reaction. "Not far from my parents' house. Nice neighborhood, and just enough space for me and Jamaal. I wanted to get your thoughts."

Jahmad seemed lost in thought for a brief moment before he spoke up. "Kimmy, I want you to do what you got to do. If you're trying to guilt me—"

"I'm not trying to do anything," I snapped, suddenly angry because he knew that was exactly what I was trying to do. "I'm just saying this is an important decision that affects all of us. Not just me. We have Jamaal to think about. Excuse the hell outta me for trying to be considerate, Jahmad."

Jahmad rubbed his hand over his beard, an obvious display of his frustration, but I didn't care. Shit, I was frustrated too. He was making this more difficult than it needed to be.

I took a breath and tried a different tactic. "Baby, listen," I said, my voice softer. "I want us to be in this together. You know how I feel about us, and you know I want us to make this work, but I don't want to pressure you. What do you want, Jahmad?" I didn't realize I was holding my breath until my chest tightened. I released it through clenched teeth, praying he gave the response I was hoping for.

"Who was that in the parking lot, Kimera?"

Shit. That was definitely not the response I was hoping for. "Who?" It was a weak stall but a stall nonetheless. I averted my eyes as my mind went into overdrive, fumbling for a realistic answer other than the truth.

"The parking lot," he repeated as if I hadn't heard him. "At the hospital. You were taking so long and I looked out the window to see you having a conversation with some dude."

I tried to lace as much agitation into my sigh as possible. "Is that what this is about?" I asked. "Because some guy was trying to talk to me? Really, Jahmad?"

"So you didn't know who that was?" His voice was softer now, like he wanted to believe me. But still, those traces of doubt I heard had me rising and moving to sit next to him. I sat close, our thighs touching, and I rested my chin on his shoulder.

"I don't know what's wrong with us," I murmured. "But I know I want us to get back on track. I want to be with you and only you, Jahmad. I want Jamaal to grow up with both of us. I want that happily ever after like my brother and Adria. Like my parents. Is that too much to ask?"

"I'm being considered for a promotion," Jahmad said simply.

I pulled back in confusion. Where the hell had that come from? "Okay," I said speaking carefully. "Congratulations."

"It's back in Texas."

I felt my temper rising as he waited, one second, then two, all the while watching for my reaction. Good, because I was damn sure about to give him what I knew he was expecting. "And you're actually considering this, Jahmad? What the hell?"

"It's not just an easy decision like that, Kimera." His calm attitude only heightened my anger, and I stood to pace the living room.

"The hell it's not. What about me? What about Jamaal?" Now I was full-blown yelling and I didn't care.

"Kimmy, lower your voice." Jahmad glanced at the baby monitor, appearing satisfied when the sleeping noises continued coming through the speaker. "I have been thinking about you and the baby. That's what's been on my mind for a few weeks now."

"Why didn't you tell me then?"

"Because look how you're acting."

I crossed my arms over my breasts, my lips in a pout, because, dammit, he was right. But still, I had a right to be angry. "I don't see how this is even a consideration," I snapped. "I mean, damn, what's in Texas?"

"It's a good opportunity," Jahmad said. "One that I wanted before I moved back here. I would be lying if I said I haven't been considering it."

I rubbed my hands through my short hair, cupped them on my neck, willing myself to calm down. I inhaled, then slowly released a breath, expecting the best but preparing myself for the worst. "So?" I spoke carefully. "What are you going to do?"

Jahmad waited a beat, then shrugged. "Like I said, it's a lot to think about. And I don't have to make any type of decision now because we don't even know if they're going to offer me the job. I'm just in the running for it."

"But what if they offer it to you? Then what, Jahmad?"

He stood now and, crossing to me, placed his hands on my forearms. "Then we'll cross that bridge when we get to it," he said. I sure as hell was not comforted by those words. That meant it was still a possibility. His ass should have been trying to convince me he didn't want the job, had no intentions of taking it, had already told them to hell with the position because he had his family here, namely his girlfriend and son. What the hell was there to cross? There shouldn't have even been a fucking bridge to come to.

"I know you just mentioned the house you found," he went on at my continued silence. "And if you want it, I won't stop you. But I've been tossing another idea around. Since Jamaal is home, I really don't want to be shuffling him back and forth. At least not now. Spend the night here, spend the night there. I want him to have that stability of a two-parent household. So how about you stay here with us."

I sighed. Not exactly the rationale I wanted to hear, but at least we had agreed for me to move in. I just couldn't help the disappointment that he wasn't thinking about me, Kimera his girlfriend, but Kimera his child's mother. We still hadn't addressed the main issue. What about us?

But perhaps with me living here, Jahmad would remember all that, would be reminded that I'm the one for him, forgetting all that shit in the past. Maybe then he would be encouraged to forget that damn job offer altogether because he saw how good we were together as a family. It was what I wanted for sure, and I knew it was what he wanted, no matter how hard he tried to pretend different.

I nodded my agreement. I sure as hell would move in and

spend my time working on getting us back to where we needed to be. After a few months, I was sure I would have this man dropping to his knee and having me looking at wedding dresses. There was no doubt in my mind.

⇒•⇐

With everything going on, I didn't realize how much I had missed my girl until she breezed through the door and threw her arms around me. She smelled of the sand and sea, and she still carried etches of the islands in her crochet halter top-and-pants suit, showing her sun-kissed complexion and tiger-like stripes of the tan lines from her bathing suit.

I stood back and noted the grin splitting Adria's face; she must've eaten damn good because she looked like she brought back a few extra pounds with her. She was certainly glowing, and it looked amazing on her.

"I'm so glad you're back," I said, and I meant it. She had come over to watch Jamaal while I ran some errands, but now I didn't want to leave. We had so much to catch up on.

"Girl, I'm glad to be back," she said and flipped her curly bangs from her face. I was loving the natural look on her loose, kinky curls that framed her round face. "You know I brought something for you and my nephew." Adria offered me a shopping bag, and I accepted it with a slight groan.

"Adria, you know you didn't have to do that."

"Shut up. Don't tell me what to do with my money." She looped her arm through mine and steered me to the living room where I had work papers strewn across the coffee table and my laptop on the couch where I had been diligently working before she rang the doorbell.

Jamaal lay in his swing, a pacifier in his mouth, his eyes seemingly engaged by the flickering images from the muted TV, though it was probably all a blur to him.

Adria made a beeline in his direction, already fumbling with the buckles to unhook him from the seat. "How is my baby, huh?" She lifted him into her arms. "Did you miss Auntie? You missed Auntie, didn't you?"

"How was Jamaica?" I asked.

"Fun. Beautiful. And exhausting," Adria admitted. She sat down, snuggling the baby tight in her arms. "What about you? What's new? Where's Jahmad?"

I didn't realize I'd released the heavy breath I'd been holding.

"Aw, hell." Adria stopped rocking the baby as worry creased her forehead. "I don't like the sound of that."

Yeah, and I didn't like forming my lips to speak on this foolishness either. "It's just one thing after another," I admitted. "We are so up and down and all over the damn place, Adria. And just when I think we're good, he springs some bullshit on me out the blue that's got me questioning whether this man even loves me at all."

"Girl, you make it sound like some *Young and the Restless* shit. What did he say?"

For some reason, reflecting on his words again, his seemingly nonchalant attitude about me and our whole dilemma, had tears stinging my eyelids. I couldn't bear the thought of losing this man again.

I had a brief flashback of my brother announcing Jahmad was moving to Texas all those years ago. Keon just mentioned it so casually over dinner, and my heart had stopped. No, Jahmad and I weren't in any type of official relationship. Hell, we weren't even sex buddies like we had been before. I was only in love with him and that idiot just hadn't realized. Or if he had, he hadn't cared.

So imagine how distraught I was when he returned last year engaged. And so was I, for that matter, but I was in it for the money. Jahmad was in it for love, and that hurt, knowing someone else had captured his heart.

But that was then and this was now. He had broken up with CeeCee for me, which proved he did love me. But could I say that now? Would he even be considering leaving if I still had his heart?

"He's being considered for this job back in Texas," I murmured, trying my best to make the news sound more minor than it felt.

"Are you kidding me?" Adria's elevated tone had Jamaal flinching in her arms, and she quickly soothed him again. "No, for real, are you fucking kidding me?" she repeated, her tone lower. "Since when is this a thought? Keon ain't said nothing about it."

I shrugged. "Keon may not know. Or if he did, girl, y'all have your own business to tend to. Not sitting up worrying about me and Jay. And he said it was just a consideration," I added, trying to make myself feel better. "Nothing's set in stone."

"He has you and a child here. What the hell is there to even consider?"

My thoughts exactly, but I couldn't let Adria send me into a panic. She shared my feelings on the issue, and rightfully so. If no one else had my back, Adria did. But if I fed into these crazy-ass emotions, I wouldn't be able to do shit but worry. And that couldn't be my focus right now. I had a child and a business to take care of.

"He asked me to move in," I added, trying to defuse the conversation. "So I'll be over here now."

"Until when? He decides to move again?" Adria snapped, shaking her head. "I swear. Men ain't shit."

I couldn't help it. The scowl on her face, the anger I could tell was brewing had me laughing out loud. She was dead serious.

"Men ain't shit?" I echoed, relaxing into more laughter. "Says the newlywed fresh from her Caribbean honeymoon."

Adria smirked. "Keon ain't shit either. Hell, none of them are. You have to just settle on the least 'ain't shit' ones and deal with it."

"Okay, and how was your trip with your 'ain't shit' husband?"

And just like that, the angry tension over the Jahmad conversation was done. I listened to Adria gush over the way Keon had wined and dined her the entire time. He had even managed to get her big ass on a jet ski—her words, not mine. Each new memory she spoke of had her face lit, radiating that glow of a woman genuinely happy and in love. I smiled as I listened, knowing now would probably not be a good time to mention Leo like I had thought. It felt good to just sit and laugh, carefree, with my best friend. Why ruin it? Because I knew when and if I did mention how Leo wasn't really dead, had been sending me child support, how he was stalking me, demanding to see my son, how now I was afraid what this man was capable of because it certainly didn't seem like he was going away, I knew all hell was about to break lose.

Chapter 8

I stared at the computer screen, but my mind was everywhere but the company website mock-up I should have been reviewing.

It had been like that for days now. I was just going through the motions. Before, I had tried to use work as a crutch, a welcome distraction so I could keep my mind off my personal issues. But since Adria had been back, she'd dived headfirst back into preparing for our grand opening and taking control of a lot of the responsibilities. "You should be spending time with Jamaal," she kept insisting. And she was right, but still. Between my mom and me, we were able to handle watching Jay all day. But when I was home alone with nothing but the baby to keep me company, I was so immersed in my own thoughts it was depressing. And after what I'd found last night, I didn't need to be alone with my thoughts or I might do something crazy.

Over the past few days, I had slowly made my way into sleeping in Jahmad's bed. That at least was a plus, but, hell, it might as well have been separate rooms. He wasn't rude or anything. Just . . . cordial. Polite. Like I was just a roommate and nothing more. There was no cuddling, no kissing.

It started last night with me trying to have sex. My body was on fire and I felt starved. Damn, I needed this man and his hands on me. But he had made me feel so ashamed, like I was trying to rape him or some shit, I knew I wouldn't have the nerve to try again.

"Kimmy, come on now." He had looked up at me, a frown marring his handsome face. "It's late."

I had been on top, straddling his waist, the slinky lingerie I'd purchased sliding down my shoulders, revealing plenty of skin for my intentions. "What do you mean, Jahmad?" I asked, trying to keep the frustration from my voice.

"I mean, it's late. I'm tired, you're tired. And I'm on JayJay duty tonight." He flipped his eyes toward the baby monitor. "You know he'll be up in a few hours so I need to catch a little bit of sleep."

Trying to change tactics, I massaged his chest and leaned down to kiss him. I could feel his body responding, his bulge hardening between my thighs, so why the hell was he fighting me? "Just let me love you, Jahmad," I whispered before slipping my tongue between his lips.

For a brief moment, it felt like he would cooperate, and I deepened the kiss. But then he pulled back and turned a bit, nudging me off his body. I slunk to my side of the bed.

"Jahmad. Do you even still love me?" I had asked.

He leaned up and pecked me, not kissed but pecked me on my lips and then my forehead. "Why you asking questions you already know the answer to?"

But did I know the answer to that? Did I really? And as he rolled over again, I watched his back and realized he hadn't answered the question.

Then, to make matters worse, I couldn't sleep, so I'd gotten up to check on Jamaal. He was sleeping just fine, just like Jahmad. Apparently my mind was the only one keeping me awake.

I had come back into the master bedroom to find Jahmad's phone illuminating the darkened room. I glanced at the clock next to the phone on the nightstand, narrowed my eyes at the digits flipping to 11:23 p.m.

I tried to swallow the suspicion, but my feet carried me closer to his side of the bed. By now, his screen was black again, but still the missed call notification light blinked in the corner of the phone. I looked at Jahmad, still sleeping soundly, and without another thought, I swiped a quick finger over the screen to bring the device back to life.

Two missed calls and a text message I couldn't read. The contact had been saved as "Baby" with a heart emoji. I stepped back, not knowing if I wanted to cry or take the bedside lamp and bash it over his damn head. Either way, I had slept in the baby's room, and as soon as morning light broke, I'd called my mother and asked if she could come over and babysit so I could work from the store today. She'd known something was wrong, but she didn't ask, and I hadn't volunteered.

Now, it was nearing ten a.m., I had this website to review and return to the designer, an interview for a cashier coming in at lunch, model calls this afternoon, and I hadn't done a damn thing but harp on the same question over and over until it burned in my brain. Who the hell was Jahmad's "baby"? The second thought, which probably hurt even worse, was that Jahmad was back to his cheating, womanizing ways. He hadn't changed a damn bit. And damned if it didn't hurt. My love, *our* love was not enough to keep him out of another woman's arms.

The knock on my door snapped me from my mini nervous breakdown, and I blinked back tears. I put on a professional face, hoping to mask the sadness. It was futile, I knew, because if it was Adria on the other side of the door, she would be able to tell easily.

"Come in."

Thank God. It was Tyree. Adria and I had agreed that the man had been doing such a good job that now that she was back, he needed to stay on as the store manager. Neither of us had to worry about much because we knew Tyree had it. He was truly a god-send.

He stepped into my office, a folder in one hand, a glass of wine in the other. "You looked like you could use this, boo," he said, setting the glass on my desk.

I couldn't help but chuckle. "It's ten in the morning."

"I know I should've brought it by earlier," he said before handing me the folder. "Your interview is here."

I took the folder, not realizing I had let a heavy sigh slip from my lips.

"You know what? How about I take care of this for you?" Tyree said gently.

I looked up, grateful. Lord knows I didn't feel like interviewing. Or really doing anything other than sitting alone in my office wallowing in my sorrows. "You sure, Tyree? I can—"

"Chile, I got it." He took the folder back. "No problem. Let me be the store manager. You, you just sit there and look pretty, boo."

Now I knew he was teasing because as hastily as I'd thrown on some jeans and a blouse, not even a lick of makeup, I knew I looked anything but. Still, the compliment had me grinning anyway.

Tyree left me, and I took a grateful sip of the white wine, letting the flavors settle on my tongue.

Picking up my cell, I dialed my mother's number for the third time that morning.

"He's fine, Kimmy," she greeted. "I told him Mommy wouldn't be able to go long without checking in again."

I smirked. "What is he doing?"

"I was going to have him change the oil in my car. What do you think he's doing, sweetheart? He eats and sleeps. These are the golden years, so if I were you, I would enjoy. You won't get more until after he turns thirty."

"Well, tell him Mommy said hey and I love him."

"Say 'hey, Mommy,'" she cooed, and I could hear him sucking

on his bottle. My smile widened, picturing his large, curious stare at the phone my mom was probably holding to his face.

"I'll be leaving here soon," I said, glancing at the clock on my wall. Not even noon yet.

"Don't rush on my account," my mom insisted. "I checked in with your father. He's at home resting and says he's fine. So we're good here."

"Is Daddy any better?" I said, worry filling my voice.

"He's getting better now that I've convinced him to stay home. That man is so stubborn, I swear."

"And here I was thinking Keon and I got it from you."

That startled a laugh from my mom. "Girl, I was about to read you some scripture. Goodbye." I hung up the phone and shook my head. "Read me some scripture" meant curse me out in my mother's language.

I was thankful she seemed to be in better spirits. Both of my parents, actually. Every time I brought up them selling the church, they both would get tight-lipped before shutting down the conversation. But it seemed their decision was final.

Thanks to me, and no, they didn't place blame, but I knew it was absolutely because of me, my dad's church had lost credibility. Even the assistant pastor wanted to venture elsewhere to start his own church, disassociated from them, because everyone felt my poly relationship with Leo was completely hypocritical. What was left of the congregation had already been encouraged to seek other church families to become involved with because my parents would be selling the church building and using the proceeds to fund other congregations to support mission work. My mom did mention there was an interested buyer who wanted to turn the building into a headquarters for international refugee assistance programs, which I guess was a good thing. But it did little to make me feel better, no matter how much my folks tried to shed light on the bright side. "Oh, your dad will be able to enjoy retirement. Oh, it will give us more time to travel and be grandparents. Oh, it was only a matter of time, Kimmy. We knew this time would come sooner or later." Yeah, they both had shared their comfort, and the guilt had been eating me up even worse.

Another knock on my door brought me out of my daze. Tyree strolled back in already shaking his head.

"What?"

"Glad we didn't waste your time with that one, boo." He tossed the folder in my shred pile. "She was most certainly not what we were looking for."

I nodded absently, not really caring. I had three more interviews scheduled for later that week anyway.

Tyree frowned at me. "Is everything okay?"

"Not really," I admitted. Between Jahmad and my parents, I knew I was no good right then. My only reprieve was that I hadn't heard from Leo since the day I brought Jamaal home from the hospital. I really didn't know if that was a good or bad thing, though.

"You should go home," Tyree suggested. "I got things here. Plus I think Mrs. Adria wanted to stop by later."

I nodded. I sure as hell wasn't being productive, that's for sure. That damn number in Jahmad's phone was fresh on my mind. Now I distrusted everything the man was doing or saying. Hell, was he even at work? Part of me wanted to drop by his job just to see for myself. Maybe I could cover it up by pretending I wanted to drop by and bring him lunch. But then again, the mature part of me was afraid of his reaction, more afraid of what I'd find. But curiosity, or was it determination, apparently outweighed that fear because I was already pushing back from the desk. Perhaps I needed to prove not Jahmad wrong but myself.

Jahmad worked on the north side of Atlanta, in a mid-rise IT building nestled among other stuccos in a corporate complex with huge windows and atrium lobbies.

I wheeled my car into the crowded parking area, already scanning the lot for Jahmad's truck. When I didn't see it, I parked, sighing in relief when I read the clearly marked Visitor Parking sign at the entrance. He must be in some off-site employee parking. I grabbed the Subway bag I had stopped to get along the way and headed for the building. I had never been to Jahmad's office but the name of his company along with a simple Google search had me in the right place.

The female security guard at the front desk tossed a bored look in my direction as I breezed through the glass doors.

"Good morning. I'm looking for Jahmad Washington," I said. She waited as if I was supposed to tell her more. I held up the Subway bag. "Just want to bring him lunch."

"Sign in," she instructed, sliding the clipboard in my direction. I did as I was told, scribbling my name on the sheet of paper. A thought crossed my mind, and I looked at the woman's plain face, still sagging with nonchalance.

"Hey, I'm opening up a cosmetic store," I started my pitch while reaching into my purse. "And I'm trying to build up some interest. You know how it can be for us black women." I held out my card in her direction. "Not sure if you're into makeup, but if you are, my grand opening is in two weeks. I would love for you to stop by, and I will definitely give you a discount on some of my products. Even a makeup session if you want." As expected, that had her face brightening as she happily accepted my card.

"Girl, thank you," she gushed. "Yes, I will surely be by. It's so hard to find time to pamper myself as a single mother with four kids."

I nodded my understanding. "Absolutely." Then I went in for the kill by adding, "Would it be too much trouble for you to call and see what floor Mr. Washington is on? Please?"

My plan worked. The little makeup chat had warmed her up,

and she quickly snatched up her desk phone. "Girl, of course. No problem."

I waited patiently as she called around, taking in the light traffic through the lobby. People bustled by in and out of the elevators, heels clicking on the marble floor.

I heard the guard hang up, and I turned to the desk once more. "Sixth floor," she revealed. "But his secretary says he's off today."

The news had my mind flipping back to this morning. Had he said he was off? I remembered him getting ready for work as my mom showed up and I was leaving the house. No, he hadn't said specifically he was going to work. But his work clothes were laid out on the bed, and he was up at six a.m., like usual on a Thursday morning. Where else would he be going?

I thanked the guard for her help and left the building, throwing the food away in a nearby trash can with every ounce of anger I was feeling.

———※◦⟶———

A distant car door slam had me unfolding from the couch and running to the window. Sure enough, Jahmad was getting out of his truck. At 8:26 p.m. at that. He stood outside for a few moments longer, wrapping up a call. And by the look of his smile, obviously a pleasure call. The bastard had some nerve.

I had left his office earlier and had been calling the man nonstop since. The first few times it would ring before going to voicemail until eventually it didn't even ring. He was ignoring me and he had only fueled my anger. Now, the baby was fed and asleep, I had poured one glass of wine too many, so whether I was overreacting or not, Jahmad was about to catch all of this hell.

"Where were you?" I snapped before he had even closed the door behind him.

Jahmad seemed surprised to see me standing there in the entry-way. "Kimmy, what are you talking about?"

"I came to your job today. Call myself being a sweet girlfriend and bringing you lunch," I tossed in there to make it sound good. "And lo and behold, you weren't there. I've been calling you like crazy and you haven't been answering." I heard the slight slur in my words, and obviously he did too because he smirked and shook his head.

"Get some sleep, Kim. We'll talk about this tomorrow."

His nonchalant attitude only heightened my anger. I stood in front of him, jabbing my finger in his chest. "No, we are going to talk about this shit right now. I'm tired of you half-assing this re-lationship."

I heard my phone ring somewhere in the living room, but stub-bornness had my feet planted right in his path.

Jahmad took hold of my wrist, his grip gentle but firm. "Kimera," he spoke calmly. "You need to calm down and sleep off whatever the hell has got you trippin'."

I snatched my arm from his fingers. "Why weren't you at work?"

"I never said I was going to work."

"Well, where were you? With 'baby'?"

I couldn't tell whether the confusion was genuine or an effort to hide his shock that I knew about the mystery caller. "Yeah, I saw your phone last night, Jahmad," I went on, growing even more fu-rious when I felt the hot tears soaking my cheeks. What the hell was I crying for? "You're cheating on me again, aren't you?"

Now it was Jahmad's phone ringing, and he pulled it from his pocket as I barreled on. "Oh, is that your precious baby? Your precious bitch?"

He turned, putting the phone to his ear, and it took everything in me not to beat my fists on his back.

"Hold on," he said and held the phone out to me. "Adria has been looking for you. She says it's an emergency."

I had a few more choice words for Jahmad on the tip of my tongue, but I bit them back and took the phone. "Hey, girl."

"Kimmy, where have you been? I've been calling you like crazy. We have to get down to the store. There was a fire . . ."

Chapter 9

Flames licked the sky, illuminating with bright orange and red that lit up the area like the Fourth of July. A population of spectators collected on the street watching as firefighters worked to hose down the enflamed building. My building. The reality had me choked up. Or perhaps it was the smoke. Either way, I could only watch in horror as the fire ate Melanin Mystique down to charred wood.

Adria had met me on the scene, and she now stood beside me shoulder-to-shoulder with only a jacket over her negligee to shield her skin from the night air.

"Damn, what happened?"

I turned at the panicked voice as Tyree jogged up to stand beside me. Though it was night, he was fully dressed, evidence that he'd come straight over from the club or some nighttime rendezvous.

"I don't know. I was going to ask you. Did you close?"

"No, I did," Adria spoke up, shaking her head in disbelief. "Tyree had plans, so I sent him on early because I knew I had some things to finish up. I left about six-thirty."

My mind flipped to everything inside. Completely destroyed. Every piece of makeup I had hand-selected, spent months finding a place, then stocking everything inside. Hell, it would be another six months or longer before the store was up and running. And I knew I probably should have been more appreciative that no one, especially Adria, had been harmed. But all I could see was our dreams billowing up into thin air like the smoke in front of us.

"Babe." Keon walked up and wrapped his arms around his wife. Instinctively, Adria leaned into his embrace on a sigh. "Maybe we should go sit in the car."

"I'm okay. I think they're going to come talk to us in a little bit."

"Sis, you need anything?" Keon turned to me and reached over to rub my arm. Yeah, Jahmad to comfort me like that, was what I wanted to say. Instead, I just shook my head. That may have been selfish. Jahmad was at home with the baby, as I had insisted. The last thing I wanted to do was wake my mom up this time of night to come see about Jamaal. She would be worried enough as it was because I was sure Keon had already called her.

We stood in silence for a moment longer, the heat from the fire slowly subsiding as the flames were completely extinguished. In their place was a pile of blackened rubble, nothing of which I recognized. And just like that, all our hard work, all our efforts were gone.

"Good evening, folks." The firefighter walked up, a clipboard in hand, soot blackening his face and uniform. His eyes flipped between all of us huddled together. "Who is in charge here?"

"Me," I spoke up and nodded to Adria. "And my best friend Adria here. The place was ours."

"First off, let me say I'm sorry this happened."

"Have you determined the cause?" Adria asked, her voice laced with worry.

The firefighter glanced at the notes on his clipboard. "It's too soon to tell, but it appears like it may have been some electrical wiring that shorted out."

I shook my head in disbelief. "That's impossible," I murmured, almost to myself. "We had the building inspected months ago. Everything was fine."

The man nodded, clearly unsure. "I'm sorry," he said again. "This is just a theory, but the officers will be able to give you more information when they investigate."

"Investigate?" Now it was Keon's turn to speak up, and he stepped forward, almost as if to protect us from whatever truth was slowly being revealed. "What is there to investigate?"

"Just standard procedure," he said with a comforting smile none of us felt. "Probably should just stick around to speak to them so they can wrap it up quickly."

I nodded, not realizing I was shuddering until I wrapped my arms around myself.

My phone vibrated in my pocket and I stepped to the side, pulling it out to view the screen. A little glimmer of relief coursed through me when I saw it was Jahmad.

"How is everything?" he asked as soon as I answered.

I sighed, struggling to keep the tears from falling. "Some kind of electrical fire," I murmured, quoting the firefighter.

"Well, thank God no one was hurt," he said. "Are you out there by yourself?"

He sounded legitimately concerned which, I had to admit, did lift my spirits. A bit. "No, Tyree, Adria, and Keon are here. We are really just waiting around now. They've already put out the fire. I think the police want to talk to us too." I paused before continuing. "Hey, Jahmad, about earlier—"

"Don't worry about all that now," he stated simply. "We'll talk, just not now. Handle your business, and I'll see you later."

I hung up the phone. He was right. As much as I wanted to have that conversation, I couldn't worry right now about Jahmad or his little hush-hush phone calls with some mystery woman.

Again, I turned my attention to the remnants of my dreams lying in a pile of rubble in front of me. For some reason, it felt symbolic. And I knew it wasn't just my business that was crumbling before my eyes.

⟫•◦•⟪

I was so tired that it took a few moments for my eyes to register the white envelope taped to the front door of Jahmad's place. I frowned, eyeing my name scribbled hastily across the front in thick red ink. I didn't even have to open the little package to know it was from Leo. Damn, and here I was thinking he would go on about his business and leave me alone. But no, that was too much to expect from Leo.

I ripped the envelope from the door and shoved it in my purse. Thankfully, Jahmad hadn't seen Leo's little gift.

He had left a hall light on for me, but otherwise, the house was dark and quiet. I carried myself upstairs, peered into the empty master bedroom before making my way to the nursery. The visual had me halting in the doorway on a smile.

Right there, at that very moment with only a sliver of moonlight casting a faint glow on their sleeping faces, right there I could've put money on Jahmad being the father. They looked so much alike, all the way down to their slightly parted lips that had a light snore wafting throughout the room. Jahmad had placed the baby on his back on the futon, surrounded by four pillows to create a makeshift barrier, even though the baby was too young to roll off. Still, the extra precaution was too adorable. Jahmad lay next to the pillows, using one arm to support his head and the other a gentle hand on Jamaal's tummy. Compelled to capture the moment, I pulled out my phone and snapped a picture.

Part of me wanted to wake up Jahmad. I had so much frustration about the whole fire ordeal just sitting like a weight on my chest. Even more, I certainly wasn't done confronting him about my suspicions that he was now trying to reclaim his little playboy card. But my love wouldn't allow me to disturb the peace.

I would have kicked off my shoes and snuggled right there with them, but Jahmad's frame plus the baby pillow wall already dominated the full-size futon mattress. So I just left the door cracked and made my way back into Jahmad's room.

The stench of smoke was heavy and had me quickly peeling out of my clothes and tossing them in a pile on the floor. I caught a quick glimpse of my figure in the mirror, and I sighed at the slight bulge in my belly. Faint stretch marks adorned my stomach and hips, but other than that, I had managed to bounce back to my little pre-pregnancy weight. My finger caressed the thin incision from my C-section.

It pained me to know I had complicated this situation so much. But in my heart of hearts, I wanted to believe Jahmad was Jamaal's father. I wished Leo would just disappear and leave us alone, because I'm sure he didn't want to be a father to my son any more than he had wanted to be to Leo Jr. What was the difference? What was the big damn deal? And why the hell was he so hell-bent on making my life so difficult?

Suddenly remembering, I pulled the envelope from my purse and turned it over in my fingers. I was tempted to just rip up this little check. Maybe that was the hold Leo thought he had over me. But I wasn't the money-hungry little girl he could manipulate and dangle his millions in my face to make me obey. Sure, that was before. But now, now I knew what I deserved. Even still, something pushed me to tear open the flap and pull the contents of the envelope into view.

Not a check. No, not this time. Hesitantly, I unfolded the single sheet of paper, my eyes scanning the contents, trying to decipher the jargon. A lot of it I didn't understand, but one thing was very, very clear as the results fell from my limp fingers: the paper was one sheet of a paternity test. A paternity test for my son. For my son with Leo Owusu.

Chapter 10

"Hello?"

I listened to the breathing on the other end, my panic slowly rising. "Hello?" The word came out in more of a pleading whisper. This was getting out of hand. Ever since I had received the paternity test results, the paper that I had stuffed into an empty purse and shoved to the back of the closet in Jamaal's room, my anxiety level had certainly elevated. All I could think about were the results: 99.6 percent positive that Leo was the father. How the hell had he managed to test my child? And what the hell would Jahmad do if he found out?

I had dismissed the thought as quickly as it had come. That I couldn't let happen. Jahmad and I were already rocky, especially since he was considering this random-ass move to Texas. And whoever he was keekeeing on the phone with the other night, the mysterious "baby" in his contacts, the news of my son would send that man packing quicker than I could manage an apology.

And now this? The fourth call this week from some unknown number that I tried to ignore but would only call and call until I finally answered, only to be met with his heavy breathing. I knew it was Leo. It had to be.

"Leo, stop this," I spoke again, lowering my voice even more.

"Please, I just—" *Click*. I pulled the device from my ear, looking at the screen to confirm the person had indeed disconnected the call.

I thought again about the paper I had hidden, then glanced at my phone where I had saved the picture of Jahmad and Jamaal sleeping as my screensaver. I didn't want to believe, couldn't believe it was true. Leo could fake his own damn death. Surely he could fake some paternity test results.

I shook my head and pushed the thought from my mind. For now, I turned my attention back to my dad. Thank God my mom had finally convinced him to go to the doctor. He claimed he was feeling better, but that wasn't enough to appease my mother, especially when another Sunday rolled around and my dad was still too weak to make it to service.

"He's going to the doctor," she had said. "Even if I have to hog-tie him to the bumper and drag him to the office like some 'Just Married' cans."

I laughed, but knowing my mom was good and serious, I insisted on going with them, more for my dad's sake than anything. He needed someone on his side against my mother.

As if on cue, I spotted Adria's car pulling into the driveway outside of the window. I stooped down to kiss Jamaal on the cheek and smile as he just stared at me, his pacifier moving with each suckle.

"Mommy will be back," I said as if he understood. "Let me go make sure Grandmommy doesn't give Granddaddy a heart attack." Jamaal let out a little gas in response, and I rushed out to meet Adria at the door.

"Your nephew left you a little surprise," I teased, then immediately frowned when I noticed her troubled expression. "What is it?"

Adria stopped on the porch and held up a finger as she continued listening to something, probably a message, on her phone. A few seconds more, and she shook her head and shoved the phone in her pocket.

"What's wrong?" I asked again.

"I'm not sure. That was from the police. Some message about needing more information about the fire."

I shrugged, not sure what else they needed but probably something routine. I didn't see anything strange about that. "Probably just needing to tie up loose ends," I assumed with a wave of my hand. "Especially because of the insurance having to pay for the damages."

Adria nodded slowly. "Yeah, probably," she murmured. "Let me know what happens with Dad. Where's Jahmad?"

"Work," I said, though I wasn't even all that sure anymore. "I guess too we need to come up with a game plan for the store. Got to get everything started again."

Adria sighed, a direct mirror of how I felt. "Damn, I don't feel like doing all that shit over," she admitted. "I mean that was a lot."

I nodded. She was right. And the idea of tackling every single task again, duplicating each and every effort to get this business up and running strong, it was discouraging.

Adria looked like she wanted to say something else, but instead she just nodded. "Let me see what 'surprise' my baby left me," she said with a smirk.

I watched her walk in the house and paused for a moment myself. With everything else that was going on, I hadn't wanted to bring up to Adria my predicament with Leo. At least, that was the excuse I was using for the moment.

By the time I made it to the doctor's office, my dad had already gone back for a battery of tests. The nurse showed me to his room, where my mom was waiting patiently, thumbing through a magazine.

"Anything yet?" I asked, taking a seat in the chair next to her.

"Not yet. Other than him fussing the whole way here. I swear that man gets on my nerves." I could tell she was trying to exaggerate some faux irritation to hide her worry.

"He's fine, Mama," I said, tossing her a comforting smile.

"I'm not about to let your father worry me into an early grave," she said, turning accusatory eyes on me. "Him. Or you."

I frowned. "Me?"

"Keon told me about the fire, Kimera."

I rolled my eyes. Of course he did. "It's no big deal, Mama. Just a little electrical thing."

She narrowed her eyes, clearly doubtful. "If it was no big deal, why didn't you tell me?"

"I didn't want you to worry," I admitted. "You have so much going on right now."

"And you don't?" My mama rested her hand in mine, gave it a gentle squeeze. "Listen, I know you don't agree with the decision for the church—"

"Mama—"

"No, listen. I know you're beating yourself up because you think it's your fault, but I don't want you stressing yourself out trying to keep from stressing me out. Because, frankly, that stresses me out."

I laughed. "Yes, ma'am."

"I'm serious." She narrowed her eyes. "Now is there anything else you need to get off your chest?"

A collection of images flashed in my mind: Jahmad, Texas, mysterious calls, Leo, a question mark over the faceless father of my son. I forced a smile and mustered up as much confidence as I could in my lie. "Everything is fine, Mama."

Thankfully, the nurse wheeled my dad into the room in a wheelchair, and his face broke into a wide grin when he noticed me in the chair. I couldn't help but smile too. I heard what my Mama said but I had to admit, my dad certainly looked better. Thank God.

"There's my baby girl." With the nurse's and my mom's assistance, he positioned himself on the bed, the paper gown rustling under his weight.

"I couldn't leave you here alone," I said, tossing a wink in my mom's direction. "You know you're no match for Mrs. Davis."

"And he better be glad I love him like I do," my mom said, crossing her arms over her chest. "If it was left up to him, he'd be in a casket still talking about 'it's not that serious, baby girl.'" That prompted a laugh from all of us. And it felt damn good. For a moment, a brief moment, all was right with the world. I didn't mention anything about the fire to my dad and thankfully, my mom didn't either.

Eventually the doctor, an older gentleman with kind eyes behind small-framed glasses, entered the room with a laptop in tow. He greeted each of us as he slid onto a rolling stool at the foot of the examination table.

"Tell 'em, Doc," my dad said. "Tell 'em I'm one of your healthiest patients so I can get this woman off my back."

Dr. Moore didn't join in the joke. In fact the creases in his face seemed to deepen with concern. "Well, for the most part your tests came back fairly regular, but we did detect traces of arsenic in your urine."

The doctor's words seemed to chill the air about eighty degrees. My mind stumbled over the news, trying to make sense of the obvious.

"Like, poison?" My mom spoke up first, piercing the silence. While it hit me and startled me and my dad into stunned silence, it was clear my mom was pissed, as if the doctor had just confessed some forbidden sin against her family.

Dr. Moore nodded. "There are only small traces as if the poison is being flushed out. But I'm deducing this was what was making you sick, pastor."

"How did arsenic end up in his body?" I said now, fear gripping my words. It was as if they were strangling me. "How could that have happened? How could he not have known?"

"Relatively small doses over an extended period of time," Dr. Moore answered gently. "Perhaps mixed with food or a beverage of some kind. It's really hard to pinpoint the exact source, but can you think back to food you've ingested and from where?"

My dad shook his head, more from disbelief than actually responding to the question. I knew what he was thinking. My mom typically cooked for him. That opened up another can of unknowns. Because since we knew my mom would never, could never, then who? And how? Why the pastor?

"Lucky for you, there appear to be small remnants of the drug," the doctor reassured us. "And you're acting like you feel good. So chances are whatever it was, it's over now."

My parents exchanged confused glances, and I could only think about the string of bad luck that seemed to be happening. And if it was who I thought it was, then no. It was far from over.

Dr. Moore glanced between us, his brows creased with worry. It was obvious he had something else to say, just didn't know how.

"What is it?" my mother pressed at his continued silence. "Is there something else?"

"It's just . . ." His sigh was heavy. "Cases like this are normally referred to the police for criminal investigation."

"No." My mother's tone was brisk and final with the objection.

I frowned. "Mama, what do you mean?" I turned bewildered eyes in her direction. "Someone did this to Daddy. We should find out—"

"Is there any way this could have been some kind of accident?" my mama interrupted, directing her question to the doctor.

Dr. Moore sighed again, the brief turn of his head enough indication that he felt this instance was anything but. His expression brought on feelings of panic and worry.

"You know you have been my pastor for many years," Dr.

Moore went on. "My family and I have nothing but the utmost respect for you and Word of Truth."

"The feeling is mutual, Doc." My dad's voice was gruff in sincerity.

"That is why I don't want to do anything to jeopardize your health. I have not only an obligation as your doctor, but also as a caring member of the congregation."

"We will handle it," my mom spoke up again. She inclined her chin. I recognized the gesture. A silent dare. When the First Lady had her say, it was as good as the gospel. "I don't want any kind of negative publicity on the church or the pastor, especially as he is recuperating. The last thing we need is some sort of investigation taking place, on top of . . ." She trailed off and averted her eyes. I winced, knowing exactly what she meant. On top of the publicity with my scandal. Yeah, it was bad enough already. Let's not make it worse. "We will handle it," my mother repeated, this time laying a hand on my dad's arm. I watched the silent exchange, my dad's hand coming up to pat hers reassuringly. Always the united front.

Dr. Moore hesitated before he gave a quick nod and left the room. I certainly hoped the effort to keep trouble out of the limelight hadn't left the door open as an invitation for more of it.

Chapter 11

"Mama, I think I changed my mind."

My mama paused in the middle of packing Jamaal's bag, a stack of diapers in hand. "Oh, no, Kimmy, we are not doing this."

I sighed, turning my attention back to the task at hand.

"Maybe it's just a little too soon," I murmured, almost to myself.

"Kimmy, he's older now. Didn't you say yourself his checkups have been good?"

They had. In fact his pediatrician had been slightly surprised at how well he was progressing given his prematurity and complications. But it was one thing to go to the doctor and back. It was an entirely different consideration when you're talking about having a baby's day outing.

It had taken a lot of convincing on my mother's part. And compromising, also on my mother's part. But I did settle on her taking Jamaal up to the church for an hour or two. My mom was right. Jamaal needed air. No matter how much I wanted to, I couldn't very well keep him in the house the rest of his life. Besides, it wasn't long. Really just enough time for me to grab some lunch with Adria. And bring her up to speed on the shit I had been going through.

I was still reeling from the doctor's news from the previous week. Arsenic? How in the hell did that happen? Sure, now he was almost 95 percent better, but what disturbed my mom and me was that he had gotten sick in the first place.

My mom had been nearly delirious when I'd spoken to her after the visit. "He's not going back to the church," she had said, pacing the living room. I couldn't help but notice the slight trembling, despite her arms wrapped around herself. "He's not. Forgive me, Lord, but I am wishing for a drink right about now."

"Why is he not going back to the church?" I asked.

"Kimmy, where else can someone be doing something to your father?" she asked like it was obvious. "Of course he hasn't ingested any poison here. The church is the only other place he eats. All those dirty women from the church bringing him food all the time, the pot lucks at the executive board meetings. Where else could he have gotten it from?"

I bit my tongue to keep my mouth shut. Mainly because I was racking my brain to come up with my own logical explanation, because I was still in denial about the same conclusion that kept circling in my mind. Leo. I didn't know how. Hell, I didn't even know why. But he damn sure was the common denominator. But I couldn't very well tell anyone that. Not only was I riding on proofless assumptions here, but blowing the lid off Leo would blow the lid off everything dealing with that man. Including the true paternity of Jamaal. As if I could trust that test right now.

That was why I had made a decision to get my own test done on my son. I didn't want to, but I had to know for sure. Maybe then I could reveal what I already figured was true, what I hoped and prayed was true, and Leo would just go away. Because without Jamaal, he had nothing. No stake, no claim, and certainly no me. At this point, I couldn't even dwell on if the results came back and proved him right.

It was apparent now this man would go to any and all lengths to get what he wanted. I would have been angry had I not been so scared. I had to admit that I had absolutely no idea what this man was capable of. And even more scary, how he was able to pull it all off. It was too unbelievable, too farfetched, but too much of a coincidence to ignore. He was doing his manipulating from afar, and it was working. I had wanted to call him, beg him to stop—even if it meant returning every damn dime I'd acquired from him. But I knew Leo, and no number of promises or amount of tears would work on this man. That's why I needed solid evidence. I just prayed it would work in my favor.

I picked Jamaal up from the changing table and cradled him against my breast. "Mama, please don't have my baby around none of those sick folks at the church," I said, following her downstairs.

She turned, gingerly taking the baby from my arms. "Kimmy, I know you don't believe this. But I have raised two kids before. I think I know a little about what to do and not to do."

Understood, but this was my baby. And my baby was delivered several months early, thanks to Tina. He was still technically a newborn. Still growing and developing. But I kept that piece of talkback to myself and simply nodded.

"Just be careful, please," I said and gave them both a kiss.

After she left, I tried to call Jahmad, not really expecting him to answer. Of course he didn't. I wasn't sure if he was ignoring my calls or if I just conveniently caught him at the most inopportune times. I did have to remember that, unlike me, he worked a full-time job. But still, the man didn't take breaks or lunches? He suddenly forgot how to text?

I left a quick message. "Just wanted to hear your voice. Going to lunch with Adria. If you feel like chatting, call me when you get some downtime." I hung up, knowing his "downtime" probably wouldn't be until he came home tonight. And maybe not even then.

I had just finished throwing on a long maxi dress with a jean jacket when the doorbell rang. I glanced out of the bedroom window, frowning when I didn't recognize the white Infiniti truck in the driveway. Apparently, I was taking too long getting to the door because just as quickly as the visitor came, the person stepped into my view, her phone to her face, sashaying back to the car. A woman. Petite from the looks of the high heels she wore to give her toned legs a bit more length. Because she was walking away, I couldn't see her face, just a mass of beautiful curly hair she'd left to style itself in the wind.

I quickly ran to the front door and threw it open, just in time to catch the tail end of her vehicle as it reversed back out of the driveway. The glare combined with a slight tint from the windshield obscured her face so I couldn't make out whether she actually saw me standing in the doorway, attempting to wave her down. But whether she did or didn't actually notice me, she kept going, reversing out of the driveway and taking off down the street.

I stood for a moment longer, unsure how to take the woman's presence. Why was she here? Why did she rush off? A new thought entered my mind as I quickly scanned the porch. Was this the woman Leo was sending after me to drop off his little packages? Who was she?

Satisfied that she hadn't left any package or letter of any kind, I closed the door, mentally evaluating the little visit again. I thought about the woman's attire, well, as much as I could see from the upstairs window. She appeared to have on business clothes, pinstriped slacks and a blazer. Perhaps it was business-related. I just couldn't be sure. And the uncertainty was causing mounting anxiety.

I called Jahmad again, swallowing my anger when the call went straight to voicemail. I called my mother next. She picked up immediately, her voice hollow, making it clear she was in the car. "Mama, is everything okay?" I asked.

"Of course. Why, what's wrong?"

I opened my mouth to tell her about the mystery woman, but

quickly shut it again. The last thing I needed to do was worry her even more. Especially on top of what had happened with my father.

I put as much humor in my voice as I could muster. "Nothing," I lied. "You know this is Jamaal's first little outing. I think I'm just worrying myself too much."

"He's fine," my mom reassured me. "Everything is fine. If it makes you feel better, just come by the church after lunch."

I agreed, then hurried back upstairs to finish getting ready. I needed to see Adria. Now.

———— ➤•◄ ————

Adria had told me about some seafood restaurant in Decatur that supposedly had the best fried lobster and even better drinks. She was already seated when I arrived and, thankfully, had a strawberry mango margarita waiting for me on the table on a monogrammed napkin. I hadn't even slid all the way in the booth before I lifted the glass and took a grateful sip.

"I know the feeling," Adria said with a wistful sigh.

"Girl, please, what feeling? You are all happy and in love and ain't got single folks problems anymore."

I paused as the waitress walked over and set two appetizer plates on the table, one with fried lobster and the other with crab cakes over some kind of cabbage.

"Anything else I can get for you ladies at this time?"

"This is fine for now," Adria said with a smile and didn't waste any time digging in.

"You good?" I asked as she forked some of the crab cake into her mouth.

She nodded and waited until she'd polished off the food before she spoke again. "An Officer Terry called me the other day. Said they were doing an investigation on the fire."

I frowned. "What is there to investigate? It was an electrical issue."

"That's what I said. Apparently, she says there were signs of some of kind of accelerant used, and they are concluding arson."

"Arson?" I sat back in the booth, the gravity of her words hitting me like a ton of bricks. "So they think someone intentionally set the fire?"

"Looks that way. And I spoke to the insurance adjuster," she added at my continued silence. "She says they're not paying out anything on our loss until the investigation is complete. Just a precaution to make sure we didn't start the fire. You know the insurance scams."

I shook my head, torn between shock, anger, and confusion. Intentional? That's all that kept swirling around in my head as Adria excused herself to the restroom and left me to digest the recent news. Intentional. Someone set that place on fire, on purpose. Thankfully, no one was inside. But what if we had been? What if I, or Adria, or Tyree had been working late, as we had so often done in the past in preparation for our grand opening? First, my father, now me. Someone was actually trying to harm, perhaps kill. The thought sent a shudder up my spine, and I had to look around, suddenly feeling as if eyes were on me right that moment.

"What is it?" Adria settled back into the booth across from me, her face furrowed in concern.

My sigh was heavy. "Girl, just . . . everything. My dad, Jahmad, now this."

"What happened with Dad?"

I bit my tongue. I had assumed maybe Keon had told her about the test results.

"Didn't Keon tell you?" I asked cautiously.

"He said Mom said something about food poisoning."

I would leave it at that. "Well, that had me worried, of course. And now this issue with the business."

"Don't let that worry you," Adria said with a shrug. "I just chalked it up to somebody's badass kids. Maybe a gang or something. You never know nowadays."

She was right. You never know.

"Now what about Jahmad?" she pressed. "Did you talk to him?"

"We barely talk," I admitted sadly. "He's in and out. Work and whatever else he's doing. I mean he sees about JayJay, but that's about it. I think he's going to go ahead and take that job."

Adria shook her head. "Stop assuming the worst, because we know how you get. Besides, Keon mentioned they chatted about it and he was leaning toward staying."

That piece of inside information did give me a spark of hope. Just a spark.

"He wouldn't leave his baby, Kimera. Come on now. Jahmad can be stupid, but I don't think he's that stupid. He loves that boy."

I nodded, not really appeased. He may not leave his baby, but he would leave me. I was sure of that now. And what if, by another stroke of bad luck, Leo really was my son's father? Would Jahmad leave then?

I took a breath as my chest tightened at my next admission. "Jamaal may not be his."

Adria stopped chewing, her eyes ballooning at my words. "I thought—I mean I knew it was a possibility because of what happened with Leo, but didn't you and Jahmad get all that sorted out?"

I shook my head. "I told him the baby was his. I just wanted him to be so bad and I just kept insisting it was true because the dates only add up with him. And Jahmad, he just believed me and never pushed the issue."

"So why the hell is it coming up now as an issue? Did Jahmad say something?"

"No." I took another breath. "Leo did."

Adria sat back, a mix of confusion and horror masking her face. "What the hell are you talking about, Kimmy? You're not making any sense."

My mind went into overdrive, trying to see how I could give as much information as possible without revealing that I had been hiding this secret from her.

"Leo's not dead," I started, picking through each word as it came to mind. "Tina tried to kill him, and he ended up faking his death. No one knew."

"Wait." Adria sat back, her mouth nearly frozen open in shock. "Tina tried to kill him?"

"She was working with this doctor, who I thought was Leo's friend. But they both were snakes, just trying to come up on some money. The doctor had this gambling debt and Tina, well, she was just being a jealous, selfish bitch. They're the ones that killed Lena, remember Leo's second wife? And those two were working together to frame me for killing Leo, which was why I went to jail. To make a long story short, Leo came to me at the hospital about Jamaal and told me everything. Now he's saying he knows the baby is his and I keep telling him it isn't true. That Jahmad is the father. Then he shows me some paternity test results confirming he is the father. So now, now I just don't know what to do, Adria." My voice cracked, and I blinked back tears threatening to erupt. This whole thing had me on an emotional roller coaster. And it was only getting worse.

Adria stared at me in disbelief. "I can't believe this shit," she murmured over and over.

"I can't let Jahmad find out."

"No, Kimmy, don't do that again," she snapped. "Don't start all that lying and shit. You have to tell him the truth. Tell him what's going on, because you already know it's going to come out."

"Not if I can get the real test results."

She narrowed her eyes. "What do you mean, the 'real' test results? I thought you said Leo—"

I shook my head, waving off her statement. "The man faked his own death, Adria. He has money out the ass. Do you really think he couldn't fake some test results? Plus, when did he test my child? That doesn't add up."

I saw my words fitting together in her head and Adria finally nodded, agreeing with the logic. "Okay, fine. You test Jamaal, and then what? What's the end game?"

"If Jahmad is the father, I can tell Leo, and he can get the hell out of our lives. At this point, it just seems he wants something to dangle over my head. And as long as he thinks he's the father, he has something."

Adria nodded again, this time almost whispering her next question. "And if Leo is the father? Then what?"

I pursed my lips. I honestly did not know. And that was what scared me.

The rain had just started to come down when I pulled up to Word of Truth. I sighed, wishing I had decided to just have my mother bring Jamaal home instead of me coming to the church. There probably weren't many people at the daytime bible study, but the effect was just the same. My dad had done his best to make this place feel like a welcome home, open for fellowship and love. It hardly felt like that now, that's for sure.

The little DNA test box snugly wrapped in the CVS bag in my purse had me quickening my pace. It was interesting. When I stopped by the store after leaving Adria to pick up the test, just seeing the box on the shelf almost brought on a wave of nausea. Damn near my future rested on the results of this little test. It would be my glory, or my downfall. Now I just needed to get home, swab my son's mouth, and send everything off to the office so they could compare it to Jahmad's DNA. I wasn't a hundred percent sure how I would even get Jahmad's DNA just yet, but I would come up with something. What choice did I have? At this point, all I could do was pray for the best.

I stepped out of the car, lifting my umbrella to brace against the downpour. A roll of thunder rumbled, followed by the flash of lightning that illuminated the sky. I was honestly glad Adria and I had decided against the little shopping excursion we had originally planned. But after the lunch discussion, neither one of us was in the mood, so we said our goodbyes and parted ways. Adria insisted I make a point to talk to Jahmad that night because there was so much we were letting linger. I agreed, but though that was a priority, it wasn't my main priority. Especially considering it was already on my mind to stop by the pharmacy and grab the test. One thing at a time. I would get everything settled with my baby, and then Jahmad and I would once again become my focus.

By the time I entered the Fellowship Hall, the small midday bible study service was already done. Still, a few members were lingering in the aisle, laughing and talking among themselves. They immediately became quiet when I entered the doors, and a tension fell over the room that had the awkwardness riding high and thick.

"Is my mother here?" I asked no one in particular.

The immediate silence afterward had me questioning whether these holy rollers were actually ignoring me. It was clear everyone assumed the others would respond. Then, "Downstairs," one woman answered. "In the nursery."

I thanked her and turned around, just as the woman whispered, "I'm surprised she doesn't catch on fire when she sets foot in here," followed by low chuckles and murmurs of agreement.

Bitch. I quickly winced when I remembered my surroundings. All the more reason to hurry up and get out of this place, I mused, quickening my pace. Maybe it was a good thing they were selling the church.

With the exception of a good-size cafeteria, the childcare center dominated nearly the entire downstairs floor. My mom had taken the liberty of personally decorating the area, from its pastel yellow and blue walls, to the alphabet wall-to-wall carpet littered with toys and learning gadgets for a variety of ages.

A handful of children were scattered throughout the room as I walked up to the doorway, closed off with a Dutch door with separate top and bottom half. The bottom half had an extended tabletop where the sign-in/sign-out sheet now rested on top.

One of the center volunteers, a young college student named Chloe, glanced up from where she was playing on the carpet with a child.

"Hey, Kimera," she greeted, rising to open the door for me. "JayJay is absolutely adorable. He is getting so big."

Per the rules, I reached over to the large sink right inside the door to wash my hands. "Thank you, Chloe. Is the First Lady here?"

"In the baby room." She gestured toward one of the rooms and eased back down next to a little boy who looked to be about two.

I paused when the boy lifted his head, his eyes roaming the floor for another Lego piece to add to the pile at his feet. It couldn't be. There was no way. But that face, I couldn't mistake those eyes, those cheeks. Sure, I hadn't seen him since he was a few months old, but the time since had only defined his distinct features. Features that I knew so well.

It took a minute for me to find my voice, my question coming out in a strangled whisper. "What's that child's name?"

The volunteer looked up at me before turning her eyes in the direction of my gaze. "Oh, he's a newbie," she said, giving the boy a little tickle to his neck. His giggle erupted, and my heart hit the floor. I knew it. Even before Chloe's lips parted to voice the name, and I whispered it as she spoke it out loud. "Leo Junior."

Chapter 12

It was like watching a ghost.

The number of months since I saw her last couldn't erase the fear nor the anger of our previous encounter. The one where she tried to kill me.

I could still remember her pointing that gun at me. Her sinister look as she openly admitted arranging the car crash with the intent to kill Leo and, ultimately, staging the scene to frame me for the crime. Leo's first and true wife, Tina Owusu, had been the master manipulator, the puppet master who had orchestrated everything that had happened to me in an attempt to destroy my life. And if it hadn't been for one little unforeseen circumstance, my pregnancy with Jamaal, she would have been successful, and my ass would have probably been rotting up in some women's prison somewhere. And she, well, she would have probably been laid out on some Caribbean beach enjoying the fruits of her malicious labor. Instead here she was, in the flesh, signing Leo Jr. out of my father's church's childcare. It was too much of a coincidence to ignore.

The last thing I remembered was fighting over the gun and blacking out once Tina had delivered a painful blow to my stomach, sending me into early labor. Leo had admitted he had shown up to my rescue and "taken care of Tina" so I wouldn't have to worry about her again. I had assumed he'd had to kill her, or at least paid to send her far away from Georgia. Maybe even jail. He hadn't said, and I hadn't asked questions. I just figured he had stayed true to his word and I wouldn't ever see her again in this lifetime. But nope. Here she was. And I was damn sure worried.

Time certainly had changed her physically, but she did carry an eerily familiar look. Her hair was cut short and curly, a pixie cut I'd been wearing for the longest time. She still reeked of luxury with her sleeveless silk blouse and slim-hugging dress pants cropped at the ankle to reveal red-bottom stilettos.

I peered out from the baby room, watching as she scribbled her name on the sign-out sheet and scooped Leo Jr. into her arms. She exchanged brief pleasantries with Chloe before disappearing, toting a grinning Leo Jr. on her hip.

"What's wrong, Kimmy?"

My mom's question had startled me because I hadn't even known she'd come to stand by my side and peer over my shoulder. I hadn't even realized I'd been staring, debating whether I wanted to follow her and see where she was going. Was she meeting up with Leo?

"Nothing, Mama," I lied, turning my back to the door to steal her attention. I had settled on trying to sneak away so I could tail Tina, but my mom quickly intercepted that plan as if she knew my sneaky thoughts.

"Come upstairs and let's go through some of those files in the storage," she said, resting Jamaal in a nearby crib. "JayJay will be fine here with Chloe."

And that had been the end of it. I had been tempted to ask my mom about Tina, but I didn't want to raise her suspicions. I would have to do my own digging. Now that I knew Tina was around and in such close proximity, I was revaluating everything. My dad's sickness, the fire, the paternity test, the phone calls.

Maybe it wasn't Leo after all. It was her. And that thought frightened me. Leo I could perhaps manage. With Tina there was no consideration of trying to contain or control the situation, or working the odds to fall in my favor. The bitch had tried her damnedest to have me convicted of murder, and then she herself had tried to kill me. There was no type of limit on what she was willing to do to get what she wanted. Now here was the dilemma. What *did* she want?

I tried to keep from harping on that, but as the week ended and the sun rose on Saturday, I would be lying if I said the shit still wasn't riding heavy on my mind.

I hadn't slept much at all and apparently neither had Jahmad. The clock read a quarter until seven, but the shower was already running behind the closed bathroom door.

I rolled over to where JayJay was now stirring. He had been so fussy last night that I had risen and brought him in to sleep between me and Jahmad. Apparently his weariness had caught up with him, because he whined a bit before he was again letting out a gentle snore.

My mind flipped for a brief moment to the DNA test still stuffed in an inside pocket of my purse. I had done some research because I knew getting permission for a sample from Jahmad was out of the question. I could use a special sample, like his toothbrush. No, it wasn't quite as conclusive, and yes, it would require some more money, but hell, what other choice did I have?

I heard the water stop, and a few minutes later, Jahmad emerged, still wet, a towel slung low over his hips. He stopped, almost in surprise, when he saw I was awake.

"Good morning," he murmured, heading to the dresser.

I sat up against the headboard, taking care not to move the mattress too much to keep from waking the baby. "You headed to work?"

"No, not today," he said simply.

I sighed, this time easing from the bed. I walked up behind Jahmad and circled my hands around his waist, rested my cheek on his wet back. "Jay, can we please talk?"

"Kimera, we—" The irritation was already in his voice, so I quickly changed tactics.

"Okay, we don't have to talk now," I said quickly. "How about we do something together today? Just me, you, and JayJay? I feel better now that my mom has taken him out the house so maybe we could go somewhere for a few hours. Have some lunch. Just enjoy each other."

For a brief moment, I felt the tension in Jahmad's spine. Slowly, very slowly, he seemed to relax, and finally he turned, placing his hands on my shoulders. His smile was tiny, but a smile nonetheless. To my surprise, he agreed. "Sounds good," he said. "Let me make a quick call first." He paused for a moment, then added, "And you're right. It's time we talk. Later."

I nodded as he strolled back into the bathroom, I was assuming to talk in private so as not to wake the baby. It sounded like he had made a decision. Good or bad, I didn't know

But I would try not to think about it. Just enjoy the day with him. That might be the one of the last times we had together.

⟶•◄⟵

I knew it had been too good to be true. I pretended to be completely engrossed in feeding Jamaal while I not so subtly watched Jahmad text someone on his phone. Whoever it was, they were certainly persistent, because I'd counted him ignoring seven notifications before he finally responded.

I watched his face for any signs of, hell, I couldn't even be sure what I was looking for. Excitement? Glee? Lust? But he just kept his eyebrows drawn and face blank as his fingers played across the phone's touchscreen keyboard. In my arms, Jamaal's eyes drooped, and when I felt the bottle go slack, I gently pulled the nipple from his lips.

It had started out well. We had decided to grab some brunch to go from IHOP and eat it lakeside in the park. We had shared a few laughs and exchanged a few calm pleasantries in the serenity of the park, but to be honest, that was just as fulfilling to me.

When we got in the car, I expected him to steer it in the direction of the house, but instead he had detoured to the mall. "Let's get a few more things for Jay," he had suggested lightly.

"As if he needs anything else," I teased, thinking now on the nursery closet jam-packed with diapers, wipes, clothes, and other essentials to last well into his toddler years, I was sure. But I didn't object when we pulled into the mall parking lot.

We had strolled in and out of stores, alternating between toting the carrier. We didn't get much shopping done before the baby got fussy and we detoured into the food court so I could change and feed him.

Now we sat at one of the tables while I struggled to ignore Jahmad's distraction. I swallowed my temper and tried my best to keep the air between us light. "Everything okay?"

Jahmad glanced up and scanned the crowd, clearly looking for someone. "Yeah, I think a friend of mine is supposed to be here." He rose, spotting the person, and my eyes grew in recognition.

The woman who had come by the house. The mystery woman whom I thought had stopped by for me. She still had the big hair, her petite frame accented by another professionally sexy business skirt suit. The same heels she'd worn to the house were again on her feet, bringing her height to Jahmad's shoulder. But more than when she came to my house, something else was familiar about this woman, and the fact I knew I'd seen her before had suspicion marring my face so strongly I could almost taste it. Friend? What the hell kind of friend? And why was this chick wearing a business suit in the mall? The fact that she was outshining me in my casual black leggings and oversized knee-length button-up shirt had me even more irritated.

"Hey!" The woman was a little too excited and too much in Jahmad's face for my comfort as they shared a friendly hug. "I was afraid I wouldn't be able to catch you again before my flight."

Jahmad turned to me, gesturing toward the woman. "Kimmy, you remember CeeCee, don't you?"

And then it hit me like a sucker punch to the gut. CeeCee. Jahmad's ex-fiancée CeeCee. The one he'd left for me. I blinked back my shock, slowly feeling it begin to boil to rage. What in the entire hell was going on here?

"It's good to see you again." CeeCee spoke up first, her smile spreading as she clearly saw the pieces clicking into place. "Kimmy, right?"

"Kimera," I snapped and turned my attention back to Jahmad. I'm sure every bit of my emotions were playing across my face, but Jahmad didn't seem fazed. Or at least he didn't show it.

"CeeCee had to come to town on business," he offered at my continued silence.

"And you know I couldn't leave without seeing you again." She nudged his arm, somewhat flirtatiously. "And this little handsome guy here. Hi, JayJay. I've heard so much about you," she cooed. I rolled my eyes. The bitch was clearly pulling every trick to get under my skin. And it was working.

I readjusted my body to shield my son from her gushing. "Let me go change him," I said, putting the diaper bag on my shoulder. It was a lie, a clear one considering I had just changed Jamaal and now he was good and asleep. But hell, I'd make up some excuse about needing to change my damn self if it meant getting out of this otherwise awkward interaction.

I escaped to the bathroom, allowing a good twenty-seven minutes and thirty-three seconds to pass before I reemerged. Just as I hoped, little Miss CeeCee was gone and Jahmad now sat alone, fumbling on his phone with one hand and sipping a smoothie with his other.

I didn't even sit. "We need to go," I said. "Now." Not bothering to wait for a response, I walked briskly to the exit. I felt my steps damn near burning a hole in the floor and I knew I needed to hurry and get to some privacy before I exploded. CeeCee's words were on rewind in my head, like some kind of taunt. Couldn't leave without seeing Jahmad *again*? Heard so much about my son? That was some karma for my ass.

"Care to explain that shit?" I started in on Jahmad as soon as we made it back home and I had laid JayJay in his crib. I now stood in front of Jahmad as he sat on the bed, fumbling with his shoes.

"Nothing to explain."

"Oh, really?" I folded my arms across my chest, bracing myself to keep from trembling. "You expect me to believe your ex-fiancée just so happened to be in the mall? The mall *you* suggested? That's some bullshit-ass coincidence."

"I didn't say it was a coincidence," he said. "Yeah, I told her she could meet us there. She had some time to waste because her flight was delayed."

"So apparently you've spent time with her since she's been here."

"What's wrong with that?"

"She's your ex for a reason, Jahmad." Frustration had me dragging out each word like I was speaking to a first-grader. Was he clearly clueless, or just feigning his ignorance to get a rise out of me?

Jahmad rose and pulled his shirt over his head. I ignored the fact he was now standing in front of me half naked. At least I tried to ignore it. My body certainly wasn't.

"She was helping me, Kimmy," he finally admitted wearily. "It's not what you think."

"Oh, really?" I said doubtfully.

"There is nothing between me and CeeCee anymore," he reiterated, his eyes sharp on mines. He could have very well been telling the truth. But I was no dumb bitch. And it was clear, more than clear that CeeCee didn't feel their relationship was as innocent as he was alleging. And that was a big problem for me.

Not able to stand still anymore, I began to pace, my feet moving across the carpet in rapid succession. "Helping you with what? That's what you have me for."

"It's different." Jahmad's sigh was heavy. "You don't know this, but CeeCee and I met while I was in Texas. We worked together. I came back to Atlanta because she got a promotion within the company and me, well, I took a little pay cut. It was a mutual agreement. Well, after we split, she went back to Texas, but we kept in touch. Just settled into a friendship."

I wanted to tell him he was stupid as hell if he thought CeeCee was just content with being friends after she was about to marry the man, but I just remained quiet.

As if reading my mind, Jahmad said, "She just wants to see me happy, even if it's not with her. She loves me that much." I winced. Was that a shot at me? I ignored it, for now.

"Okay, so now what?" I pressed.

"Well, she was the one that recommended me for the Texas promotion. So while she was here on business, we were just trying to hash out the pros and cons. That's it."

My legs suddenly felt weak, and I sank to the bed. So that was her game? Wanted to get him back out to Texas and back into her arms. Well, I'll be damned. Smooth. Real smooth.

"But she's 'baby,' in your phone." I hadn't wanted to reveal my discovery, but what he said was making entirely too much sense. And shit, now I felt stupid for thinking otherwise.

He nodded. "That's my fault," he admitted. "I've just never

changed it from when we were together before. But I swear it doesn't mean anything."

I sighed, detecting every ounce of his genuineness. "Well," I asked, my eyes closing, "what did you decide about the job? Texas?" Me? I held my breath, anticipating his answer.

I heard him move, and suddenly his presence was in front of me, the light remnants of his cologne tickling my nose.

"Look at me, Kimmy." Jahmad's gentle voice prompted the first few tears to trickle from my lids. I felt his hand caress my face, and obediently I opened my eyes, tears blurring my vision.

"I'm not going," he said, gently swiping his thumb over my face to smear my tears into my cheek.

I nodded, relief coursing through my body, and I leaned in to kiss him. I thought he would stop me, but instead he deepened the kiss. I wrapped my arms around his neck, savoring every moment. It had been so long. Too damn long. But this man had my body responding on demand, waking up parts that had been put to rest a long time ago.

"I love you," I murmured, my words muffled against his lips.

Jahmad pulled back, temporarily cupping my face in his hands. "I love you too," he said.

"And us?"

He stared at me for a moment longer, searching my eyes for something. "Is there anything you need to tell me, Kimera?" he asked.

My heart quickened. Did he know something? Was this a setup? Some kind of trick question with the future of us hanging in the balance like a pendulum?

I took a deep breath, mustering as much sincerity in my words as I could. "No." I kept my eyes level. "Nothing."

"No more lies, Kimera," he said, his voice firm with the request. "No more secrets. If we're going to work on us, we both are going to be all in. Me included. Can you promise me that?"

I nodded, already regretting the lies as they fell from lips, compounding on top of each other like a Jenga game waiting to collapse and break. Leo, Tina, the baby, and now CeeCee. It seemed every aspect of my life was one big lie. But still, I voiced what he wanted, no, needed, to hear. "No more secrets," I vowed. "No more lies. Just us, Jahmad."

He smiled his satisfaction, and I moaned as he lifted me in his arms and carried me to the bed.

I had to admit, perhaps it was because of me that we had been fighting so much these past few months. I had washed my hands of Leo and I was ready to dive in headfirst with Jahmad now that I had, supposedly, left everything in the past. To me, it was as if none of that bullshit from before had ever happened. I was pressuring him, I knew. He wasn't ready and, dammit, I wanted him to be ready, because I was. But as he had so clearly expressed on more than one occasion, he had trust issues. I guess I shouldn't have felt so hurt about his considering the Texas job because, honestly, he had those trust issues because of me. But, hell, so did I.

"I'm sorry," he whispered, resting his forehead on mine.

My eyes fluttered open. "For what?"

"I guess I was just scared," he admitted. "I just wanted to make sure you weren't up to that same stuff from the past. I was scared to give up my life if you weren't all in."

I pressed my lips against his, pushing every ounce of passion I felt into the kiss.

"I am all in," I murmured. At least that part was true.

He laid me down, the sheets cool against my back, sunlight spilling through the blinds and casting us both in a hazel glow. His touch was soft as he began undressing me. My skin felt like it was on fire, and I wanted him so bad my body was throbbing in tune to my quickening heartbeat. Jahmad took his time, replacing his fingers with his lips, then tongue. He moved slowly, delicately, like we had forever.

"Jahmad." His name seeped through my lips in a quivering whisper as he gingerly spread my legs. I grimaced at the initial shot of pain, slowly opening as he worked his way in inch by inch. And soon, the pleasure pierced my insides and left me startled, gasping for mercy.

His moan filled my ear as I opened for him, wrapping my legs around his waist, clinging to him like a lifeline. And when we both came, it felt like the first time, and my body trembled as I fell in love with him again. We were starting over. This was us, and I was ready to give myself completely, openly, and honestly. Well, for the most part, I reconsidered as we lay cuddled together, spent, our skin slick with our juices an hour later.

Noting he had fallen asleep, I quietly pulled from his loving embrace and rummaged through my purse on the dresser, the sunlight spilling onto the DNA test. I took one quick look at him and ripped open the box, praying this would solve our problems. And not add to them.

Chapter 13

I turned into my subdivision and had a brief moment of panic when I spotted the police car in my driveway. Hell, I was already on edge because I had had to leave the house this morning so I could drop the paternity test off at the post office under the excuse that I was running to the grocery store to get some breakfast food. Now the two Publix bags in my front seat validated my story, but my anxiety had kicked in as I'd dropped the package in its return envelope in the mailbox. Especially because Jahmad and I had made up, repeatedly, last night and this morning. And I'd vowed to be upfront and honest with him. So it was guilt that had me picking out all his breakfast favorites along with an "I love you" card, though it really didn't make me feel any better.

Now to see the police car brought on that same feeling from before, when the police showed up to tell me Leo had been in a car accident. Then again when they came to arrest me for the crime. But my temporary fear was quickly replaced by panic when I remembered this time was different. This time my son was in the house and there could be a problem.

So I sped the last few blocks and parked by the curb, not bothering to grab the grocery bags as I ran up to the house.

I fumbled with my keys for a few seconds before Jahmad opened the door, and I urgently pushed past him. "Jamaal—"

"He's fine." He quickly stopped me before I took off up the stairs to the nursery. I breathed in relief, waiting for the news to calm my heart. Jahmad gestured toward the living room with his eyes. "I tried to call you and let you know. She's here for you," he said, obviously referencing the cop.

"I was in the grocery store. I didn't hear my phone." Then I remembered and added, "Can you go get the food out the car? I'll talk to her."

I headed toward the living room where the officer, a blond female who looked like she was better suited for the high school cheerleading squad, rose to greet me. A flashback to my arrest had some PTSD shit going on because I paused at the door, looking for the handcuffs.

"Kimera Davis?" she asked.

Comfortable she wasn't about to cuff me and toss me in the back of her squad car, I nodded, extending my hand to shake hers. "Yes. How can I help you?"

"I'm Officer Terry," she said, flashing the badge attached to her belt. "As I'm sure you are aware, we are investigating the fire at your business property. It appears to be arson, so we are needing to question all parties involved. I already spoke to your friend and business partner, Adria Davis, and I just wanted to ask you a few questions."

I relaxed even more and nodded. "No problem. Whatever I can do to help."

I sat down on the couch as she resumed her seated position on the oversize chair across from me. Officer Terry then flipped her little notebook open, studying her notes.

"You were at the business property on the day of the fire?"

"Yes, I went to work earlier that day."

"And about what time did you arrive, and what time did you depart?"

"I guess it was about seven when I got there and I left around ten or eleven. It was definitely before noon."

She scribbled on her notepad as I spoke. "And who all was there when you left?"

"Just Tyree," I said. "I think we were scheduled to have some models come in later, but they hadn't gotten there yet. We were preparing for our grand opening."

"And Tyree is?"

"Tyree Nixon. He's our store manager."

She spared Jahmad a questioning glance as he came into the room and sat down beside me, putting an arm around my shoulders. Grateful for the support, I leaned into his embrace.

"And what about Adria Davis?" Officer Terry went on and I shook my head.

"I think she came later, but no, she wasn't there when I left."

"And what did you do when you left the store?"

I paused, thinking it best to skip over the part where I made a pop-up visit to Jahmad's job only to find he wasn't there. Clearing my throat, I masked my hesitancy by pretending to be deep in thought.

"Let's see," I stalled. "Just went to get me something to eat and then came home. My mom was watching my son, so I just came on back so she wouldn't have to be here all day with him."

Officer Terry closed her notepad and stood. "I think that's all I have for the moment. Except one more thing. Do you know anyone who would actually want to burn your place?"

I tensed as the image of Tina and Leo came to mind. I had deduced it was one, if not both of them. There was no other logical explanation.

I felt Jahmad's eyes on me, and I had completely forgotten his arm was draped on my shoulders. I prayed he hadn't felt my body tense.

"Not that I know of," I murmured and rose as well to break the contact. "Adria and I figured it was just some teenagers probably playing and it got out of control. Maybe someone smoking. But do you have a card or something? I'll call you if I think of something else."

I couldn't tell if she believed me, hell, my paranoia had me not believing my damn self, but she merely reached in her pocket and passed me a card anyway. "Yes, please do." Her eyes turned to Jahmad. "Both of you."

"Definitely. I'll see you out."

I let him walk the officer to the door, and I headed upstairs to check on Jamaal. He had fallen asleep in his swing, some faint lullaby wafting from the speaker. I gently moved him to his crib and watched him for a minute, not rushing to address Jahmad when I felt his presence.

"Is he asleep?" he whispered.

"Yeah," I said, turning to walk by him. "Still want some breakfast?"

He grabbed my arm and guided me into the hall, shutting Jamaal's door behind us. "You didn't tell me they were looking into arson."

I shrugged away his concern. "Because I don't believe it was arson."

"Oh, yeah? 'Cause it sure seemed like you did when she asked you if you knew somebody."

So he had felt it. I tried to pull my arm away but his grip was firm. "Jahmad, it's not a big deal. For real."

"No secrets, no lies, Kimera." Jahmad's voice was laced with restrained anger.

I sighed. He was right. But if I couldn't lie, and I couldn't tell him the truth, what the hell was I supposed to say? "I don't know if it was arson," I started slowly. "If it was, I don't know who did it. *But* if I had to suspect somebody, my guess would be Leo's first wife, Tina."

Jahmad frowned but remained quiet, urging me to continue. "I hadn't seen her since what happened when she almost killed me," I went on. "But that was months ago. The other day, I just so happened to see her at my dad's church. She was picking up her son from the childcare."

"Well, hell, Kimera, that's more than just a coincidence. Why didn't you tell me? Why didn't you tell the cop?"

"Because I didn't want you to worry," I said. That much was true. "And I don't want to go pointing fingers over something that's probably nothing."

"Kimmy, she tried to kill you," he snapped. "Tried to kill my son. That is hardly nothing."

I rested my hands on his shoulders. I had to admit his compassion was turning me on.

"Babe, I'm sorry. I'm not trying to minimize the situation, but I really don't want to jump the gun here. Look at how you're feeling now. You see what I mean?"

Jahmad sighed, and I could tell he was trying his best to calm down, but the vein near his temple and his clenched jawline made it apparent he was failing miserably.

I leaned in to kiss him, working my lips against his until they softened and his arms circled my waist. "I'm not letting it slide," I murmured, resting my forehead against his. "I'm going to look more into it myself. And if I find anything funny, I promise I will tell you."

"And we are going to the police," he added.

"Deal."

He kissed me this time, and I let him pull me into the bedroom to get a little snack before breakfast.

⇒►◄⇐

The phone snatched me from my sleep, and I groaned. Jahmad and I never did make it to breakfast, so now I was starving after two rounds of sex.

I sat up, allowing the sheets to pool at my waist just as the ringing stopped. The space next to me was empty, and I struggled to clear the fogginess from my brain.

Keon. That was it. Jahmad had mentioned meeting up with Keon and a few of their friends for a little bit. I had snuck a text to Adria confirming that story while he was in the shower. Then I checked on the baby before climbing back in the bed and dozing off. A quick look at the clock showed it was now 5:37 p.m., so he hadn't been gone but for a couple hours. I rose to check on Jamaal, figuring he must be almost awake by now.

My phone rang again, and this time I reached for it, because frankly the noise was irritating as hell. "Hello?" I answered, clearing the sleep from my throat.

"Hey, boo," Tyree greeted. "Did I catch you at a bad time?"

"No, I needed to get up. What's up?"

"I was actually wanting to see if you and Adria had discussed the new store."

"No, not really. Not yet. I think we were just trying to see what happens with the insurance, since they're doing all of this investigating."

"Yeah, a police came by to question me," he revealed. "But I just wanted to see what your thoughts were, because I didn't know if I needed to start looking for another job or what. But when I asked Adria, she said y'all probably weren't going to open another store."

I frowned at that. "No, maybe she just misunderstood you. We are definitely going to open another store. Just a matter of getting everything together and seeing where we stand with the investment, finding a new location, and just starting all over again. Just going to take a little time, but as soon as we sit down and get everything finalized we'll for sure keep you in the loop, because we need you onboard."

"Sounds good," Tyree said, relief evident in his lighter tone. "And, Kimera, thanks again. For everything. You don't know how much it means to me to be part of this."

I smiled. "Same here."

I hung up with him and tossed my legs over the bed. I chalked it up to misunderstanding, but for some reason, Tyree's words about what Adria might have told him settled heavily in the pit of my stomach. I would see about my son then call her about it. I sure hoped she hadn't made a serious decision like that without first consulting me.

I knew something was wrong as soon as I stepped foot into Jamaal's bedroom. Something about the air in here; it was cooler, thicker. The first thing I noticed was a teddy bear in the middle of the floor. Well, what was left of a teddy bear, I think. Someone had slashed the thing until all the stuffing lay spilling out on the carpet. I stepped closer to the crib, peering over the rails, and let out a scream.

Chapter 14

My baby was dead. At least, that was the thought that kept circling around in my mind since I'd seen him. I couldn't stop shaking. No matter how much I tried to calm myself, tried to rationalize what had happened, my body felt like it was going into some kind of epileptic seizure and no longer could I control myself.

Seeing the torn teddy had already instilled the first few bits of fear. But peering into that baby bed and seeing my son's warm brown complexion tinted blue with his lack of oxygen had me in a state of panic.

I was hysterical as I fumbled with the phone to dial 911. All I could do was pray. Please, Lord. Please don't let my baby die.

"911, what's your—"

"Please help me," I cried, hysteria jumbling my words. "My baby! He's not breathing."

"Okay, ma'am. I'm sending paramedics right now. How old is he?"

"Five months."

"Is he unconscious?"

I looked at Jamaal's motionless figure and sobbed. "Oh, God, yes. He's not moving. Please don't let him die." How long had he been like this? Had my son died while I lay in there sleeping? He still had a few minor health issues, but I had been faithful with his treatments and medication. What the hell had happened?

"Okay, I need you to put the phone on speaker and give two rescue breaths." Her voice was calm and soothing, and I appreciated it. It did bring a little comfort. A little. I did as she instructed, trying my best to stop my shaking fingers.

"Tilt his head back slightly, lift his chin, and cover his mouth and nose with your mouth. Breathe in twice."

I sobbed, delivering two quivering breaths, watched his tiny chest rise and fall.

"Any response?"

"No!"

She spoke on urgently. "Start administering CPR. Paramedics will be there shortly."

And that's how they found me: sobbing over my child's limp body. By the time they had arrived, he had started breathing again; at least I think he had. I couldn't tell if it was actually him or my quivering hands, or the life I was struggling to breathe into him. They carried him into the ambulance and sped up the street with me doing a hundred miles per hour right behind them.

It was all a blur. I don't remember calling anyone, but I must have, because shortly after we burst through the emergency room and they left me in the lobby alone, they were arriving in rapid succession, first Adria and Keon, then Jahmad, and last my parents.

Someone's arms wrapped around me to bring comfort, but I was numb. My body was there, but my mind was elsewhere: back in the room with my child while he fought for his life.

"He's strong." I held my dad's words from before, when he was first having birth complications. "God's got him." I clung to that in desperation.

A cup was shoved into my hands, and I looked up to see the arm belonged to Adria. I shook my head and put the little Dixie cup down on a nearby table. It was just water, I knew, but the thought of putting anything in my stomach made me nauseated.

She sighed and eased onto the chair beside me, the plastic creaking under her weight. "Have you heard anything?"

I shook my head, not bothering to hide the tears wetting my face.

"He's fine," she assured me, rubbing my arm.

My nod was more of an acknowledgment than an agreement. All I could think about was my son's face with its slight blue hue and his body so still. Why hadn't he been moving?

Everyone took turns trying to comfort me, and when they saw I just stayed in my daze, they turned to comforting each other.

Finally, a doctor emerged from the back and walked in our direction, his face neutral. "Ms. Davis?" He turned expectant eyes on me. I nodded, feeling Jahmad grab my hand.

"How is my son?" I whispered.

His eyebrows drew together in concern. "He's alive," he started, and I released a grateful breath. "He is stable, but given his delicate state, we would like to keep him overnight for observation. It appears to have been some kind of choking event."

I shook my head. "That's impossible. We don't keep anything in the bed with Jamaal. Not even a pillow."

"Well, he could have gotten hold of something," the doctor offered. "It looked like a piece of a stuffed animal or something. Maybe he grabbed hold of it in his hand. It's really hard to say with babies, but we would still like to keep him overnight. The fact that he was a preemie and had to have oxygen just makes us want to take the extra precaution."

The idea of my baby being back in this place instead of home where he belonged had me wanting to oppose. But Jahmad squeezed my hand, silencing the words on my tongue.

"Of course, doctor," he responded. "Whatever you all think is best."

The doctor left us alone, and everyone huddled together, digesting the recent news.

"We'll stay," my mom offered. "You and Jahmad should go on home and get—"

I was already shaking my head. "No, I'm not leaving him."

"We'll both stay," Jahmad said gently. No one else objected. "I'll go home and get us something to wear."

I then remembered the teddy bear I'd seen, and I pulled him to the side to speak in private.

"Can you look in the nursery when you get there?" I whispered. "There was some kind of teddy bear . . . It scared me at first because it wasn't there before. At least I don't . . ."

"Was it his?" Jahmad's face crinkled in confusion.

I tried to think back. Had I seen it before? I couldn't be sure. But either way, how did it get so cut up?

"Just look around and tell me what you think," I said. Then I added, "Please." Prickles of fear begin to inch its way up my spine. All I could think was, how did that teddy bear get there? Someone must have put it there. Which meant someone was in my house. In my house with my baby while I slept a few yards away. That reality sent me into a panic. But, on the off chance I was overreacting and there was some logical explanation I couldn't really think of right now, I would remain calm and just focus on that.

The look on Jahmad's face made it obvious he wanted to say more but he didn't.

"Let me ride with you," my brother spoke up, and I nodded my agreement with the idea. Just in case something was wrong, I felt more comfortable knowing they were both there.

They left then, and I suggested my parents leave shortly after. My dad suggested we pray first and we held hands in a circle, right there in the lobby, while he sent up words of praise and glory and asking God to protect our little Jamaal.

Adria remained quiet as we sat together in the lobby, now alone. I could tell she had something on her mind.

I glanced at her. "What?" I prompted.

"What happened, Kimmy?" Her eyes turned to mine, and for the first time, I saw they held the same uncertainty and fear I was feeling.

I shook my head. "I'm not sure," I admitted.

"Was it Leo?"

"I don't think so." And I really didn't. No, I had a new suspect in mind. One with more motive. One who had tried it before and, therefore, was more capable.

I told Adria about Tina, from the time I saw her all the way up to the point I'd confessed it to Jahmad. Adria was clearly speechless.

"So, you told Jahmad about Leo?"

"Not Leo," I said. "Just Tina. He thinks we should go to the police."

"Uh, hell yeah," Adria said it like it was obvious. "Especially now with JayJay. I mean come on, Kimera. This shit is getting out of hand."

I nodded. She was right. I knew it. I just hated to admit it, because it was looking like everything was getting worse and not better.

"Kimmy." Adria's voice was filled with compassion as she touched my hand. "I'm for real. Don't put us through that shit again. You almost died and so did Jamaal. This is serious."

I nodded. "I know. I'm going to take care of it."

I still couldn't call the police. Not yet. But there was someone else who could get that bitch on a leash. Leo.

Jahmad startled me awake, pulling me from my nightmare. I lifted my head from the side of the bed and looked around, trying to remember what had happened. The beeps and whirrs of the machine hummed like a soft melody as Jamaal lay sleeping, his tiny body seeming to disappear in the hospital gown. But he was breathing. That's all that mattered to me. His color had come back, the familiar brown complexion making him look like a tiny china doll in the crisp, white sheets. I sighed in relief, not wanting to remember the stark images that played in my dreams. Images of my child with Tina, her vindictive laugh as she held my son tighter and tighter until he had lost consciousness. I blinked until the vision faded away.

"How is he doing?" Jahmad whispered.

I sighed, grateful. "He's fine," I said. Remembering, I suddenly glanced around, noticing the room was empty with the exception of us. "Where is Adria?"

"She left with Keon when we got back." Jahmad set the bag down and took a seat beside me. For a moment we just sat in silence, both of us lost in our own thoughts watching Jamaal sleep. Interesting how we had shared the same moment only days earlier, but the difference was he had been in his crib in his nursery, safe. And we weren't afraid then.

I broke the silence first. "Did you find anything at the house?" I asked, afraid of his answer.

"No. Nothing."

Confused, I looked at his profile in the darkened room. "Not even the teddy bear? It was on the floor with all the stuffing. You couldn't miss it."

Jahmad shook his head. "I didn't see that."

My mind tried to process the information. It didn't make sense. None of it made sense. I shuddered to think someone had been in our house, but that was the only logical explanation. Of course there had been a teddy bear there. I wasn't imagining things, and what more proof did I need than my son lying here in a hospital bed from choking on a piece of it? But where was it?

Had Tina come back and taken it? Was this her fucked-up idea of some kind of sick mind game? That was certainly what she was known for, but why now? She clearly saw I had moved on and wanted no part of her husband. What was her end game?

Jahmad must have been thinking my thoughts exactly, because he spoke up and said, "As soon as we get out of here we are going to the police."

I did not respond, just continued staring at my son's sleeping figure. I knew he was right, and that was what I was afraid of.

I waited patiently for Jahmad to go to sleep, and when it finally looked like he dozed off, I grabbed my phone and snuck from the room. The reception was horrible on this floor so I took the elevator down to the hospital entrance and dialed Leo's number.

Of course, I did not expect him to pick up, especially on the first ring. But his voice came through the speaker as if he had been waiting for me to call. "My love," he greeted. "What a welcome surprise to hear from you. I've missed you."

"We need to talk," I said, his pleasant demeanor almost making me angry. Here my son was laid up in a hospital bed because of his wife and he had the nerve to act like this was some sort of courtesy call. Like two old friends getting together for drinks. The bastard. "Where is Tina?"

Leo paused as if shocked or confused by the question. "What do you mean?"

I rolled my eyes. "What do you mean 'what do I mean'? You're the last one that saw her before you told me she was out of the way and I wouldn't have to worry about her again, remember? Well, now I've seen her at my dad's church, and she was in my damn house." I conveniently left out the part about Jamaal. No need to add all that and overcomplicate an already complicated situation. "I think your bitch is stalking me," I went on. "And I'm telling you she needs to back off or I will go to the police and press charges."

"Okay, my love. I understand, but it's not that simple."

"And why is that?"

"We need to talk in person," he said quickly. "I will text you an address, and we can meet tomorrow."

"No," I snapped. "There is nothing—"

"My love, just hear me out. There are some things you need to know that I can't say over the phone."

I started to object again but heard the text message notification in my ear. It was Jahmad asking where I was. I quickly typed back that I had come out to get some air and was on my way back up. Then I put the phone back to my ear. "Fine," I agreed. "Text me and we'll meet tomorrow." I thought for a moment, then added, "Don't bullshit me, Leo. I'm not about to play these games with you and Tina. I'm not y'all's wife anymore." And with that, I hung up the phone and hurried back up to Jamaal's room.

Chapter 15

Tears stung my eyelids as they placed my son in my arms. He was grinning, looking and reaching for my face as if nothing had happened. And that was how I wanted to act: as if nothing had happened. I didn't want to harp on the what-ifs, because Lord knows I had beat myself up enough lingering on those, one scaring me more than anything. What if Tyree hadn't called when he had and woken me up? I would have slept on while my baby lay dying. The dreaded thought had me holding on to Jamaal just a little longer, just a little tighter, inhaling a little deeper the fresh baby soap scent that clung to his skin.

"Mommy missed you," I murmured. I kissed his still-damp hair, creating little soft ringlets that made him look more like a baby doll, before placing him carefully in his car seat carrier.

I half listened to the doctor about Jamaal's discharge instructions and follow-up care, partially because Jahmad was taking it all in like he was studying for an exam, but mainly because I was thinking about meeting up with Leo later.

He had texted me, sure enough. He wanted to meet at the Decatur downtown district; why I didn't know. So now my mind was flipping through all sorts of lies and excuses I could use to get away from Jahmad without looking suspicious. And I prayed he wouldn't hold to his suggestion we go to the police. Not yet.

Leo's words from yesterday echoed in my head, and I couldn't help but wonder what was so important that he needed to tell me in person.

"Ms. Davis?"

I turned at the voice, throwing a warm smile at the doctor when I realized he had been addressing me. It was obvious my mind was everywhere but here. "Take care of my little man," he repeated. "Next time I see him let it be at his first birthday party."

I nodded. "Absolutely, doctor, and thank you so much for everything."

I let Jahmad take the carrier from my hand and lead the way down the hall. He had something to say for sure. I could tell from his demeanor, from the brisk strides he took that seemed to maneuver him across the floor in half the time, even the tight grip he had on the carrier's handle.

We waited at the elevator, and I turned to him, resting my hand on his arm. "What is it?"

He shrugged off the contact. "Nothing."

"No secrets, no lies, remember?" I tossed his phrase in his face as I followed him onto the elevator.

"Maybe you need to start taking your own advice."

Shit. My mind went into overdrive, playing through the past few hours. What had happened? Had he found out about my meeting with Leo?

"And what is that supposed to mean?"

Jahmad didn't respond, just kept walking to my car. I waited while he secured the baby's car seat in the backseat before I spoke again. "Jahmad, what the hell is supposed to be your problem now?"

He didn't answer but glanced to his phone when it rang, piercing the tension between us. I crossed my arms over my chest.

"Oh, who is that? Your precious little CeeCee?" I snapped.

He faced me now, and my eyes widened. What little bit of rising anger I had was snatched clean and replaced with fear by the

pure rage I saw across his face. But underneath that was something else. Hurt, raw and jagged.

"Jahmad—"

"Follow me to the house," he said. And with that, he turned
and walked across the parking lot in the direction of his truck.

My heart quickened. Yeah, he must have found out about Leo,
I deduced. How? I didn't know, and at this point it really didn't
even matter. What mattered was: how was I going to explain my
deception?

I felt like I was driving down death row. Hell, even the cars I
passed felt like the passenger's eyes were on me, tsk-tsking at the
"dead bitch driving."

By the time I pulled up behind Jahmad in the driveway, I still
hadn't come any closer to a logical rationale for me not telling him
about Leo. None other than the truth in that I was scared it would
make him question my fidelity. And I sure as hell couldn't admit
that because, no matter how true it was, I knew he wouldn't believe
me. Even still, there was nothing else I could say.

As I parked my truck, I spotted Jahmad's neighbor, Patti,
stooped over a collection of manicured bushes, her short frame
bent as she stood starring at the shrubbery, a brimmed hat shielding her warm face from the spill of sun. Her shih tzu, Pokie,
sniffed eagerly through the grass at her ankles, stopping every so
often to lift a bark of attention to his distracted owner. I watched
as Patti pushed up the sleeves of her sweat-stained blouse and
shook her head.

Jahmad had already disappeared inside, and I took my time
getting JayJay out of the truck.

"Morning, Kimmy," Patti greeted, her rich southern accent
hanging like honeysuckle on each syllable. "Oh, you got that baby.
Let me see him."

She didn't wait for a response, just crossed the yard and

peeked into the carrier in my arms. "My, my, he's certainly getting big, isn't he?"

"Yes, ma'am."

Patti's smiled faded as she glanced to Jahmad's house. "I saw
the ambulance and police out here the other day. Everything
okay?"

Not wanting to rehash the situation, I simply nodded. "Yes,
ma'am. Everything is fine. Looking for something?"

"Snakes," Patti replied on a defeated sigh. "Or possums or
something. For days now the flowers over there"—she pointed to
a small garden on the bit of lawn dividing her and Jahmad's properties—"have been trampled on."

I eyed where she was pointing. "What do you mean?"

"Like flat. Like some cat or something is stepping on 'em. I
probably just need to call someone to come out here and spray or
set some kind of trap." A few more of Pokie's anxious barks and I
couldn't resist leaning over to scratch between his ears. His appreciative licks slapped wet streams of saliva against my wrist.

I took my time trying to digest what Patti was saying about the
flower garden. Something about that didn't sit right with me. And
considering what had happened and my conclusion that someone
had to have been in Jahmad's house, well, that certainly had me
riding high on all kinds of paranoia.

"Ms. Patti, have you noticed something around the house?" I
asked, readjusting Jamaal's car seat. "Like, I don't know. Someone coming around more?"

She frowned. "Like when y'all are gone? Nothing out of the or-
dinary, I suppose. But I can certainly keep a lookout if you want
me to."

I shook my head and plastered on a polite smile. "No, that's
okay. Since you're talking about the flowers being trampled, just
had me curious."

Patti murmured in agreement, pulled off the brimmed hat to

wipe the sweat pearled on her forehead. The gesture had her silver ringlets spilling from their neat perch to brush each shoulder. She stooped to scoop up Pokie, who was amusing himself by biting and growling at my shoelace. "It's those damn possums," she said, shaking her head. "Or raccoons, cats, or something. But anyway, let me get back inside. You call if you need anything, you hear? Don't you be afraid to call me." She looked at me with a sternness that reminded me of my mama.

I nodded with a smile before turning to walk toward the door. Just to make sure, I did pause to take a closer look at the flower garden Patti had indicated. Sure enough, the flowers were flattened, and there were even slight impressions of something in the soil. Of what, I couldn't make out.

I heard Jahmad in the kitchen when I stepped inside. Damn, he hadn't even bothered to grab the carrier and help me with the baby this time. But I knew whatever ice I was on, it was thin as hell, so rather than call him on it, I just headed up the stairs.

For a brief moment, I had a little post-traumatic stress entering the baby's room. My eyes immediately landed on the empty carpet, expecting to see the torn teddy bear. But Jahmad was right, there was nothing. And by the look of the open closet, he had gone searching for it, which did make me feel just a little better. It meant he believed me. Which also meant he too figured someone must have been in the house.

I set Jamaal's carrier down and did my own little mini search of the room to put my fears at ease. I peeked in the empty closet, then dropped to my knees and checked under the crib, half expecting to see Tina's crazy ass hiding in the shadows.

Even after checking around, something about putting my son back in the crib where I'd found him near death left me uneasy. Plus, he had fallen asleep, his head bobbing against the cushions of his seat. So I picked him up and carried him back downstairs and placed his carrier on the dining room table.

I caught Jahmad rummaging through mail while sipping what looked to be Hennessy at the kitchen counter. He spared me an absent glance.

"You not laying him down?" he said.

"He's fine."

I caught sight of something on the back door. "You got a new lock?"

"Yeah."

"Why?"

"Because the other one was broken."

He didn't have to say anything else for me to put two and two together. Teddy bear or no teddy bear, it was more than clear Tina had broken in and tried to harm my child. Which meant she had started World War III.

"We're getting a security system," I said. "And new locks on—"

"Kimera, what is this?" Jahmad interrupted, holding up a sheet of paper.

I frowned, more from his off-the-wall question in the middle of our discussion than the actual junk mail he was holding out to me. Still, I stepped closer and took the paper from his hand.

It was as if time stood still, painfully still. As the light-headed feeling clouded my brain, I wished like hell I could rewind time. Before the baby's accident, before CeeCee's pop-up visit, before the fire. Before all that shit. And maybe then I would've gone with my first instinct about ripping up that damn paternity test Leo had sent me as opposed to stuffing it in a purse in the nursery closet. The one that said that Leo was Jamaal's father. He must have found it when he was searching Jamaal's room for that damn bear like I had asked him to.

The paper slipped from my limp fingers and fluttered to my feet, resting faceup to display the results like an engraving: 99.6 percent. I was already shaking my head to deny the results, but more so to deny what I knew Jahmad must be thinking of me and Jamaal.

"It's not true," I whispered, my voice trembling over the words. When he remained quiet, I rushed on, seizing the opportunity to explain. "Someone sent this to me, but there's no way they could have tested Jamaal. That's how I know it's not real."

"Who would have faked some paternity test results, Kimera? And why?"

I was sobbing then, feeling like the walls were closing in on me. One lie after another and now I was strangling on them. I hadn't noticed when Jahmad pushed another stack across the counter so hard that they slipped off and fell to the floor in front of me. "You say that shit is fake? What about those? Are they fake too?"

I shut my eyes against the couple of checks Leo had sent for child support. Usually I would just deposit them into Jamaal's little savings account, but I guess I had been so stuck on stupid, just asking to be caught with my hand in the cookie jar, because these last two checks I hadn't bothered to deposit. Not yet, anyway.

"Who's writing you checks, Kimera?" Either fueled by his anger or the liquor or a combination of both, Jahmad was yelling now. "Or is that Tina too? I guess Tina is burning down your store, breaking and entering, trying to choke Jamaal, leaving teddy bears, and sending you money too. Is that it?"

I sighed. Frankly that did sound absurd as hell. "That's not what I'm saying—"

"Get your lying ass out of my house."

"Jahmad, you don't understand. Leo—"

I stopped short when Jahmad took the glass and hurled it across the room, the shattering startling a scream from my lips as well as Jamaal's. Instantly, the baby's cry filled the air, vocalizing exactly how I felt.

Jahmad didn't seem to care. He snatched the keys from the counter and stormed out, slamming the front door so hard the walls shook with the impact. I wanted to crumble to my knees, but I forced my trembling legs to move, stumbling to the door and yelling his name over the baby's wails though I knew it was useless.

I opened the door as Jahmad wheeled his truck through the lawn, his tires digging mud trails into the grass in an effort to get around my car, which was blocking the driveway. He tore up the street, and I watched him disappear, and this time, no matter how I tried to deny it, this time I knew it was for good.

Chapter 16

I heard the knock, loud and clear, but I still didn't bother to answer. This early in the morning, it could only be one of my parents on the other side of the door, and I figured maybe if I pretended to be asleep they would go away.

I really wasn't in the mood for conversation now. They hadn't bothered asking me questions when I showed up at their house last week, bag and baby in hand.

I'm sure they had been trying to mask their excitement I was moving back in, because now they could spoil their grandbaby. Never mind the fact that Jahmad had just kicked us out and had discovered, quite possibly, my child wasn't his. Never mind the depression that seemed to settle on me, thick and suffocating, so that all I had the energy to do was drag myself between the bathroom and the bed.

I had called Jahmad so many times he had blocked me and I hadn't even bothered leaving messages anymore. I'm sure he received all thirty-four of them along with the twenty-seven text messages. What probably pained me even more was that he had basically written JayJay off. No type of communication to see if he was doing okay. It was as if those results had hardened his heart, and any connection with my son was a connection to me, which he had made it good and clear he didn't want. He hadn't even let me explain. He hadn't even let me tell him the test was fake, at least that's still what I was hoping, and I had gotten a real one done with true results on the way. And the checks, well, I had done it for Jamaal, slowly building up his little savings account. Couldn't he see it wasn't about me? Or did he not care at that point?

Then, and I had to admit this was what really ripped at my heart, was Jahmad just making an excuse? He had given up Texas for us, for our family, but had he been looking for a reason so he could still go? Maybe it wasn't even me at all like I was beating myself up for. Maybe it was CeeCee. Jamaal and I were just collateral damage.

So now my child was without a father. And I couldn't lie, I was in no better shape myself as his mother; I might as well have been just as absent. I was fortunate my parents loved on him so much I'm sure he didn't even have time to register my absence. In my condition, that was probably a good thing.

The knock came again, gentle but persistent, and I finally mustered enough strength to pull myself from the pillows. The sweaty t-shirt and oversize sweat pants were now on their fourth day of wear and by the slight smell, were obviously overdue for a wash. Squeezed in my tiny bedroom was not only my stuff but Jamaal's, and we had officially taken over the rest of the house as well with toys and baby essentials cluttering the floor and furniture. My room was too small for a crib, not that that would've mattered, so my dad had gone out and gotten him some kind of convertible pack-and-play with the bassinet, changing table, and playpen that they had insisted be put in their room. I appreciated them stepping in. I hated to admit I couldn't see about my son like I wanted to right now with my heart hurting.

"Kimmy." My mom had apparently got a little fed up with me not responding and gone ahead and cracked the door. She poked her head through, noticed I was sitting up in bed in a daze, and opened the door all the way. She carried a gurgling Jamaal on her hip, who had found deep interest in the teardrop earrings she wore. "I just wanted to make sure you were awake."

I nodded and glanced at my cell phone for the umpteenth time, though I knew exactly what it said. Hell, I had been staring at my screen for the past hour, waiting on something, anything from Jahmad. Still nothing but the clock reading 7:52 a.m. and a fully charged battery.

"I'm up," I answered and held out my arms for Jamaal so she could hand him over. "How is he?"

"He is fine. We just had a bottle. Changed his little stinky butt." My mama paused and narrowed her eyes at me. "What about you?"

I shrugged, stalling. "What about me?"

"Don't play with me, child. You know what I mean."

I sighed my answer, struggling to keep the tears from falling. "Jahmad and I just had a little fight," I said, skirting around the whole truth.

My mama kept her eyes level with mine. "Was it your fault?" she asked bluntly.

That stung, mainly because she was right on the money. "How do you figure it was my fault, Mama?"

"I'm just asking. You don't have the most pure of track records here recently."

I knew she wasn't meaning to, but it felt as if she were digging the knife in further. First Jahmad, then the church, and now my mom. I smacked my teeth. "Everything is not on me. You know your little golden child Jahmad is not perfect either." My mind flipped back to CeeCee, whom I was sure he had called up before I'd even had a chance to pack my shit good.

"I'm not saying he's perfect," my mama said. "But I am saying that man loves you and especially Jamaal and he wouldn't put you out unless he felt you were to blame for something."

Damn, she was right. But still . . .

"He didn't put me out per se. My leaving was a mutual decision." I'm sure that sounded like the half-ass lie it was. A mutual decision to leave wouldn't have found me back at my parents' house but at a place of my own. I highly doubted the townhome I had wanted was still on the market so I would need to start my search over again. I would need to start picking up what was left of the pieces of my life. I really had been putting it off. It would make the end of my relationship that much more permanent. I hadn't been ready to admit that. But now, hell, I didn't even know anymore.

"Kimmy, just remember it's not just about you anymore," my mama said. "You have a son to think about."

"I am thinking about my son."

"Are you? Because if so, you need to stop being so damn selfish and start keeping Jamaal in mind when you make decisions. Whatever you do doesn't just affect only Kimera anymore. You're not the only one without Jahmad. Jamaal is too. Now what?"

My head dropped to my son lying on the bed in front of me. He was now occupied with his own feet, sucking his pacifier hard like he expected milk to come out. My mom's last question echoed in my head. I had asked myself the same thing repeatedly. Now what?

My mom backed toward the door, pausing in the frame. "Your dad and I are going out for a bit. We got an interested buyer on the church. Take care of my baby."

I nodded. "I'm taking care of him, Mama."

"I'm talking about you now," she said and closed the door behind her, leaving her words in the room.

I had missed calls, but these weren't the ones I was waiting for. Disappointment clouded my heart as I swiped through the notifications. No Jahmad. All Leo.

I honestly had forgotten all about meeting him after my argument with Jahmad. And now, just seeing his name come up on my phone screen sent waves of anger coursing through my body. It was because of him I was in this shit. Sending me that damn test in the first place let me know he was just trying to stir up trouble. Him and Tina's ass. Hell, probably both of them together. Our last conversation played in my mind.

He had said he needed to talk to me in person when I brought up his wife. He sounded . . . what was the word? Hesitant? Worried? I couldn't put my finger on it. But whatever personal shit he had going on, I couldn't care less. All I knew was he had ruined my damn life, before and now that I had left his ass alone. I knew I wouldn't be able to contain my rage if I saw him.

I put the phone back down and resumed packing Jamaal's diaper bag. Adria was on her way so we could go house hunting. She said she kept bringing it up because she and Keon were looking, but I knew that was an excuse. I knew it was to get me out of the house and out of my little funk. So I agreed, not really expecting any results from the search.

The doorbell rang just as I finished changing my little man, for the third time, and I carried him and his bag to answer it. She stood on the other side in her burgundy maxi dress and blue jean blazer, her natural curly 'fro pulled up into a high ponytail. Immediately, she took Jamaal from my arms and sprinkled his plump cheeks with kisses. She then pulled me in for a hug.

"How you holding up, sis?" Her face crinkled in genuine concern.

I nodded, putting on my best fake smile. No use verbalizing a lie so I didn't push and neither did she. I was grateful. Adria just knew me like that, when I needed her opinion or when I just needed her. Now was the latter.

We packed into the car, strapping Jamaal into his car seat before heading down the driveway.

"I've been talking to Tyree," Adria started cautiously as she eased the car onto the expressway. "About Melanin Mystique. Just trying to come up with a game plan."

I frowned. "Tyree? Why not me? Last I checked I was your business partner." At Adria's sigh, I quickly regretted my words. "I'm sorry."

"No, it's cool. I just meant he called me trying to see what we were doing. He's been holding off on looking for another job because he thinks we'll be back open soon." She hesitated before speaking again. "I told him I thought he should probably go ahead and look for something else."

I nodded, my mind drifting. I tried my best to swallow my nonchalance but honestly, Jahmad had taken precedence over the store. But maybe I needed to realign my focus. I needed to keep busy. Without my business and especially without Jahmad, I felt like an empty shell of myself.

Adria had her head cocked in my direction, obviously studying my reaction. "Well, I don't think the investigation will take too much longer," I said. "As soon as they realize none of us had anything to do with anything, the insurance will release the money so we don't have a complete loss. Until then, I still have some money we can use to—"

"Kimmy, no, you're not putting up another eight hundred fifty thousand dollars. Hell, we weren't even done with hiring and marketing yet. Shit, after the grand opening, we're looking at well over a million plus. And that's not including what you lost with the fire." I opened my mouth to counter her argument, but she kept on. "Besides. I'm not sure we have the time and energy,

Kimmy. That was crazy hectic and not at all what I expected. I think it was too much, honestly."

"So what are you saying, Adria?" I shifted in my seat to look at her straight. "Too much for who? You?"

Adria didn't respond, even after she pulled her car up to a brick two-level home with a "FOR SALE" sign embedded in the soft, freshly mowed lawn. She shut the car off and squinted through the window.

I took the opportunity to glance around, noting the spacious lots. Nice neighborhood, gorgeous house, but entirely too big for what I needed.

"Come on," Adria got out of the car, nearly bursting in excitement. "Get JayJay and let's take a look at this place."

Obediently, I stepped out of the car and opened the back door. Of course Jamaal had fallen asleep, little droplets of drool trickling down his chin. I leaned, carefully unbuckling his seat belt when the vehicle caught my eye through the back windshield. I frowned. Now I knew I wasn't crazy. I pulled Jamaal from the car, all while keeping my eyes on the white Infiniti parked not so inconspicuously a few blocks down. The same truck that had been parked in my parents' neighborhood and even at the townhome I had been looking to purchase a while ago.

My feet remained planted on the pavement, and if it wasn't for JayJay in my arms, I would've stalked right up to the vehicle and demanded the bitch come out and try and take me now. No guns, no pregnancy, no sneak attacks. Just a good ole-fashioned ass whooping. Tina was clearly asking for it.

I then thought about marching into the house and giving Jamaal over to Adria first so I could handle this unfinished business. But no sooner had the thought crossed my mind than the engine revved up and the truck bent a curve to take off on a different street. The collection of random letters and numbers on the license were just that, random and meaningless. But I did notice the tag was clearly out of state. Which one I wasn't sure, but definitely not Georgia.

"Hey." Adria appeared at my side, her eyes following mine to land on the now empty street the truck had just disappeared on. "What's going on? You okay?"

I wasn't. Questions cluttered my mind about Tina's intentions. But I nodded my response to Adria, immediately wiping the concern from my face as I used my hip to close the back door.

"Just looking at the neighborhood," I lied. "It's pretty, but I don't know, Adria. The house is a little too much."

"I figured for you and JayJay, yeah," she agreed, leading the way up the drive. "But Key and I decided we needed the space."

I opened my mouth to acknowledge her comment, closing it again when my brother suddenly appeared in the doorway of the house. "Hey, sis," he greeted and, as customary for all my family, took the baby from me. He leaned in and pecked me on the cheek before sharing an intimate kiss with his wife.

"Keon, I didn't know you would be here."

He smirked and glanced to Adria. "Why wouldn't I?" Noticing the confusion registered on my face, he said, "Oh, my bad. You don't know yet."

"Know what?"

They each waited a beat, exchanging knowing smirks. Then finally, Adria spoke up. "The sellers just accepted our offer on this house. We close next month."

A grin split my face, the first one I knew in a long-ass time. I threw my arms around her neck as she let loose the mini scream she had obviously been holding in. "Congratulations! I'm so happy for you both." And I genuinely was. Their happiness was contagious and for a moment, I had forgotten my own sorrows. I gave my brother a playful punch on the arm. "Look at my brother actually getting his grown man on."

"Come on, let me show you around," Adria said, snatching my arm.

Their new home was beyond gorgeous, from the gourmet kitchen to the floor-to-ceiling windows that opened the living room to the sunroom and in-ground pool in the fenced backyard. Hardwood floors swept throughout the house, adding the perfect touch of modern masculinity to offset the feminine charm in the chandeliers and crown molding.

Adria pointed out each unique feature like a proud homeowner, making sure to add what they planned to do in each of the rooms we toured. When she took me upstairs, we saw the large master bedroom along with three more bedrooms, one of which Adria was sure to inform me was Keon's "man cave."

"He can have his little space," she was saying, pushing open a door to another one of the spare bedrooms. "I'm going to have plenty to keep me busy."

"I'm sure," I said, peeking through the blinds to look over the front yard. "You're about to spend up all his little coins to decorate all this space."

"Yes. Especially this nursery."

I turned, just in time to see Adria nod in affirmation and put her hand to her stomach. Now it was my turn to let out a scream.

"I guess congratulations again," I squealed, instinctively placing my hands on her belly, already feeling for movement. "Why didn't you tell me? How far along are you?"

Now it was more than obvious, I wondered how I hadn't noticed before. I mean, yeah, it looked like she had picked up a couple pounds, but I had assumed her ass was just happy laid up with my brother and living her best life. But her glow was in her eyes, her smile, and it looked damn good on her.

"Like seven weeks," she revealed. "But it's the early stages, and I know how miscarriages are common in the first trimester, and I don't want to get Keon's hopes up yet—"

"Wait. You haven't told him?"

She shook her head. "I'm going to," she added. "I'm just scared. I don't know how Key is going to take it."

"What are you talking about? He's going to be thrilled."

Adria sighed, letting her arms fall to her sides. "That's one way to think of it," she murmured. "He could be excited and something happens and I could be getting his hopes up. On the other hand, what if he thinks it's too soon? We've only been married . . ." She paused and winked. "Seven weeks."

I grinned at the revelation. Typical conception-on-the-wedding-night story. These two were a fairy tale. "Adria, my brother is going to be so damn excited none of us will be able to shut him up for the next nine months."

She nodded, tears glistening on her eyelashes. We both giggled. "These damn hormones," she said, crying and laughing at the same time. I had to admit, I wanted to do the same thing myself. But for different reasons. And unfortunately there were no hormones to which I could attribute my own slew of emotions.

Chapter 17

I had to blink several times to make sure I was reading the correct name on the screen. But there it was in plain sight. Jahmad was calling.

As I sunk to the couch, my fingers shook as they hovered over my phone. Then, scared he would change his mind, I quickly swiped the screen to answer the call and put the phone to my ear.

"Hello?" I greeted and held my breath.

"Hey, Kimera." His voice was flat, his tone formal. Like he was making a business call. But beggars couldn't be choosers. After all this time, at least he was calling. Eighteen days, to be exact. I had damn sure been counting.

I let out my breath in a stuttering sigh and squeezed my eyes shut. "Hi." I didn't realize I was whispering and I cleared my throat. "I've been trying to reach you. I'm glad you called."

"How is Jamaal?"

His abrupt tone stung. But I had to look at the positives. He had called about the baby. Despite whatever hatred he had for me, he had still called.

I looked to Jamaal having a little tummy time on his play mat on the living room floor. His head was lifted and bobbing with the effort to keep it up.

"Missing you," I answered for myself. The silence prompted me to continue. "Jahmad, we need to talk. Please. I'm sorry for what happened but I need to explain." Another pause and I felt my heart racing in anticipation of his response.

"Yeah, we can talk," he agreed. "I'll come over there later."

I jumped up, unable to contain my excitement. "What time?"

"Later," he stated stiffly. "I'll text you." Then he hung up.

I wanted to scream for joy. Dancing to Jamaal, I bent and scooped him up, planting noisy kisses all over his face. He cooed and giggled in response, reaching his hands to my face.

"Good to see you back to your old self, baby girl." My dad padded into the living room on a stifled yawn and immediately made his way to the kitchen for his morning coffee.

"I'm happy," I said with a smile. "Jahmad is coming over later so we can work things out. I'll probably move on back in with him." Granted, that was wishful thinking, but I was being optimistic. Speaking things into existence, like my father would say.

The welcoming scent of coffee beans filled the air. Hinges squeaked on opening and closing cabinets and drawers as my dad went about taking out his mug, sugar, and spoon.

"I'm praying for you two," he said. "You know, you both together with that grandboy of mine makes my heart smile. Now once you two get married, I can die a happy man."

"Stop that, Daddy. You know I don't want to hear you saying anything about dying."

"I meant that figuratively, baby girl. You know I'm not going anywhere." He poured the coffee in the mug and turned to kiss us both. The fresh steam from his cup warmed my cheeks.

I then noticed he wasn't wearing his pajamas but some slacks and a button-up. "Where are you headed?"

"Just need to go to the church for a bit," he said. "Get some paperwork."

I frowned my disapproval. My mom had been adamant on not letting him return to the church, at least not alone. But she'd left about an hour ago to run some errands, so she certainly wasn't here to object.

Dad chuckled at my expression, obviously reading my thoughts. "I'm okay, baby girl. I won't be long. Besides, you see I'm completely fine."

That much was true, but I still felt uneasy. "Let me just call Mama and let her know."

"I don't need your mother's permission to do anything," he said, puffing out his chest. "There is nothing wrong with me going to the church that I oversee. I'm not scared of your mother."

He strolled past me toward the door, then stopped and turned. "If she calls and asks, just tell her I went out to run some errands please, baby girl."

I laughed. "I thought you're not scared of her?"

"I'm not," he said. "But I'm no fool either."

———⟶◦⟵———

Jahmad's text came through at exactly 1:32 p.m. I'd been anxiously awaiting the notification and I eagerly opened the message to read it. "4:00," was all it read. Good. That was all I needed.

I'd already gone shopping and picked up cute little matching outfits for Jamaal and me, distressed white jeans with a royal blue top. He'd been fed, burped, and I took care to change him even when his diaper was clean for fear his little Pampers would flood onto his nice pants. I had to make sure we looked the part, the family Jahmad was missing and longing for.

At thirty minutes until four, I changed Jamaal one last time and laid him on his baby gym floor mat. When he started hollering, I immediately picked him up. "Daddy's coming," I whispered in his ear. As if he understood, his little cries subsided into tiny whimpers. I grinned at the calming reaction. "I know. I miss him too."

The doorbell had both of our heads whipping in the direction of the front door. I waited a brief moment before making my way over, not wanting to appear too anxious. Another ring filled the empty house, this time a little longer. Taking a breath, I clicked the locks out of place and swung the door open.

I'm sure shock registered all over my face as I stared at the visitor. Not Jahmad at all. What the entire hell was she doing here?

CeeCee didn't bother waiting for an invitation, just stepped past me into the living room. I didn't know what was more dominant, her perfume or her attitude, so clearly expressed by the scowl on her face as she looked first around the room, then to Jamaal in my arms, and finally at me.

"Listen, I'm going to make this quick," she said, planting her hands on her hips. "I know what you're trying to do and that shit ain't going to work."

I rolled my eyes. Whatever she thought I was trying to do, I would rather her keep thinking it than give her the satisfaction of knowing I didn't know what the hell she was talking about. Whatever it was, it was obviously pissing her off.

"You need to back off," she went on. "Stop using that damn baby to get to Jay. He won't fall for it."

"Oh, you mean his son?"

CeeCee smirked. "Don't even try that shit. Jay already told me the baby is not his, so your cards are up. I mean that was real cute how you tried to pass a child off as his. Desperate, but cute. But now that he knows, you have nothing left. So get the hell over it."

It was obviously a blessing I was holding Jamaal because otherwise I would've knocked the bitch backward off her little stilettos. My grin was just as condescending. "So if it's over, why are you here?" I taunted. "Seems to me you feel threatened because you think that maybe, just maybe Jahmad still loves me. And you're afraid."

CeeCee flicked her hand at my comment, as if she were waving away a pesky fly. "Jahmad has been keeping me informed of y'all's issues. Why do you think I never went back to Texas? He asked me to stay here and wait for him until he was ready to take that promotion. Now he can come back to me."

I struggled to wipe away the surprise on my face. That wasn't true. It couldn't be.

"Hey," she added with a pitiful smile at Jamaal. "At least you still have your child, so you won't be totally alone. And Jahmad,"—she lifted her hand to her own flat stomach—"well, he has ours. So it's a win-win."

Nausea settled in the pit of my stomach, and I suddenly felt so weak I had to brace against the wall so I wouldn't drop my baby. CeeCee breezed back out the front door, leaving it open wide for me to see her hips sashaying toward a white Infiniti truck. So this had been the bitch stalking me? This whole time? Not Tina, but CeeCee? Damn.

She had parked at the end of the driveway so she hadn't quite pulled off when Jahmad's truck pulled up. I watched curiously. I wondered if any of her story had validity. I guessed this would show it.

Jahmad climbed from his truck and immediately started for CeeCee's vehicle as she stepped back out of the driver's side. I couldn't make out what they were saying, but they appeared to be yelling and clearly talking about me with the way they both were gesturing wildly in the direction of my house. Good. That's what the hoe got.

Jahmad glanced up and briefly his eyes met mine. I quickly scurried to close the door so I could continue watching from the privacy of a window. JayJay began to feel warm and heavy on my hip so I switched sides, not daring to put him down and step away from the action. I wanted to see Jahmad put this bitch in her place.

By the time I pulled back the curtains in the living room, CeeCee was back in her car, shielded in the tinted glass. Jahmad was leaning on the door. The two seemed much calmer, which had my panic slightly rising. What were they talking about so cool and composed?

The warm, wet sensation, now followed by a stench, had traveled to my other side, and I looked down. Pee and poopoo seeped from Jamaal's white pants and had transferred onto not one but both of my sides from where I had him perched on each hip. The smell was enough to have me gag as yellow and brown splotches stained the white denim fabric.

"Dammit, Jay!" Irritation had the words dripping from my lips before I had time to stop them, coincidentally right when Jahmad pushed open the front door. Silence, then Jamaal erupted into fitful sobs.

I wanted to cry right along with him. I know I looked and smelled a hot shitty mess, not at all the impression I wanted to give Jahmad when seeing him again for the first time. My own tears seeped from my eyes, fat, sloppy rolls that streaked makeup down my cheeks.

"What happened?" Any trace of apathy was gone from Jahmad's voice, now replaced with compassion. Genuine and utter compassion. That made me cry harder. Damn, I missed this man.

He came forward, and gentle hands took Jamaal from my arms. That was all the baby needed, because he quickly stopped crying and immediately reached for him with soft whines.

"Whoa there, little man." Jahmad held the baby out in front with extended arms. Jamaal's little feet dangled, and the shit that collected in the seat of his pants and ran down his legs made it obvious those clothes were completely useless. It was also obvious he didn't have a shred of diaper on his ass.

Jahmad turned JayJay around so he could see, clearly coming

to the same conclusion. "Where is his diaper?" he asked. "Why you got him out here balls-free, pissing and shitting everywhere?"

I threw up my hands. "I guess I didn't put the diaper on tight enough when I changed him last," I admitted, swiping the tears from my damp face. "I'm sorry, I was waiting on you, and I—"

"Just go get cleaned up," Jahmad suggested, his tone now gentle. "I'll handle Jamaal."

The situation was far from humorous, but I felt the chuckle bubble up in my throat before spilling out to full-blown laughter. Two pairs of eyes landed on me, and I'm sure I looked as ridiculous as I felt.

Jahmad shook his head. "What?"

"I look like shit," I said for lack of anything else.

He nodded. "Damn sure do. And you smell like it too."

I don't know why, but that little snide-ass joke comforted my heart. He might as well have told me he loved me.

I only wore a towel as I journeyed back in my room, my body still wet from the shower. Jahmad was seated on my bed with a now clean Jamaal wrapped in a red onesie and blanket, a bottle to his lips.

I smirked, watching him for a minute. "You would think he's had enough milk." I felt Jahmad's eyes on me as I leaned over to kiss the baby's forehead. "Mommy is sorry for yelling, baby." And because I knew Jahmad was still watching, I took my time bending and squatting at the dresser, pretending to look for clothes to put on.

"I'll meet you back up front," he said suddenly, almost as if he was frustrated. He rose and left the room.

More to prolong the inevitable, I took my time changing into a t-shirt and some baby shorts. By that time, Jamaal was nodding off, so I picked him up and rocked him the rest of the way to sleep. I then carried him in my parents' room, placed him in his crib, and mentally prepared myself for the war I knew was waiting for me.

Jahmad slipped his phone in his pocket as I reentered the living room and joined him on the couch. "Where are your folks?" he asked.

"They went out earlier. Running some errands and handling church business."

"My fault about CeeCee." He nodded toward the door. "I didn't know she was coming over here. Hell, I didn't even know she knew where you stayed."

"She's been stalking me, Jahmad," I said. Now was as good a time as any to play the sympathy card. Especially if what she had said was true and they really were back together. "She came in here with all this bullshit about y'all, popping off at the mouth about Jamaal. I mean why is she even still here in Georgia?"

"I'll talk to her," Jahmad said simply. His voice held the tone of finality, like he was done with the topic, but no way could I let it go.

"She says she's pregnant," I whispered, studying his reaction. I should've known better. Jahmad had an out-of-this-world poker face, and I couldn't tell if the revelation was true or if he even knew for that matter. He just kept his face blank and stared ahead. I thought about the sequence of events that had happened, leading up to the most recent. "She probably was the one that hurt Jamaal," I mumbled.

I peered at Jahmad just in time to see his frown of disgust. "That's real fucked up if you believe that shit, Kimera," he snapped.

"I'm just saying, who else could have done it?"

"Maybe you need to stop blaming shit on everybody else and own up to the fact that you fucked up."

"Me?"

"Yeah. JayJay was in there near dying on something, and what was your ass doing? Sleep. That's some neglect for your ass."

I was all the way on a hundred now. How could he even part his lips to say some shit like that to me? "You know what? Fuck you, Jahmad." I spit out each word with every piece of rage that was now coursing through my body. I was hurt, and shaking at the revelation that something like that would even cross his mind. I collapsed on the sofa, willing the tears away that were threatening to fall. Not to mention my head was throbbing with such force it was almost making me nauseated.

"I didn't mean that," Jahmad finally spoke up again, breaking our strained silence. "That was fucked up for me to say."

You damn right was what I wanted to say but didn't. I just nodded in response. Then I thought about the question that had been sitting on my heart. I didn't want to ask but I had to know. "Are you going back to Texas?" I whispered. At first, I wasn't even sure he heard me, but he leaned forward and rubbed his face. He looked as stressed as I felt, that was for damn sure.

"Probably so."

Those two words felt like a knife to the gut. I didn't think it would hurt as much as it did. The bitch had been right. Whether she was having his baby or not, perhaps she could've been lying to add insult to injury. But hell, even that paled in comparison to right now. Bottom line, she was in Texas, and he was going back. And leaving me and Jamaal.

"I've tried to think about this from every perspective," Jahmad mumbled, almost to himself. "Yours, mine, Jamaal's. I can't see anything other than your lies and deceit."

I shook my head. "Jay, no. It's not like that."

"You told me he was mine, Kimera," he countered through clenched teeth. "You let me believe it. Not once did you say it could be a possibility otherwise. That shit is foul, and I can't be with a woman that would do some conniving shit like that. Not just to me but to her child." He turned disgusted eyes to me, and I felt like shit, again.

"Jahmad, I didn't know. I'm sorry. I just wanted—needed you to be. I—we love you." I chanced reaching out to touch his arm, not surprised when he snatched it back. "We need you, Jahmad. Please don't do this to us."

"Do what?" he snapped. "Not let you manipulate me? Not let you trap me?"

The tears had started flowing again, and I let them, freely. "You are his father, Jahmad. What difference does all that other shit make? You saw how he acted when you came in the door?"

"Don't—"

"That's what matters!"

"Then why did you take the money, then?"

I opened my mouth and shut it again. I really didn't even have an answer for that. "Because I was stupid," I blurted out, my voice cracking. "Because part of me felt that man owed me for everything he put me through, so I was willing to milk it. I'm sorry."

"Sorry for being a gold-digging bitch?"

The words slapped me, and I had to look at him to make sure they had actually come from his mouth. Damn, he had never taken it that far. As if he too realized that, he dropped his head and his shoulders went slack. "My fault," he murmured. "I shouldn't have said that."

I sighed. "No, you're right." Silence. No rebuttal, no objection. Just silence.

Jahmad rose to his feet and pulled a folded envelope from his pocket. It had already been opened, the wrinkles and creases evident that he had been carrying it around for a minute.

"You snuck and got another DNA test done?"

I gasped, eyeing the return address on the envelope. I had forgotten all about that. I took it from him, my fingers trembling. The results. The real results were in. Jahmad knew the truth. "I should have told you," I admitted. "But I didn't believe those other results. The ones that you found. They weren't true."

When he didn't say anything or move, I sighed and pulled the results from the envelope. And my heart shredded to pieces. I had lied again, and I waited for some cameramen for Maury to follow me off the stage while the audience roared in disbelief. Those first results had been true. Jahmad was not the father.

Chapter 18

"The property has just been reduced." The real estate agent, I believe her name was Mandy, Melanie, or something, did a twirl in the middle of the living room, her arm gesturing out toward the quaint space. "It's the perfect size for you and little man here." As if on cue, Jamaal tossed the woman a gummy smile from my hip.

I nodded, going over the house tour we'd just finished. It was smaller than I anticipated, but for some reason it seemed to fit. I didn't need a ton of space. After all, it was just me and my son.

I moseyed to the kitchen area. It was slightly outdated so I would need to purchase new appliances, darker wood cabinets because the white was just too countrified for me, maybe do some painting. The backyard I wanted to fence in so I could sit out on the deck and watch JayJay play in the yard. Even upstairs, the two bedrooms and bonus room over the two-car garage needed some minor fixes. Nothing major, just some tender love and care. That was probably why the little home was pulling on my heart. It was a detached home and yes, a little fixer-upper. Hell, like me.

"If you want to think about putting an offer in—"

"I want to put an offer in," I decided. No need to play, second-guess, and there was certainly nothing to sleep on. If I gave myself more time, I would just get my hopes up for no reason.

The woman clapped in delight. "I'll go get the paperwork from the car. I should already give you a little sneaky congratulations. This is a very motivated seller."

I nodded. "Well, good," I said. "Because I am a very motivated buyer."

The woman walked outside as my phone vibrated in my purse, for what I knew was the tenth time. Probably Adria again. I loved my best friend and I knew she was concerned, but I wasn't in the mood right now. I was sure Jahmad had told Keon everything that had gone down yesterday, and Keon had blabbed to Adria. I was embarrassed, but more than that, I had fallen back into my state of depression.

He had left me yesterday. After he had given me the real test results, the ones that confirmed that no ounce of Jahmad Washington's DNA flowed through my son's body, that Jamaal was indeed another product of my marriage to Leo Owusu, he had left me there crying, crumbling, and begging on the floor of my parents' living room. After a while, hell, I don't even know how much time had passed, but a throbbing migraine had me peeling myself off the floor. After I downed some medicine, I packed my and Jamaal's stuff and booked myself at a hotel. I couldn't face my parents. I couldn't face anyone. I had turned my phone off and just wanted to be alone.

So I had soaked in a warm bubble bath with my baby nestled on my breast and just watched the time tick by. When the warm water had chilled and I felt Jamaal's wrinkling skin pepper with goose bumps, I'd gotten out, dressed and fed him, and laid him in the bed beside me. I knew I had to get away and, frankly, the W Hotel in downtown Atlanta wasn't far enough.

So I had stayed up researching before buying tickets to an all-inclusive island resort in Punta Cana. Impulsive, but it wasn't like I had anybody to talk me out of it. No strings holding me down. Nothing. If it hadn't been for my parents, I wouldn't have even considered purchasing a home in Atlanta. I needed a change of scenery, and I wouldn't have minded moving across state lines. Maybe Florida or Virginia. But I wouldn't dare take my baby away from my family. So the seven-day trip to the Dominican Republic would do. I already had a taxi ready to take us to the airport in a few hours. And now, if I could lock in this house I'd also found in my web surfing last night, then I would be set. Not happy. But set. That was probably as good as it would get for now.

Four hours later, I was sitting in the airport with Jamaal on my lap and a home purchase contract in my luggage. I had eventually sent Adria a text just letting her know the baby and I would be going out of town for a few days and I would call her when I returned. I had then turned my phone off knowing the news would circulate among my family and ease any worry.

The intercom called for first-class passengers and I rose, Jamaal on my hip and the handle to a roll-on carry bag in my hand. I absolutely planned to make good use of the three-hour flight, and I prayed JayJay would too. As it was his first flight, I really didn't know what to expect, but I certainly hoped for the best.

I had just settled in my window seat and shut my eyes when the leather seat next to me creaked from the weight of my companion. I didn't bother acknowledging the person, and I hoped my closed eyes would deter him or her from trying to strike up a friendly conversation. It seemed to work, but the giggles from my baby indicated that he was obviously entertained by the person.

"He's perfect, my love."

My eyes snapped open, half expecting Leo's voice to dispel with the end of what I assumed had to be a dream. But there he was, in the flesh. For a brief moment, I just sat in shock, almost hypnotized by the familiar eyes and charming smile. He was of course calmer than I'd seen him at the hospital, all traces of aggression gone, which I could only attribute to finally seeing his son. The thought made me cringe, but I just held my breath as he continued cooing at Jamaal and Jamaal babbled back like they had some secret language.

"Leo, what are you doing here?" I finally asked through clenched teeth.

He sighed and sat back, shifting in the seat to look at me. "I know what happened," he said, his voice carrying compassion; I couldn't tell if it was sincere. "Between you and Jahmad. I just wanted to let you know that all hard feelings aside, I'm here for you, my love."

"Why, Leo? Why? You're the one that ripped everything up. You sent the paternity test, remember?"

"I just wanted you to know the truth. You kept insisting he wasn't mine. Look at him."

I didn't want to, but my eyes dropped to Jamaal. He was right. When I finally got out of what I wanted to see, the similarities were undeniable.

"You know, it can be like you wanted in Jamaica," he said. "Our honeymoon. You wanted it to be just us instead of you, me, Tina, and Lena. We can have that now. Here. With our little one." He flashed a wide smile. A smile that was making my heart beat entirely too fast.

I shook my head. "Leo, please just go away," I said, not hiding the pleading in my tone. "I just want to be alone right now."

"I promise I won't bother you if you don't want me to," he said, lifting his two fingers in a mock scout's honor. "You've been avoiding me and I just want to be there for you. And my son. That's all. I love you. Don't you know that by now?"

I turned my face to the window as the plane began its taxi to the runway. I did know that. That's what I was afraid of.

———※◆※———

Leo had insisted he wouldn't bother us, that he wanted us to enjoy our little getaway and he would stay back until I called him.

I noticed how he said *until* instead of *if*, like it was some kind of guarantee. I just rolled my eyes and ignored him for the rest of the ride.

We landed in Punta Cana, and I was quick to leave Leo behind as I made my way first to baggage claim, then to the shuttle that would take us to the resort. I wasn't surprised when he later boarded the same shuttle with a duffel bag on his arm. But instead of sitting in the empty seat beside me, he made his way to the back and stuck some headphones in his ears. Of course he would book the same hotel as us. I frowned at the circumstances. I wanted to get away from everything and everyone. The last thing I had expected was to spend my vacation with my supposed-to-be-dead ex-husband lurking in the shadows.

We pulled up to the oceanside resort with its all-white, open-air buildings and beautiful backdrop of sunny skies and palm trees. It was completely gated, and after checking us all in curbside, ensuring that yes, each person was a paid guest at the expensive property, the shuttle wheeled us around the circular pathway and dropped us off right in the lobby.

Immediately, two Hispanic women in flowing sundresses came out to greet us, murmuring pleasantries in English with their Spanish accent and offering frozen fruit cocktails with paper umbrellas on a tray. I thanked the ladies and passed on the drinks, since I was carting my justification right on my hip. I did promise myself I would order some room service later and indulge in the open bar after JayJay was down for the night, though. Shit, why not? It was included, and Lord knows I needed it.

I was led outside and shown into another open-air building with two stories. Our room had an ocean view on the bottom level, with a Jacuzzi tub, marble steam shower, and a private mermaid pool right outside of a sliding glass door that instantly opened the interior hotel room to an outdoor living space.

My first thought as soon as I was alone was to power on my

phone and call Adria to let her know I had arrived safely. I immediately dismissed the idea. I didn't want to lapse into explanations and risk refuting my entire purpose for getting away in the first place. Negativity was not part of this package, and despite having one across the way in building five, which is what the hotel agents informed Leo upon check-in, I was determined not to let him or any of that bullshit back in Atlanta ruin my plans for rest and relaxation. Sure, it would all be waiting for me when I returned, but hopefully a few island days, sun, and alcohol would keep me sane enough to deal with it.

Chapter 19

Day one and two, Leo kept his word, and I didn't so much as see him anywhere. I hated to admit it, but I was specifically looking for him, just so I could avoid him, but apparently it wasn't necessary.

I tried the different cuisines, bounced between lounging poolside with Jamaal on my chest or sitting on the pool steps and letting him get his little feet wet, and catching a few of the live resort shows. They had an onsite childcare center, which I didn't even bother to try. I kept my baby saddled to me like my lifeline. No, Leo wasn't on any of my paperwork, but I didn't want to chance anything.

We didn't make it out to the beach until day three. Jamaal and I were playing out in the sand, well, mainly I was playing, he was watching in amazement, when a guy walked near with parrots on his shoulders. He gestured toward me with the digital camera in his hands. "Let me take your picture, *mami*," he offered in his thick Spanish accent.

I smiled my apology. "No thanks," I said.

"Here, take mine," Leo said, walking up to us.

I eyed him from behind my sunglasses; his swim trunks riding low, his bare chest glistening from his obvious dip in the ocean. Damn, the man was still fine as ever.

The photographer excitedly transferred the birds to Leo's shoulders and began snapping away. I watched in amusement as Leo struggled not to appear frightened by the creatures, even made a few funny faces; I didn't know if they were for my enjoyment or the camera. Even Jamaal appeared to be giggling at the mini show.

At one point, one of the parrots obviously flapped his wings too close to Leo's face, and he let out a startled holler that had me doubling over in laughter. "Oh, man, I'll give you a hundred bucks to send me that one," I told the photographer.

Leo hid his embarrassment with a shy smirk. "I'll give you five hundred dollars to destroy it." And just to prove a point, he quickly dipped in his pocket and pulled out several wet bills.

I shook my head as the photographer, clearly pleased by the sale, accepted the money and headed off farther down the beach for more customers.

"I needed that laugh," I murmured, appreciating how much better I felt, just that quickly.

"I needed that too," Leo said. I could tell he was debating whether he should sit beside me. He didn't. His eyes dropped briefly to Jamaal before flicking away as if he had been caught doing something he shouldn't. "I didn't mean to disturb you two," he murmured. "Just wanted to put a smile on your face, my love."

Before I could comment, he left me grinning as he walked off farther down the beach, his black skin shining like onyx crystals in the sunset.

On day four, Jamaal was a little crankier than usual, and I was trying my best to balance his squirming figure and my breakfast tray at the same time. I didn't realize Leo was even there until I saw his hands take the tray from mine.

"I got it," I said. That was a lie. I clearly didn't have it, and I probably looked very pitiful with my crying baby in one hand while keeping a firm grasp on my tray of blueberry waffles, eggs, and Canadian bacon in the other.

Leo ignored me and took the tray anyway, leading me to a nearby table. "Want me to get you something else?" he asked as I sank into the booth.

I smirked at him. "Since when do you wait on me, Mr. Owusu?"

"A lot has changed, my love," he said. He winked, briefly looking at Jamaal once more, before strolling off to prepare his own breakfast.

By the time he returned, I had gotten Jamaal a lot calmer and managed to get down a fourth of my waffles. I didn't object when Leo sat at the table right next to me. I couldn't help but sneak side glances at him as he ate in silence.

"He looks just like you," Leo commented, keeping his eyes trained on his plate. I looked down at Jamaal in my arms, searching for any traces of my features in his baby face. I didn't see any.

"Thanks." I should have been cussing this man out with every piece of anger I'd been harboring, but for some reason I was at a loss for words. Wasn't I supposed to be pissed at this man? This man who had damn near destroyed my life, both while I was married to him and even after? Why was I so comforted by his presence? I sighed, recognizing that Jahmad had left such a big hole in my heart, I was searching for any semblance of normalcy, of familiarity. Damn, I was a pathetic mess.

Leo polished off his meal and turned in my direction. I could read the conflict of emotions that played on his face, but still, he kept his mouth shut.

"What is it?" I finally prompted.

He paused, then said, "May I hold him? Just for a minute?"

Instinctively, my grip on Jamaal tightened. I remembered the test results, the real ones, that no matter how much I tried to believe it wasn't so, this was indeed his son. There were 99.6 reasons why I couldn't deny that much.

I nodded, watching Leo's every movement as he rose, slipped his hands underneath Jamaal's armpits, and lifted him into his arms. He stood still as if he were holding his breath, afraid to move. To my surprise, JayJay didn't cry. He just watched him as intently as I was, the question, I was sure, playing on all three of our minds. Now what?

A beat passed, then two, and just as slowly, as if he didn't want to push his limit, or maybe it was mine, Leo held the baby back out to me. He let out the breath he had been holding as Jamaal settled into my arms once again. "Thank you" was all Leo said, and again, he left before I responded. I snuggled Jamaal closer, smelling Leo's lingering scent in his hair.

Later that day, I felt more comfortable using the in-room child-care service for Jamaal just for an hour or two while I took a peek in the spa. I should have been surprised, though I wasn't, to wander into one of the indoor rooms to find Leo neck deep in the Jacuzzi under the dim glow of the intimate lighting that cast a soft illumination on his downcast face. I wondered what he was thinking about because damned if his expression didn't match my entire mood for the past few weeks.

Without a second thought, I entered the room and took a seat at the lip of the Jacuzzi, placing my feet inside. Leo looked at me, and his face warmed a little. Or perhaps that was just the steam from the water. I couldn't tell. For a moment, we remained silent, neither wanting to address the elephant in the room while a speaker played a soft jazz melody that added to the relaxing aura and lightened the tension between us.

"We never did get to talk before," he started. "I tried calling you."

The heat from the water on my legs was beginning to warm my entire body. "I guess it doesn't really matter now," I murmured. "I thought Tina was stalking me. But I found out it was . . ." Jahmad's little sneaky bitch, CeeCee. "Someone else," I finished with a shrug.

"Why would you think Tina was around you?"

"I saw her at my dad's church, Leo," I reminded him. "That's hardly a coincidence. I mean what was she doing there?"

"I don't know," he admitted with a sigh. "After what happened with you, I don't see much of her."

The news brought a wave of confusion. I frowned. "But she has Leo Junior. What about him?"

"Leo Junior is not my biological son," Leo said, looking up at me with saddened eyes.

I shook my head. That didn't make any sense. "But Lena—"

"Was pregnant, yes." Leo nodded his affirmation. "But not by me. Not like I thought. Tina told me afterwards she'd arranged for Dr. Lin to get her pregnant with a sperm donor. Apparently, I wasn't getting her pregnant, at least not fast enough for Tina's liking. By that time, Lena had just had the baby, I was dealing with her death and then the death of my mother. It was like that on top of everything else."

Shock had my mouth wide open as I struggled to process this new information. Never had I expected that. I thought back to Leo's detachment from Leo Jr. initially. I had often wondered why he wasn't more involved and had just handed his baby to Tina on a silver platter, but I had just chalked it up to all he was going through. But now it made sense: Leo Jr. was never his baby to begin with.

And Dr. Lin, Lord, I couldn't even process how much he had been involved in this whole ordeal. I originally thought he was Leo's good friend. And now here was Leo revealing that, in fact, there was indeed more to this man's deception, with Tina being the master ringleader. My mind was completely blown.

"Wow," I murmured, for lack of a better reply. "Just wow. So did Tina tell you this or did you find out?"

"She told me after the fact," he said. "We were arguing and she just blurted it out. I don't even know if she meant to tell me. She said she had sworn Lena to secrecy because there was still a chance it could be mine, and really, what did it matter, she said. By then, I had signed the birth certificate, and like I said I was flying out to take care of my mom before she died, so I really didn't have a chance to get everything cleared up before . . ." He trailed off. But he didn't have to say the rest. I knew. Before Tina tried to have him killed and he went ahead and faked his death.

Slowly, the other pieces of the puzzle clicked into place. I could never figure out why it was that big of a deal with my son. I kept wondering why Leo was so hell-bent on being in JayJay's life considering he already had a child. Because really, biologically, JayJay *was* his only child. Damn.

"You sent test results," I said, remembering the little envelope he'd left taped to my door.

"I wanted you to know," Leo admitted. "It was nothing to have him tested in the hospital. One of the NICU nurses owed me a little favor. But you just wouldn't listen. You wouldn't let me be in his life. I need to be in his life."

His last comment sent a slight chill up my spine. How was this supposed to work now? We were just supposed to co-parent like everything was normal? Like *we* were normal? I was so deep in thought that I didn't notice at first that Leo had moved closer to me, and his arm now brushed against my leg underneath the water. I couldn't tell whether it was accidental, but I didn't object.

"Someone tried to hurt Jamaal, I think," I revealed, studying Leo's reaction. "I was asleep and when I woke up, there was a stuffed teddy bear in his room that had been cut up so the stuffing was everywhere. Jamaal was choking and had stopped breathing. We had to rush him to the hospital."

He looked genuinely alarmed. "When was this?"

"Few weeks ago. They didn't find the stuffed animal. And it

looks as if I'm lying. Like maybe it was just neglect. At least that's what people are saying." And by *people*, I meant Jahmad. But honestly, his opinion was the one that mattered. And the shit still hurt.

"I know you wouldn't do that, my love," Leo said, his voice soft. "You're a perfect mother. A perfect woman. I just didn't appreciate you as much as I do now."

His words sent electric shocks through my body, and I had to blink my surprise. How did we suddenly get off of Jamaal? Leo was being gentle; all the things I had gotten from him before we got married. Before he changed. And he was showing that tender compassion that I had been lacking for so long from Jahmad.

My mind was foggy and cluttered with confusion. Even after he leaned to my face while pulling me into the water to meet him, the bubbles tickling my skin and the pressure causing my sundress to rise up until it was floating on top of the water around us like a sea of floral cotton. I don't even know who kissed who, but I did feel his soft lips against mine, coaxing them apart with his tongue. He swallowed my moan, wrapping his arms around my naked waist, pressing my body against his.

I broke the kiss, only for him to pull me closer as he devoured the sensitive flesh on my neck. "Leo, we can't . . ." My mind suddenly went blank, and I sighed at the welcome bliss.

Chapter 20

What the hell was I doing? I couldn't help but ask myself this question repeatedly as I watched Leo down the beach, lifting Jamaal in the air. The pair looked to be thoroughly enjoying the little playtime, their laughter muffled by the crash of waves against the shore.

I sighed as I readjusted my hat to further shield my forehead from the sun. My eyes narrowed behind the dark sunglasses. I couldn't take my eyes off of them. They both looked so . . . happy. But where did that leave me?

Leo loved me. He had made sure to voice that numerous times both during the intimate spa encounter yesterday, and even after when he called my room later that evening. I woke up just as confused as I had gone to bed.

My heart belonged to Jahmad. At least I thought it did. The way he had up and shattered it into pieces, I really didn't know which piece to follow. But my head, my head settled on pure logic. At this point, what was wrong with being with Leo? No Tina. No poly anything anymore. Just us. And our son. That's how he had presented the idea, and to be honest, it sounded too rational to ignore. Jamaal would have his father, his real father. Because no matter how much I had tried to will it so, Jahmad was not it, nor did it appear that he wanted to be. He sure had made that clear. So I guess that old saying could apply: if I couldn't be with the one I loved, I could love the one I was with. Jahmad had insinuated I was being selfish before. But actually considering being back with Leo, just for the sake of my son, was probably the most selfless thing I could do. Maybe I couldn't prove it to anyone else but myself. Maybe that would have to suffice.

I rose from the beach towel, brushing the few traces of sand from my tanned thighs. In one fluid motion, I lifted the fishnet cover over my head, revealing the black mesh one-piece that hugged my curves. I tossed the cover, my hat, and sunglasses to the ground and made my way to the water.

It was cool, the gentle currents lapping farther and farther up my body as I eased out hip-deep into the ocean. I hated this. Here I was trying to get away to solve my problems, or maybe I was running. Shit, I was big enough to admit it. But I had done nothing but add to them. I smirked, picturing my parents', or hell, even Adria's reaction if I told them I might possibly get back with Leo. Holidays were about to be complete shitstorms.

"What is it, my love?"

Leo appeared by my side, clutching Jamaal tight in his arms. I tossed a sideways glance at the father and son, surprised when Jamaal didn't bother reaching for me but entertained himself with Leo's massive beard.

"Just thinking," I admitted, casting my eyes back out to the distance.

"I've been thinking too," he said. "I'm sorry if I am making you feel pressured. I know this is all unexpected." *Damn right it is*. He paused for my response, but I merely nodded instead of voicing my thoughts. "You don't have to decide now. Just enjoy the rest of the vacation. Get home, get settled. And can you just promise me you'll give it some thought?"

My nod was slight, but a nod nonetheless. I certainly had several thoughts to consider. Perhaps it was divine intervention, because I was terrified if he had asked for an answer now, he would have seen my mind was already being made up.

He brought his face toward mine, kissing me over the top of Jamaal's head. He lingered longer when I didn't push him away immediately. I just felt embraced by the gentle affection, as if he was giving me reassurance. Validation.

Leo sighed as he broke the kiss first. "Wouldn't it be nice if we just stayed here?"

My heart skipped a beat. Eerie, the exact thought had already crossed my mind. Damn, it must have been something in this Dominican Republic air, because no way could I be acting this senseless. None of it, not me, him, and certainly not us made any piece of sense. And yet still, the thoughts lingered.

We headed back to our things on the beach and began packing up. The sun was already beginning to set, settling a brisk chill in the air that had me shivering. Leo handed Jamaal to me and promptly wrapped a towel around both of us. He paused with his arms around my shoulders, as if he was going to say something else, when a ringing cell phone pierced the silence. Leo glanced at me, and I gestured toward the beach bag on his shoulder. "Yours," I answered his curious look. "Haven't turned mine on since we got here."

A mask of worry creased his face, and he sighed before digging into the bag and pulling out the noisy device. He eyed the screen before swiping to decline the call. It was quick. Very quick. But I was able to make out that the contact's name was T. Of course he would still be fucking with Tina.

For some reason, that angered me, and I stomped away like I had a damn reason for acting like some betrayed lover. Wasn't I still in my feelings about Jahmad?

Leo caught my forearm. "What is it, my love?"

It seemed silly to assume it was her. After all, she had tried to kill him. But at the end of the day, the woman had been his wife. Was some foolish, stupid love still there between them? "Are you sure you're still not seeing Tina?" My question was more accusatory, but at that point, I really didn't care.

Leo frowned in confusion, then slow realization as he put the pieces together. He shook his head. "It's not what you think—"

"Because I can't do this again, Leo." I was near hysteria with bottled emotions. "I've been down this road with you, and it almost got me killed, not to mention thrown in jail. And the abuse and the secrets and, just, everything. I can't do it."

Leo hugged me, sandwiching Jamaal between us. "Sssshhh, you don't have to," he said calmly. "I'm sorry. For everything."

That broke me. I let the tears fall as he cradled my head on his shoulder. I cried for everything and nothing at all. I cried for past, present, and future. I cried certain tears of uncertainty and crystal clear confusion that left me completely exhausted. And meanwhile, Leo kissed my damp cheeks, murmuring his apologies that I knew in my heart he meant, but I was still afraid of the forgiveness.

I let Leo stay in my room that night. Sex aside, because, hell, at this point, I wouldn't have been able to get my kitty wet if I submerged her in the tub. No, my mind was cluttered, my heart hurt, and my body was exhausted, so it felt damn good to lie in Leo's arms and just *be*. He had always been protective, aside from the abuse, but there was no question I immediately felt comforted by his presence.

"You said you haven't turned on your phone since you got here?" Leo asked suddenly, bringing up my earlier statement on the beach. His deep voice echoed in the darkened room.

"No."

"What about your folks? Do they know you're here?"

"No."

He sighed, and I immediately felt guilty. "They're probably

worried," he said. "And your friend. I know you all are very close."

"I know," I admitted. I didn't even want to begin to think about the missed messages I had waiting when I finally turned that thing back on.

"I'm leaving out early in the morning. I have some things to take care of."

I swallowed the slight swell of disappointment. We, or at least I, had two more days left on my vacation. I had to admit, I had begun to welcome Leo's company, especially when it came to Jamaal. "We'll talk more when you get back?" He phrased it like a question.

"Yes, we'll talk," I agreed. A lingering forehead kiss, first for Jamaal, and then me, then he left me alone with my thoughts.

I got up and fixed a few pillows around Jamaal's sleeping frame. Then I crossed to my purse and pulled out my phone. It had gone cold from lack of use, and I powered it on, searching my bag for the charger because I wasn't sure about the remaining battery life. It glowed to life and one by one the notifications appeared on my screen. Adria. Adria. Mom. Keon. Mom. Mom. Adria. I swiped through the missed calls. None from Jahmad. Why did I really expect any?

I sat on the bed, listening to the voicemails. Of course, Adria was worried. Where the hell was I? Why wasn't I answering? I figured as much. I clicked through, deleting them until I came to the one from my mom that had fear gripping every fiber in my body. A message from two days ago.

It took me a moment to piece together what she was saying through the tears clogging her voice, but certain words I could make out as clearly as if she had been uttering them in the room right next to me. Dad. Hospital. Poison. Serious. Dying.

Chapter 21

I didn't understand how things had happened so fast.

The last time I saw my father, he was on his way to the church before Jahmad stopped by the house. He was happy, healthy, joking. Not at all like the shred of a man that had inhabited him for these past few months. I had been so wrapped up in everything I was going through, never did I consider the last time I saw him like that would be the last time I saw him.

Jamaal and I caught the first plane out of Punta Cana. After two layovers, lots of prayer, cranky tears from Jamaal and a number of fearful ones of my own, we landed back in Atlanta, and I was damn near on two wheels trying to get to Southern Regional. The entire way, I was toggling speed-dialed calls between my mom, Adria, and Keon. Hell, I even chanced Jahmad. Everyone's phone was going straight to voicemail, which I could only attribute to the poor-ass reception in the hospital. At least that's what I tried to focus on rather than the rising panic the more time passed by without any indication what the hell was going on.

This must have been how they felt trying to reach me while I was away, and the guilt clawed at my heart. If something happened to my father . . . I shook my head to dispel the negative thoughts even as the hospital came into view and had my heart slamming against my chest. I couldn't afford to think that way.

Several pair of eyes landed on me as I approached the waiting room on the sixth floor, pushing Jamaal's stroller underneath the large sign with the words "Intensive Care Unit" displayed. It felt like it took everything in me to make it upstairs after I had called around and discovered that was where my dad was. How did he get up here in a matter of days?

I hadn't even opened my mouth to ask the question when Keon broke from the huddle and approached me first, grabbing my forearm and steering me clear of the rest of my family.

He was scared and worried, that much was clear. But even in the midst of that I could easily detect anger bubbling under the surface.

"Key—"

"Where the hell have you been?" he snapped, lowering his voice.

"Wait, why are you mad? What happened to Daddy?"

"So good to know you finally care."

"Of course I care. What kind of shit is that to say?"

"We have been looking for you for days. Worried about you. Jamaal. But yet again you don't give a damn about anybody else but Kimera."

I was stunned silent. My brother was known for being direct and he sure didn't hold back. I knew everyone would probably be in their little feelings about me going MIA for a week, but damn. Was it that serious?

"Listen," I said, matching his anger for anger. "You worried about me getting away for a few days and I really don't care. I'm worried about my dad. You can save your little bullshit for later."

"Nah, my little bullshit is the reason why you don't even know what the hell is going on," he said, narrowing his eyes. "The ones who need to know know. You can keep doing what you been doing, li'l sis."

He turned around and headed back down the hall, stopping Adria as she passed him obviously coming in my direction.

Their exchange was brief, him stepping in front to block her path and her rolling her eyes and pushing past him anyway. About her coming to my rescue, no doubt. He would push the issue later.

"Hey, girl." She greeted me with a hug, her voice weary. Her red-rimmed eyes were glassy, and tears dried on her sunken cheeks. She looked like she had aged in a matter of days, and that shook me up even more.

"Adria, what is going on?" I questioned. "I got the message about Dad, Keon is acting like he done lost his damn mind—"

"He was worried. We all were."

"I left you a message."

She nodded as if dismissing my rationale. It was obvious her mind was on the more important issue at hand. I calmed down on a sigh. "What happened?"

Adria started quivering and biting back another swell of tears. "It's not looking good," she whispered. Her voice broke, and she took a breath before speaking again. "We are still waiting on the results from the tests. He's in a coma. They don't . . ." Adria trailed off, and I bit beck my own fear.

"How—what happened?"

"Mom rushed him here a few days ago. He was complaining of stomach pain, running off, throwing up. Fever, chills. At first they thought the flu or a really bad virus. But he just got worse. Now . . ." She trailed off and put a trembling hand to her mouth as if she were afraid of the words she was about to utter. "He doesn't look too good, Kimmy. He's lost his hair. He's not being as responsive. Like he's slowly slipping—"

I shook my head adamantly, refusing to believe her conclusion. "I need to see him."

"It's restricted," Adria said. "So only one person at a time, and it's only during certain hours." And as if knowing I needed it, Adria wrapped her arms around me, which had my body braced against hers for support.

She led me back to my family, still standing around in a circle. They were holding hands, and it was clear I had interrupted the prayer session. I was mildly surprised to see Jahmad among the faces, his expression just as solemn with the sad news.

I positioned Jamaal's stroller in the middle of the circle and stood between my mom and Adria as they again bowed their heads. I tried my best to concentrate on my mother's words, but I was murmuring a silent prayer of my own, guilt-ridden with my own absence while my father lay dying.

Time ticked on, and eventually nightfall brought a new staff with still no new news of my father's condition. Jahmad had whispered something in my mom's ear and given her a kiss on the cheek before he left without so much as a glance in my direction.

After a long while of pleading and insisting, Keon finally convinced a very reluctant Adria to go home and get some rest. She offered to take Jamaal with her and I agreed, noticing how fussy he was, whether in or out the stroller.

Now it was just me, Keon, and my mom left, and, as if she needed a distraction, she turned to me with a forced smile and watery eyes. "So Adria tells me you went out of town," she said. "Did you enjoy yourself?"

Though her question was simple enough, I still felt bad. "I'm sorry I didn't call, Mama. I just needed to get away, and I never thought—didn't think—"

She shushed me with a gentle pat to my hand. "No, of course you didn't. I'm not mad about that. You were stressed, I could tell. I was worried, but after Adria told me you were okay, I was just glad you were able to get away for a little bit."

I nodded. At least she was being understanding. That was certainly more than I could say for my brother. And Jahmad, I thought, remembering how he had ignored me.

"And JayJay? Did he do okay with the travel?"

I nodded again. "He did great." Especially considering his father was there, but I certainly saw no need to mention that part of the story.

I debated asking my next question and decided against it. My mom looked so fragile right now, and it seemed like any mention of my father would cause a nervous breakdown. It seemed like she was searching desperately for something, anything to talk about instead.

"I bought a house," I announced, though given the circumstances their initial excitement wasn't there.

My mom's smile was small, but a smile nonetheless. "That's great, sweetie," she said. "I'm so glad. We are going to miss you and JayJay around the house."

That was all it took; she cracked and began sobbing into the open palms of her hands. Keon immediately wrapped his arm around her limp shoulders and she leaned into him.

"I don't know what happened." Her voice was muffled by her hands. "Oh, God, why?"

When panic had her tone lifting, her voice echoing even louder in the waiting room, Keon hoisted her to feet and shuffled off with her down the hall, their steps slow and dragging with the weight of their grief.

They hadn't returned yet when a doctor walked toward me and leaned down, a clipboard in hand.

"Are you here for Pastor Michael Davis?"

I rose quickly and nodded. "Yes."

"Sandra Davis?"

"No, that's my mother. I'm his daughter, Kimera. Is everything all right? Can I see him?"

The doctor sighed, as if he were afraid of the answer. "Is your mother around? It's probably best if I speak to her first."

My mom shuffled back into the lobby, a balled-up tissue in hand. She stopped as she noticed the doctor, then moved hesitantly closer in our direction.

The two stepped to the side out of earshot, the doctor's lips moving, small and unreadable.

"My bad, sis," Keon said suddenly at my side as we watched them both. "I'm not really mad at you. Just the situation. We all were here. Even Tyree and that girl CeeCee. And when he asked for you and you weren't here . . ."

I nodded. Fear had us all looking for someone to blame. Unfortunately, I had no one to point the finger at but myself either.

"I just want to see him," I said, almost to myself.

"He doesn't even look like himself." For the first time, Keon's voice cracked, an outward display of the raw emotions he was trying his best to hide. One look in his eyes, the inner turmoil shown like a mirror reflection of my own.

The doctor touched my mother's shoulder and walked off, leaving her standing there in a daze. Watching her, nausea settled in the pit of my stomach. The way silent tears slipped down her face as she stared off into space like some mindless zombie, the tissue falling from her fingers and fluttering in surrender to the tile floor, we knew there wasn't any good news in our future.

Chapter 22

Sunlight seeped through the glass windows and spilled on the downcast faces of the congregation packing the pews. Such a stark contrast to the mood. Rain would have been more appropriate. The sunshine frankly was adding anger to my grief. Just another reminder that the sun had risen on another day. Yet one more day without Pastor Michael Davis in it, and life was moving on without him.

We buried my father on a Tuesday morning. For midweek, attendance was better than it had been on any given Sunday as of late. I didn't know whether that was a good thing or bad thing. I knew my father was well loved and certainly at one point well respected, but where the hell was that support when he was alive? No, they had pretty much shunned him, leaving him to fend for himself and try to keep his passion alive. All because of their judgment toward me. That pissed me off more than anything. And as far as I was concerned, they could save their condolences and phony ass tears. He had lost everything, including himself.

My mom had always been a take-charge woman. Strong like my dad. That's why the two worked so well together. One half of the same soul, they used to say. Never before had I seen her break that control. But even this was too much to handle.

He was on life support for two weeks before they laid every-thing on the table. Physically, he was here. His body was frail, his head balding from the alopecia, his skin ashen from the illness, medication, or maybe a combination of both. So, yeah, his body was definitely here, only because of the machines that pumped oxygen and simulated life to keep him hanging on for us. His mind and spirit were long gone.

I knew it from when I would talk to him in that hospital room, clutching his hand in mine. He was hollow, and my words seemed to echo around much like cries in an empty room. Yet still, I talked, prayed, held pictures of Jamaal in front of his closed eye-lids in the hopes that maybe, just maybe it was all strong enough to pull him back from his unconsciousness. But then my mama had told me with a weary voice that it was time.

I stood at the door of the sanctuary trying to be strong, but I was crumbling inside. I didn't even think it was possible to shed as many tears as I had.

One by one people filed in shaking my hand, murmuring quiet apologies, pulling me into hugs that did nothing but add to my discomfort. But I was on autopilot as I nodded my fake gratitude, wishing I were anywhere but here.

The funerals of Lena, Leo's second wife, and then Leo himself, as staged as it was, didn't touch my heart. Sad, yes, but I couldn't bring myself to grieve the lives of people I barely knew. More like co-workers in the little business arrangement. But my dad, there were no words to express my sorrow. No emotion to accurately capture the part of me that had been lost as his heart rate monitor flatlined. Whose baby girl was I now?

"I'm sorry for your loss," someone whispered, and I blinked to keep from sobbing out loud. Sorry. Loss. *Are you really sorry? Do you know how much I really lost?* You're thinking of a pastor. I'm thinking of a father, friend, counselor, mentor, provider, husband. I'm thinking of the late-night talker, the jokester. Dessert sneaker after my mom would put me on punishment when I was a little girl. Shoulder to cry on. Comforter. Protector. I had lost more than any of these people could possibly be sorry for.

Keon crossed the aisle and took my arm. He probably knew my legs were about to give out. I was trembling, or maybe that was him as we walked together to the front.

Adria immediately grabbed my hand as I sat down next to her. She squeezed as if giving me strength neither one of us had.

I couldn't bring myself to look at the casket. My mom had insisted on it being closed so "everyone could remember him at his finest." But still I couldn't help but picture his body resting on the plush cushions inside of the brown-and-bronze box. The idea of it had me nauseated. Because that's all it was: a box. My dad deserved better. Like commanding that pulpit instead of lying at the foot of it.

One of the associate pastors began the service with a welcome prayer. I bowed my head and clenched the program where my dad's smiling face looked up at me. I held my breath to keep from crying out from my soul.

When it was time for the eulogy, I stood on shaky legs I didn't trust and took delicate steps to the podium. There were so many people in that room whose eyes ripped between me and the casket I stood behind. Some eyes were completely closed to try and block the tears. Muffled cries seemed to hum together in a song, sniffs, hitched breaths, whimpers all blending together. I looked out at the crowd and saw a blur.

"To all of us, my dad was a pastor," I started, trying to remember the speech I had prepared. "But he was more than that to me. Never did I think I would have to live without him. Never did I think there would be a time I would need him and he wouldn't be here for me." I finally chanced looking down at the elaborate floral arrangement on top of the casket. The four walls of this building felt as confined as that box. "He was supposed to walk me down the aisle at my wedding," I whispered. "There was more for you to teach me, Daddy. There was more life to live. You left and took a piece of all of us with you."

I was supposed to talk more on what a wonderful man, a wonderful person my father was. I had found one of Lena's poems to read that I thought would be appropriate. I was supposed to lead the choir in a song. But I just remember my weakened legs finally giving out and suddenly collapsing to the floor, my wails like pleading calls to Heaven before I was lifted into someone's arms and carried from the front.

The pain had long since surpassed mental and emotional. It felt like my entire body was crying and aching from the tension that coursed through my muscles. My vision wavered and blackened around the edges so all I saw was the sanctuary door I was being carried toward. Then the familiar furniture of the church foyer came into view.

I was lowered to a chair and, as if on reflex, I bent over to put my head between my knees.

When I was sure I wouldn't throw up my insides all over this beautiful carpet, I sighed and leaned up, shutting my eyes against the sting of harsh reality.

My lips curved in appreciation as Jahmad's hand stroked my back. That did offer some comfort. Even more so when his lips touched my cheek.

"Thanks, Jahmad," I murmured. "I needed that."

A pause, then, "You're welcome."

My eyes snatched open. No, not Jahmad. Leo. My back straightened, and shock had me blinking several times to make sure my eyes weren't playing tricks on me.

"Leo, I . . ." Embarrassment warmed my cheeks. "I'm sorry, I didn't know you would be here. How did you . . ." I trailed off, remembering the story of my father's passing had populated every local news outlet for the past two weeks. What had been disgusting was the fact that a few had even tried to toss my own story back in the mix, interweaving the sordid truth with the lies so well it was impossible to tell one from the other anymore.

"You really didn't have to come," I said.

"Yes, I did. You needed me."

I really didn't want to minimize his compassion by correcting him that it wasn't him I needed, so I just nodded in response.

The door slid open, and Adria, Tyree, and Jahmad approached me, their steps deliberate with concern.

"Kimmy—"

"I'm fine," I said, immediately trying to dispel Adria's worry. I was far from fine, that much was clear, but Adria kept her mouth shut. She flicked a look at Leo.

I started to make introductions and just as quickly decided against it. This really was not the place nor the time. But I could see all three of the questioning gazes at the man at my side, entirely too close for casual friends.

Leo had tensed beside me and so had I, which I could only attribute to Jahmad standing there. Suddenly, I felt like I was suffocating.

"You sure you good, boo?" This time it was Tyree who spoke up, and I nodded and stood, satisfied when they didn't give out on me again.

I turned to Leo. "I have to get back in there. But thank you. I really appreciate it."

A little smile touched his lips, but he didn't comment. I did, however, feel him watching us as we made our way back inside to finish my father's service.

———✦———

Everyone had collected back at the church cafeteria for light refreshments, though I don't see how anyone had an appetite after watching my dad being lowered into the ground.

I found a little corner that I hoped hid me well as light chatter filled the air, along with the clinking of utensils as people picked from the meatballs, pasta salad, and fruit my mother had spread out banquet-style.

I was just here for the sake of being here at this point. I wanted nothing more than to go pick up my son from the childcare center and take him home so I could cry in peace. That didn't appear to be happening anytime soon.

All eyes were on me. At least it damn sure felt that way. Someone approached the table and slid a plate of food in front me, murmuring that I needed to eat. I nodded and they kept on.

Right now, I was wondering where my mother got her strength. She stood to the side surrounded by church members, and she appeared to be engaged in polite conversation. If I were her, this little gathering would have shut down a long time ago. No sense in these people trying to act like they knew how I felt.

The vibration from inside my black clutch had me reaching inside for my phone. A text from some random number. *So sorry for your loss.* I texted back a quick thank-you. Guess I would have to get used to that. I'm sure I would be getting it a lot now. Immediately, another text. *You sitting over there alone. Do you need Leo to come rescue you again? Lol.*

I frowned and looked up. As if she had been waiting, my eyes caught Tina's stare. She blended right in with her black, mid-calf dress and black pillbox hat. In fact, I almost had to do a double take to ensure it was her. But when a little smirk touched her lips and she wagged her fingers in my direction, I rose. I hadn't seen Leo since the service, but I really couldn't wait on his protection right now. This bitch knew something, and I needed to find out what.

She didn't appear fazed as I made a beeline in her direction. In fact, her smile widened. "Kimera Davis," she said as I approached, and just to piss me off, or maybe it was for show, she pulled me into a hug. I stiffened under the contact. I wouldn't dare cause a scene in my dad's church, at his funeral.

"What are you doing here, Tina?" I said through tight lips.

"I came to pay my respects. Your father was a wonderful pastor." She touched her heart. "And a very, very wonderful man." Something about the way she said it made me suspicious. What the hell was she insinuating?

"Tina, I don't know what your problem is, but you need to leave me alone. I know you've been messing with me, and the shit ends. Now."

Tina exaggerated a gasp. "The language," she said. "In the house of the Lord."

I rolled my eyes and took a step closer, keeping my voice low. "Don't play with me."

"Or what?" she taunted, crossing her arms over her chest.

A quick vision of me dragging this bitch outside and whooping her ass came to mind. Oh, the satisfaction.

"Relax, Kimmy," Tina spoke up again. "I at least thought we could be friends. So much time has passed, and here you are, still holding grudges."

"Grudges? You're the one bothering me." I thought about the fire, my son, my father. I couldn't be sure, but somehow she had to be linked to this. It was entirely too coincidental. And for what? Leo?

"Look, you can have Leo," I said. "You're trying to ruin my life over him? Really?"

Tina rolled her eyes. "Trying to ruin your life? Don't you think that's a bit extreme?"

"For you? Hell, no."

Tina chuckled. "Well, I'm flattered, really. But I don't know what you're talking about." She was lying. She didn't even bother trying to keep the sarcasm out of her tone.

Tina pivoted and walked away, putting some distance between

us before she turned back and added, "By the way, how is your baby?"

The question appeared innocent but was laced with amusement, so I knew exactly what this bitch meant. I remembered how I woke up to my son not breathing, the hospital stay. He almost died and she was up here with that humorous twinkle in her eyes.

"Mama wants you," Keon said, stepping in front of me.

I didn't answer, could only watch paralyzed in rage as Tina sauntered away. She had hurt my child. I was going to kill that bitch.

Chapter 23

It was another level of emptiness at my parents' house. The rooms felt entirely too cold, the walls too thin. The air was still and hollow. It was as if everything had died with my father.

It had been a week since his funeral, but that had done nothing to dull the ache in my heart. Of course being around his things brought back too many memories, and I often would just sit in his lounge chair and sniff the fading remnants of his cologne that had seeped into the cushions. I tried my best to be there for my mother, but, hell, I couldn't even be there for myself. The only bit of life between us was Jamaal, who continued into his easy routine with the innocence of a child, unbeknownst to him the horrors and trauma of life. Damn, if only we all had that blissful ignorance.

Keon and Adria came over every day with food that none of us had an appetite for, so stacks of Tupperware and aluminum foil–covered dishes began to clutter the refrigerator. Their brief visits usually brought a little life to my mom's eyes. Keon carried my father's smile and warm eyes and for a moment, even a small one, it was as if he was reminiscent of young Daddy.

And Adria, bless her heart, was trying to keep our spirits up with her ultrasound pictures and clothes she'd purchased for my niece or nephew. She was certainly showing more in her hips and stomach, and to be honest, it was a welcome distraction from my own turmoil.

My mom was a strong woman, had always been. But I knew this was taking a toll on her. She suddenly looked older, more frail, her eyes sunken with the weariness of heartache and too many tears. Reality was slowing beginning to set in, like a camera lens coming into focus. Daddy was nowhere, yet everywhere, and it toggled her on the edges of sanity. It was a wonder she could bring herself to sleep in the same bed now, alone.

Which was where I figured she would be this morning when I heard the doorbell ring for the third time and she still hadn't answered.

I took a peek at Jamaal sleeping in the bassinet beside me before climbing from the bed. I didn't bother with a robe to cover my oversize t-shirt. Hell, it couldn't have been any later than nine o'clock in the morning, so whoever the hell it was, they were lucky I was even answering at all.

Jahmad stood in the glare of the morning sun, and I had to squint to see his handsome face actually had a little smile.

"Good morning," he greeted. "Sorry, I didn't realize it was so early."

I nodded and stepped to the side to allow him room to enter. He carried a drink tray with cups of coffee in one hand and a Dunkin Donuts bag in the other. Whatever it was did smell good.

"Figured you ladies needed some breakfast," he said, leading the way into the kitchen.

"Thanks, but I'm really not hungry."

"Kimmy, you need to eat." He took one of the coffee cups and set it on the table with packs of cream and sugar. He looked at me and pointed to the dining chair. "Sit," he ordered. "Drink. Get something on your stomach." I did as he said, my mouth almost watering at the delicious aroma of coffee beans.

Jahmad remembered how I liked my coffee, because he had dumped two creamers and a ton of Splenda on the table in front of me. "Did Keon send you on his behalf?" I asked, ripping open the sugar packets. "Usually he and Adria do the food runs."

"No, I needed to come for myself. See how y'all were doing. Mom still asleep?"

"Yeah I'm not going to wake her right now. She hasn't been sleeping much." And I was hoping after the sleeping pills I gave her last night, she could get as much rest as possible.

Jahmad pulled two wrapped sandwiches from the bag and set one down in front of me. I knew I wouldn't eat it, but I didn't move to stop him.

"What about you, Kimmy?" he asked, sitting down opposite me. "How you holding up?"

I took a delicate sip of the hot liquid, let it linger a bit before swallowing. Anything to make sure I wouldn't bust out into another round of fresh tears. Sure I would be able to keep my composure, I sighed. "It's hard," I admitted. "I miss him so much, Jahmad. And watching my mother trying to cope is heartbreaking."

Jahmad's face went slack with the mutual emotions. "I know. Your dad was like a father to me too. Always has been, since I never . . ." He trailed off, and I knew exactly what he was going to say.

He never knew his father. His mother tried her best with the single mother thing, but she always worked so much trying to provide for herself and her only son. Her absence allowed Jahmad to run the streets, and though he never got into serious trouble, he did take pride in sexing every piece of tender ass this side of metro Atlanta. And when he joined the basketball team and met my brother, he was always around, since there was nothing at home for him. No home-cooked meals, no family time. My parents being the Christian folks they were, they eagerly accepted

Jahmad into our little family, hoping to fill the void he often seemed to be looking to fill with other females.

I remembered Jahmad hadn't been out of high school but six weeks when his mom was killed in a car accident. Of course he had been broken up, but that didn't even seem to compare with how hard he appeared to be taking my dad's death.

"Does it get easier?" I asked. Part of me thought he would lie.

"No," he said, his eyes level with mine. "But maybe one day you'll be able to think about him without the tears."

We sat in silence for a moment, both of us lost in thought, though I couldn't be sure what all was on Jahmad's mind. I wanted to ask him all kind of questions. Was he still going to Texas? When? What about CeeCee? Were they some kind of rebound-ass couple? But I kept my mouth shut. I knew this damn sure wasn't the time for that conversation.

"How is Jamaal?"

I smiled; happy my son still crossed his mind despite what had happened between us. "Getting big," I answered. "And heavy. Eating all the damn time."

That prompted a laugh from him. "Well, he's a growing boy," he said. "Wait until he becomes a teenager. You remember how me and Keon used to be."

Now I laughed, memories flooding back. "Hell, yeah. You would put in a dinner request like this was your personal restaurant, and Mama would make it. Used to piss me off because you wouldn't leave shit for me."

"I was hungry."

"Greedy," I corrected. "I used to think you did that shit on purpose. And remember that time you ate Daddy's plate by accident?"

Jahmad slapped his forehead. "Man, your dad told my ass not to come back for a month."

"And here you were bringing your ass back the next day acting like everything was fine. That man loved you, I swear, because me or Keon would've never lived that down."

All humor faded from Jahmad's eyes as he lowered them to the uneaten breakfast sandwich in front of him. "I loved him too."

I paused, and then feeling like I needed it, like we both did, I leaned over and wrapped my arms around his neck.

For a moment, I just held him, trying to offer what little bit of comfort I could. I was surprised he let me.

He pulled his head back a fraction, resting his forehead on mine. "We'll get through this," he whispered, his breath cool on my face.

I held my breath. I couldn't be sure what he was talking about. My dad's death? Or us? It was a risk, I knew, but damn, I needed him. All of him. I was broken, and it was Jahmad who could make me whole.

So without a second thought, I leaned my face closer and pressed my mouth to his. I could tell he was surprised at the action, but when he didn't immediately break the kiss, I took the liberty to deepen it, using my tongue to massage his lips until they parted in invitation.

I swallowed his moan as his arms wrapped around my waist to lift me from the chair and onto the table. He situated his body between my legs and I exhaled, his fingers snaking up my shirt and causing my body to tremble under his touch. He snatched his lips from mine to put them to my neck, and I soared. "Jahmad." His name trembled from my tongue. "Please. I want—"

The sharp sound of the doorbell piercing the air had us both jumping apart. I let out a staggering breath as I struggled to calm my racing heart. The brief intimacy had my skin suddenly feeling engulfed in heat, and by the looks of Jahmad leaning against a nearby wall, I certainly wasn't the only one.

The doorbell rang again, and I hopped down from the table.

Hopefully I could remember how to get my legs to cooperate. "The doorbell," I mumbled as if it wasn't obvious.

Jahmad nodded. "Get it. I'll go make sure it didn't wake JayJay."

His walk was quick as he disappeared up the stairs, like he was trying to escape. I didn't know whether to be agitated or relieved at the abrupt end to what was about to be some rough-ass kitchen comfort sex. Damn.

I opened the door, all lovemaking thoughts completely disappearing at the recognition of the officer standing on the front porch. She had her blond hair in a high bun and a bit more makeup this time, which only accentuated her modelesque features. As it did before, the officer's uniform made her look more like she was acting out the part instead of it being her real job. But then, I remembered how seriously she had taken her profession when she came by Jahmad's house, investigating the fire at my business. With everything that had happened since, all that seemed like a lifetime ago rather than a few short months.

The woman turned and offered a small smile. "Good morning, Ms. Davis," she greeted. "Not sure if you remember me, but I'm Officer Terry."

"Yes, I remember you." I stepped to the side to allow her to enter.

"I apologize for waking you."

I could only imagine my disheveled look and wanted to giggle at the assumption. No, I wasn't getting out of bed before she came knocking, but Jahmad and I were certainly headed there.

"No problem," I said, waving away the apology. "I probably should have been following up with you about the fire, but that really hasn't been on the forefront of my mind. I just recently lost my father, among other things."

"Yes, I'm aware. And I'm so sorry for your loss. But that's actually why I'm here."

I frowned. "About my father? What is it?"

Officer Terry's face turned grim. "Is your mother home? I would like to speak with her."

"She is asleep right now, but you can talk to me."

"I'll be more than happy to discuss this with both of you, but it's really imperative Mrs. Davis is included in the conversation."

Something about her words made me uneasy. But I nodded anyway and headed to my mother's room.

I was surprised to find my mom sitting up in bed, her longing gaze to the window. "Mama, I thought you were asleep," I said.

"Oh, sweetie, I've been up for hours," she said, exhaustion heavy in her voice. "I sleep off and on."

"The police are here."

"Police?" It was as if the word sounded completely foreign to her.

"Yes, ma'am. She said she wants to talk to us about Daddy."

That seemed to have her hustling a little faster than I'd seen her move in days. She slipped a housecoat and house shoes on before following me back to the living room.

Jahmad had made it back with Jamaal in his arms, and I caught Officer Terry shaking the baby's little hand as we entered, a huge grin on her face. "Your son is absolutely adorable," she said to no one in particular.

"Thank you," I said, taken aback when Jahmad and I spoke at the same time. I glanced at him out of my peripheral vision, wondering if that was intentional. And if so, what, if anything, did it mean?

"Mrs. Davis." Officer Terry held out her hand to my mother as she began her introduction. "I'm Officer Terry. My condolences to you and your family during this difficult time."

"Yes, officer, thank you. Please have a seat."

I winced when she sat down in Daddy's lounge chair. Obviously my mama felt the same way.

"Please, not in that chair," she said, her voice barely above a whisper. "That's the pastor's chair."

The officer quickly got to her feet. "I sincerely apologize," she said. "I'll just stand. This won't take long anyway." She pulled a notebook from her back pocket before tossing a look first to me, then to Jahmad. "Do you mind if they stay?"

"Of course they are staying." My mama seemed offended by the question. "These are my children. Whatever you have to say about my husband you can say it in front of them."

"Well, it appears Pastor Davis's case has been referred to us as a possible homicide," she started, continuing despite our questioning mumbles. "The toxicology report indicates substantial levels of arsenic in his system. And testing on his hair follicles indicate he had been given small doses for a long period of time, dating back to earlier this year up to the day before he passed in the hospital. Do you know anyone who would have wanted to hurt Pastor Davis?"

"No. No one." My mom buried her face in her palms. "Lord God, as if it wasn't enough for my husband to die. Now it's murder?"

I was just as shocked but couldn't help repeating on the officer's question. Did we know anyone who would want to hurt my Daddy? I did. And she just so happened to be at the funeral with that damn smug look on her face.

As if sensing my thoughts, Officer Terry turned to me. "What about you? Anyone who would want to hurt your father?"

I debated giving her Tina's name, then thought better of it. I paused and shook my head. "No," I lied. I would find out if it was true. Then I would handle her myself.

"Mrs. Davis, did you love your husband?"

My mom was clearly offended. She scrunched her face in disgust. "I know you're not insinuating I would have anything to do with this," she snapped, her voice coming out more forceful than it had been before.

"I am exploring all possible avenues." Officer Terry stared at my mom for a moment before turning pointed gazes to both Jahmad and me. "Right now, everyone is a suspect."

My mom rose from the couch, fists clenched at her sides. "You're right," she said through tight lips. "You're not staying long. Get your narrow behind out of my house and go find your killer. Because he is certainly not here." And with that, she stalked from the room.

Obediently, Officer Terry headed toward the door before glancing at us. "Cute kid," she commented with another smile. "You two stay safe, and we'll be in touch."

I didn't like the sound of that.

Chapter 24

"So wait. She really thinks it was poison?"

Adria's voice carried the same shock I still felt. Two days after our little surprise visit from Officer Terry, and I was still reeling from the news. Now the thing on everybody's mine was who? And just as important, why? Which is why I was on my way to get some answers. If I didn't have to commit a homicide of my own first.

I held the phone to my ear with one hand and maneuvered the steering wheel of the car with the other. I had let the windows down, hoping the warm August sun would lighten my mood. I was wrong. But at least I was getting JayJay out of the house. Adria and Keon had both made me feel guilty enough about keeping him cooped up while I dealt with my grief. This little excursion would solve that too.

"I may have to go by the church later," I said as I wheeled the car in the parking lot. "Maybe in a few hours. Meet me over there?"

"Okay." Adria's voice was filled with uncertainty. "What do you need at the church?"

"Just want to do a little research of my own," I said.

I spotted someone across the grass, and I quickly ended the

call, promising my girl I would explain more later. For now, I needed to get some answers, and hopefully he would be able to give me some.

"Thank you for meeting me," I said as I walked up, pushing Jamaal along in his stroller.

Leo looked up from his perch on the park bench, squinting against the afternoon sun. He glanced down to Jamaal and his smile widened, showing off those perfect white teeth of his.

"Thank you for calling, my love," he said. "May I?" I nodded, and eagerly Leo unfastened Jamaal from his buckles and hoisted him onto his lap.

I smoothed my sundress and took a seat next to him, taking in the scenic lake with park goers scattered across the manicured lawn, either playing with dogs, fishing, or just lying out enjoying the fresh air. I sighed as the gentle breeze tickled my cheek.

"You okay, my love?"

"My dad used to bring me and my brother to this park when we were kids," I murmured before I realized I had.

Leo followed my gaze to a playground not too far in the distance, the muffled laughter of children carrying across the lake. "I've never been here," he said, as if engulfed in his own memories. "And even in Ivory Coast, my father wasn't that kind of father. He loved me, but he was strict. Everything needed to be done a certain way. No exceptions."

I noticed the twinge of bitterness that laced his words, but when Leo made no move to speak further on it, I turned to face him, propping my arm on the back of the bench.

"Leo, I need to know where Tina is."

Just as I'd expected, he frowned and looked at me like I was crazy. "Why are you asking me that?"

"Well, I told you before she's been around messing with me. She was at the funeral."

"I didn't see her."

"Well, I did. During the little reception after the service. Leo, she's up to her same old shit."

Leo shook his head as if in disbelief. "You sure about that?"

"I think she killed my father."

Leo paused, his face wrinkled at the thought. I couldn't tell whether it was shock or concern that registered across his face. Then he stood, lifting Jamaal in his arms. "Let's walk a second," he said, leading the way across the grass.

Obediently, I stood pushing the empty stroller behind them. I didn't like the way he was acting. He was clearly hiding something.

We moved closer to the lake and began walking along the bank, not too close where the water could reach our feet, but still close enough that the dew moistened the air around us.

"The police came to my house the other day," I started when the silence had worn on. "They say my dad was poisoned."

"I understand you're hurting, my love, but think about it. Why would she do that?"

"Hell, Leo, didn't she try to kill you? Then me?" I snapped. "Don't act like this is so farfetched with your precious wife. Fact is, the woman is capable of it, and we both have almost died because of her."

"I just don't want you to jump to conclusions," he said. "Tina has endured a lot to be with me, and I have asked a lot of her. Perhaps unfairly. Not justifying anything, but it's not quite that simple. Let me do some digging and find out exactly what happened to your father."

I stopped walking and grabbed his arm so he could turn to me. "That's all well and good, but I need to know where she is myself. I have to protect my family." Then for good measure, I added, "And that goes for our son."

Leo dropped his eyes to Jamaal, who was gnawing on his little fist, drops of slobber wetting his shirt. "I'll look out for you two," he said finally, looking me directly in the eye. "I promise."

I let out a groan in frustration. "Why are you protecting her?" I knew I was yelling when a few people looked my way. I didn't give a damn.

Leo remained calm despite my outburst. "I'm not protecting her," he said. "I'm protecting you, my love. I swear."

He reached his hand to my face, probably to wipe away the angry tears stinging my cheeks. I slapped his hand away.

"It's so complicated." Leo's voice had lowered to a little above a whisper. "I wish you knew everything."

"Then tell me," I said. "Just tell me, Leo. What is she doing? Why? I know you know. I know you still talk to her, don't you?"

"Yes, but—"

"Then tell me. Did she have something to do with my father's death?"

Leo looked off into the distance but remained quiet. That was all the answer I needed.

Without another word, I snatched Jamaal from his arms, startling a gasp from both of them. Jamaal's bottom lip poked out and his eyes scrunched shut in preparation for the cry I knew he was about to let out.

"You two have crossed the line, and she better hope the police find her before I do." I paused, then added, "And, Leo, I swear to God if you had anything to do with any of this shit, you won't need to fake your own death next time."

"My love, please don't take my son—"

"Might as well tell him goodbye for good." And with that, I turned and stormed off, dragging the stroller behind me, Jamaal's cries echoing loudly in my ear.

I strapped him back in his car seat and quickly slid back in the driver's seat. I didn't realize my hands were shaking until I rested them on the wheel. I half expected Leo to follow me, so I was surprised to see him through my windshield still standing in the same place. But he wasn't looking my way. Rather he had his hand up shielding his eyes from the sun as he starred across the lake at something. Or someone.

⸺►◄⸺

As I had asked, Adria was waiting in her car in the parking lot of the church as soon as I pulled up. She saw me and was already talking as I stepped out.

"Girl, what is so important?" she asked. "You know as soon as I mentioned I was meeting you, Key got worried and wanted to come."

I leaned into the back seat to take out a now sleeping Jamaal. "Let's just keep this between us, Adria."

"You know I'm going to do that. Now what's up?"

By the time we got to the front door, I had brought Adria up to speed on my conclusions about Leo and Tina. Just as I suspected, my ass wasn't crazy.

We quickly hushed as we passed a few of the executive committee members on our way to the childcare center. "Kimmy, for real, if what you're saying is true, we need to go to the police."

I passed Jamaal across the threshold to the childcare volunteer and scribbled my name on the sign-in sheet.

"I plan to," I said, though I wasn't entirely sure if that was completely true. I had brought her here to help me search for Tina's information. It would make sense to have it on file somewhere considering Leo Jr. did attend the childcare. But even if I found something, what then? I still needed some evidence of the poisoning. What did I expect her to do? Admit to it? It would be a cold day in hell before she did that. I figured approaching Leo again wasn't going to do shit. Hell, he appeared to know more than he let on. Why? I didn't know.

Then another thought hit me as we headed to my father's office. The bastard was probably in on it. That was the only logical explanation. Why else would he be so damn tight-lipped about the whole thing unless he had something to do with it himself?

I could've slapped myself for being so damn trusting of him, letting my desperation for Jamaal to have his "father" cloud whatever good sense I had. Of course, he would play the doting father, the loving man, in my time of need. First when I was on the outs with Jahmad, now in the wake of my dad's death. How ironic he was there to pick up the pieces after he'd shattered my world himself.

"Shit," I hissed as the thought strengthened. "Adria, I'm so damn stupid."

She glanced around and I winced, remembering I was in a church. "What are you talking about?"

"I'm talking about, it's him," I said. "Somehow Leo is involved. He has to be."

"Why do you say that?"

"Adria, it makes sense. He's still talking to her. That much is clear. She isn't pulling all this off alone."

Adria pursed her lips in thought. "That doesn't make sense. I mean, I don't like him with everything that happened, but didn't you tell me he saved you from her?"

"Yeah . . ." She was right. That part didn't make sense. But, hell, neither did any of the mess I had been tied up in when it came to them. But I knew there was something else underneath. Something that was hidden in plain sight. That fact alone caused a shiver of fear to race up my spine. I couldn't put my finger on it, and that made me vulnerable. And whoever it was was attacking me in every way possible. First my business, my son, and ultimately my dad. Who was next?

My head suddenly whipped up to Adria as she stood in front of me in all her pregnant glory. "Maybe this was a bad idea," I said. I couldn't bear the thought of anything happening to her.

"No, we're going to look and see what we find," she insisted.

The uneasiness was still there, and I couldn't shake it. "We'll stay for fifteen minutes," I relented. "Then will you go home to Keon?"

"Yes. But only if you promise you'll go to the police if we find anything."

I nodded. "Deal." I took a breath and entered my dad's office.

It was as if this space had been frozen in time all the way down to the papers littering his desk. His scent still hung in the air as strong as if he were sitting in the leather wingback chair.

Without thinking, I crossed the room and picked up the frame on his desk. A picture of all four of us. One of those little family pictures my mom had dragged us to JCPenney Portraits to take one year because we didn't have any. The kind where we all dressed in the same color of various clothing styles. I looked to be about eight or nine, with two tight hair bows and a forced smile that matched Keon's, because we'd been told we better act right. Come to think of it, that was the first and last time we'd taken formal family pictures. Which was probably why my dad had framed it instead of trashing it, because the picture was hideous, if I could be honest.

Yet still, the picture had captured every piece of genuine happiness in his eyes. Those eyes I felt like I hadn't seen in entirely too long, and with the exception of memories and photos, would never see again.

Adria let me have a little moment, because she waited patiently until I'd set the frame back down before speaking. "We're going to get to the bottom of this." I surely hoped so. For all of our sakes.

She started in the file cabinet while I rummaged in his desk. Apparently everything was going according to plan with the sale of the church from what I could see by the papers. Offers, bill of sale receipts for furniture, a log of the financials. My folks had been right. There wasn't a lot of money left, and they were just about breaking even with the prospective buyer offers on the table. I surely hadn't realized it had gotten this bad.

"What is that smell?" Adria asked as we continued our search. I sniffed the air and caught the subtle aroma of stale food. Not too strong, but strong enough. My dad kept a mini-fridge under his desk. I opened it, and immediately the smell grew stronger, assaulting my nostrils. Other than a half-gallon of sweet tea that looked to be nearly gone, there appeared to be something wrapped in a grocery bag. A little investigation revealed it was spaghetti, weeks old, with mold around the Tupperware corners. "Probably should throw those out," Adria suggested, turning back to the files in the drawer.

I nodded, eyeing the refrigerator contents once more. *Poison.* The officer's words came back to bounce around my head. I couldn't shake it. I felt like I was missing something.

"Is this what you needed?" Adria pulled a folder from the drawer, stuffed tight with papers. "Childcare Registration."

I put the food out of my mind and walked closer as she examined the sheets inside, thumbing through each one. She stopped on a piece of paper in particular. "Child's name, Leo Owusu Junior."

"That's it." I reached for the paper, my eyes quickly scanning the information myself. Sure enough, she had put what looked like authentic information. A phone number, even an address. Question now, what was I going to do with it?

A knock hit the door and startled us both. Adria and I exchanged glances before I quickly folded the paper and stuffed it in my pocket. "Come in," I called.

The door opened and to my surprise, Tyree peeked his head in. I let out a relieved sigh. "Hey, boos," he greeted with a smile. "They told me I could find y'all back here."

I beckoned him into the room. "Yeah, just trying to straighten up a little. What are you doing here?"

"Well, I started attending after . . . you know—the pastor got sick. Sad to say, but I think that was my little wakeup call." His smile faded, and his forehead creased in concern. "How you holding up, boo?"

I gave a little shrug. "I'm hanging in there, I guess. Thanks again for coming to the funeral service, Tyree. And even to the hospital. It really meant a lot that you were there for me and my family."

"Of course." He looked to Adria, his smile widening again. "Baby mama over there looking hungry."

Adria laughed and rubbed her stomach. "That's always."

"Well, they just finished bible study. Y'all want to go grab something to eat?"

Adria closed the file cabinet and looked to me. I knew she was remembering I wanted her to get home to my brother. Just to be safe. Yeah, we had Tina's address, but we had no idea where the bitch was.

"Rain check," she said. "Key is waiting for me at the house, so you two go ahead. Call me later, Kimmy?"

I nodded, relieved.

"Sounds good," Tyree said. "And hey, when we all get back to somewhat normal, I've been playing with some ideas for Melanin Mystique. An investor friend of mine is in town, and he's very interested."

"Interested?" Adria and I spoke at the same time.

Tyree grinned like he was sitting on a pot of gold. He lifted his hands, palms out. "Okay, okay, don't get mad but . . ." He paused dramatically. "I may have shown him your business proposal. And he may be interested in investing."

My mouth dropped, and for the first time in a long-ass time, I saw a little peek of light at the end of the tunnel. "Wow, that is great news, Tyree," I said, still in shock. "I'm just—wow! Why didn't you say anything before?"

"Well, I wanted it to be a surprise, and I know you're going through a lot. Now it doesn't have to be some immediate decision. But I thought, when you're ready, I could set up a little business meeting, just to talk."

I looked at Adria, her face still registering just as much shock as mine. "We'll talk about it," she answered for me. "Thanks, Tyree, and tell him we are interested. Just give us some time. Kimmy just—"

"Of course, boo. I know." Tyree nodded as he grabbed each of our hands. "And that's what I told him. I just wanted you two to keep it in the back of your minds. You know I'm here for whatever you need."

I hugged him. "Thank you. For real. Now let's get out of here."

"Wait, what's that smell?" Tyree paused at the door, sniffing the air like I had just done earlier. Oh, damn, the refrigerator.

"We probably should throw that old food out, Kimmy," Adria said, wrinkling her nose in disgust.

I thought about it as Tyree headed for the refrigerator to do just that. "Just leave it," I said, stopping his movements. On second thought, maybe there was something in there. Maybe not, but still, throwing it away didn't seem like the smartest move right now. Not while my dad still had an open homicide case with poisoning involved.

We got Jamaal from the childcare and headed outside together. The sky had darkened, threatening rain.

"Please call me when you get home," I instructed as Adria hugged me first, then kissed Jamaal.

"Yes, *Mother*," she chided. She hugged Tyree as well, then left.

"So, boo, what you thinking for lunch?" Tyree asked, glancing at his watch. "Well, dinner rather," he corrected, noticing the time.

I glanced up as the first few sprinkles of rain dropped. "Let's do dinner another time," I suggested. "I'm not really hungry, and I probably need to get home before the sky opens up."

That's what my mouth said, because honestly it sounded good. But really, I had an address in my pocket. Maybe I needed to pay Mrs. Tina Owusu a little visit.

Chapter 25

I knew I was taking a huge risk being over there. It was dangerous, but, hell, I had been in worst situations. But now as I sat outside of the apartment building, I had to admit the decision to
come had been impulsive and thoughtless. What did I expect to
find?

The first droplets of rain splattered the windshield, causing the
glass to blur and fog. But still, I managed to keep my eyes focused
on the window of the first-floor apartment in building F. My eyes
dropped to the words on the paper I had unfolded. Yeah, this was
supposed to be Tina's place.

The complex wasn't anything fancy, but it was kept up nicely
and looked on the fairly newer side. I couldn't picture Tina staying here, though. Not flashy, money-hungry Tina. I couldn't help
feeling like this was more of a temporary place to lay low. Which
only heightened my suspicions. The hell was she hiding for unless
her sneaky ass was up to something?

There was a little whine from the back seat, and I glanced in
the rearview mirror. Jamaal's pacifier had dropped to his lap, and
the lack of his little soother was definitely making him irritable. I
hated I couldn't leave him with anyone while I went on this little
excursion, but I couldn't ask Adria because then she would ask

one too many questions, and leaving him with my mom right now was definitely a no-go. Who else did I have? Leo? Jahmad? Hell, no.

So as much as I didn't want to, I had gone ahead and brought him along, promising myself I would just watch and see if she was there. I could always come back later, even with the police if I needed to. I reached to the back seat for his pacifier and popped it back into his mouth.

The afternoon fell, bringing school buses wheeling through and tenants home from work. But still no Tina. After an hour and a half, I had just about given up. She probably just put some random-ass address for paperwork's sake. I should have known Tina's uppity ass wouldn't be caught even looking at apartments, much less living in one.

The crisp black Bentley caught my eye through the window, mainly because the vehicle looked fresh off the showroom floor and appeared completely out of place in the parking lot riddled with Fords, Chevys, and Hondas. Now that was more like Tina.

I frowned as the vehicle backed into a parking space and for a moment just sat there. I panicked. Did she see me? I called myself parking far enough away from the building while still being able to see so as not to look too obvious. Now I was second-guessing that decision as well. Sure, I had traded in the Porsche Leo bought me for a more spacious vehicle now that I had to cart around a car seat. But my Audi Q7 was anything but inconspicuous and just as out of place as the Bentley.

My phone vibrated in the cup holder at my hip and, keeping my eyes on the car still sitting, waiting, I picked it up and put it to my ear.

"My bad, girl. I meant to call you when I first got home to let you know I made it. I jumped in the shower real quick," Adria said.

"Okay, good." At least that eased my fears. Adria was home, safe and sound. "Where is Key?"

"I asked him to run out and get me something to eat," she said, then added, "And, Kimmy, I swear if that man comes back with anything other than Hot Cheetos and sour cream, I am divorcing his ass. Sorry in advance."

I didn't respond as the door to the car swung open and Leo emerged into view, a cell phone to his face. Apparently some heated discussion had him distracted as his mouth moved quickly.

"Girl, you okay?" Adria asked, clearly sensing my distraction.

"Yeah," I murmured. "Just thought I saw someone."

"Where are you?"

"I'm headed home." That was a lie, but not really. I would be headed home as soon as I figured out what the hell was going on with Leo. I couldn't even say I was really surprised to see him here. I knew he and Tina were still fucking around. This just confirmed it.

"Okay, well, call me later. I think Keon just pulled up anyway."

"Enjoy that nasty shit," I said, referring to her snack of choice.

That prompted a laugh. "I'll save some for you."

We hung up as Leo crossed the street to building F, his pace unusually quick. And I noticed how he kept looking around as if he knew someone was watching him.

From my position I wasn't able to get a good angle on the door, but I did see him pull out keys as he hung up the phone. I did see his smile, a huge contrast to the anger he had been displaying with the caller only minutes before. And I did see a hand grab his forearm and pull him playfully out of view. Then he disappeared into the apartment.

I sighed, deciding to go home. I was still unsettled by the unanswered questions. Leo pulled out keys, so he obviously lived there, or was very close to the person who did. That was unusual, even for him. Who was he arguing with? And who lived in the apartment in building F? Obviously by the smile on his face, someone he was very happy to see. Probably Tina, I instantly concluded. It was clear the bastard was lying. As I had figured, they were in some twisted little something together. But why bother me? Was it revenge? And did they really kill my dad?

I left with more questions than answers, and that shit was bothering the hell out of me.

———※◦◦———

I leaned on the door to the formal dining room, which my mom had made into a makeshift office. I was surprised to have found her in there, well, anywhere, really, outside of her bedroom. But here she was going through something in a file cabinet.

She didn't readily speak, so I waited patiently while she continued browsing for whatever it was she was looking for.

Finally, she sat down, a manila folder in hand. "What are you doing?" I asked at her continued silence.

"Just finalizing some things." She looked up at me. "I'm selling the house," she admitted. "And the church. I can't do this, Kimmy. I just need to—"

"Mama, I get it. You don't owe me any kind of explanation."

Mama nodded and dropped her head. "I just feel like I'm betraying him," she admitted. "By leaving. Like I'm supposed to be stronger than I am. But, I can't." She shook her head and met my gaze with tears in her eyes. "I'm not that strong, Kimmy. Your dad was my strength."

I blinked back tears of my own. "You know I just bought my house. Move in with me. I think it's too painful for us to be here. At least right now. Let's stay there for a little while and then if you still want to sell the house, I'll help." That appeased her. For now.

My mom rose from the chair. "Officer Terry came by again," she started. "Asking me all kinds of questions. Making allegations."

Anger immediately ignited in me. I thought back to Detective Vincent Wright and the investigation when the police thought I had killed Leo. Shit was infuriating and embarrassing. It hurt like hell to know my mom was going through that.

"I know something happened up at the church. I just don't know what."

I left my mom there and stormed to my room. I tried not to wake Jamaal as I rummaged through my dresser. Surprised I hadn't thrown it away, I found Officer Terry's business card and carried it back with me to the living room, dialing the number as I walked.

Her desk phone went to voicemail. "Officer Terry, this is Kimera Davis. I have some additional information on my father's case. I may know who did it. I have a name and address, so please call me back." I hung up and shoved the phone back in my pocket.

"Kimera." My mom's gentle voice startled me as I turned to face her. Shit, I hadn't expected her to hear me. "You know who did it?"

I had never explained to my mom everything about Leo and especially not Tina. As far as she was concerned, Leo was dead, and I had gotten a little hurt when someone tried to snatch my purse, reason for my bruised appearance when I went into labor with Jamaal. I sure as hell didn't need to add to what she was already battling.

"I don't," I said, choosing my words carefully. "But I don't need the police coming down on you. I found something in Daddy's office at the church."

"What?"

"Just some food in the refrigerator. Remember they said it was poison. So I just think they should take a look."

Mama's nod was slight as if even she knew I was stretching. I hugged her.

"We are going to get through this," I tried my best to assure her.

"I don't think we will," she murmured before pulling from my arms and walking back to her bedroom.

⟶•◦•⟵

I half expected Officer Terry to call me back pretty quickly. I was actually anxious to divulge my little pseudo-FBI discovery. I just hoped it was worth something. Lord knows I was just as determined to solve this case as they were. We all needed closure, and having whoever did this to my dad walking, talking, and breathing while he lay six feet under was enough to make me sick.

It wasn't until later that evening when my phone rang, and I didn't hesitate to answer without looking. "Officer Terry?"

"Hey, boo, it's me."

My anticipation fell at Tyree's voice. "Oh, hey, sorry about that."

"Is this a bad time?"

I took a seat on the bed. "No it's good. I was just—Never mind. What's up?"

"I wanted to see if you could meet with the investor today. I know it's last-minute but he just got an emergency and is flying out in the morning. He probably won't be back for a while."

I glanced at the clock on my nightstand. It was already nearing six. Sure, daylight still clearly showed through my window, but my body was already aching to lie down. Funny how the mental exhaustion was wearing on me physically.

"So he wants to meet now?"

"Well, in about thirty minutes if that's okay," he said. "Mrs. Adria is with me, and we are going now to see this possible location. I don't mean to rush you but just didn't want us to miss out on this opportunity. But if you want us to just meet him," Tyree quickly added, "I understand. It's last-minute, and I already told him you were dealing with a death in the family."

I sighed. As much as I wanted to stay, I couldn't leave my girl to handle this business meeting on her own. I was surprised she hadn't called earlier to let me know she had decided to go. But, hell, I could attribute that to the pregnancy brain because my girl, bless her heart, was forgetting her mind left, right, and sideways.

"Text me the address," I said.

"I got Chloe's number," he said of the childcare worker from church. "You need me to call her for you, boo?"

I glanced at Jamaal in his crib. I really didn't want to take him to a business meeting, but my mother was really in no shape to watch him. In fact, she had taken a few sleeping pills and gone to bed not even thirty minutes earlier. Tyree's suggestion about Chloe was a good idea, but I hardly wanted to bother the girl at the last minute like this.

"No, I got it," I answered, already pulling a fresh onesie and pants from the dresser. I would just feed and change him, and I was sure he wouldn't be too much trouble. In the meantime, I was getting a little excited to hear what this investor had to say. With everything going on, I was welcoming this little piece of good news. Lord knows I wouldn't be able to take any more of the bad news without losing my damn mind.

Chapter 26

I was already in love.

Tyree's text instructions led me to a Buckhead shopping district with a 3,000-square-foot standalone building nestled amidst a clothing boutique and spa. Tyree mentioned the person owned all three properties and was interested in a combined investment.

This prospect brought much-needed relief to my life. I was tired of being depressed, tired of the headaches and the sorrow. Tired of my heart aching in grief. I could appreciate Tyree's attempt to put a little hope back into my life. Without a bright spot, it was so easy to see how people could consider suicide.

I shook the last thought from my mind as I stepped out of the car. I couldn't bring myself to even let those malicious thoughts linger. For my sake, my mom's, and most importantly my son.

I put Jamaal in his stroller, adjusted his straps and pacifier, and wheeled him through the parking lot. The only other vehicle was Tyree's black Mustang parked close to the front. He had already given me a heads-up that we would probably be the first to arrive and we could just look around. The investor was Robert Quinn. I'd done my homework on this man and saw he'd invested in a number of black-owned start-up companies, all very profitable since he'd become their partner. Mr. Quinn was stuck in traffic but happy that Adria and I had agreed to meet with him on such short notice.

"What took you so long?" Tyree opened the door just as I pushed Jamaal's stroller up the walkway past the "For Sale" sign stuck in the grass.

"I'm not late or anything, am I?"

"No, you're good. He'll be here in about five minutes."

I tossed him a small smile. "Well, I'm five minutes early, then."

I glanced around the large open space with glistening hardwood floors and floor-to-ceiling windows that opened to the parking lot. "Wow, this place is amazing."

"I know. Beautiful, right?" He gestured widely and did a little turn in the middle of the floor. "Can't you see it here? Much better than the other space."

"Definitely." I craned my neck to a hallway going down the back. "Where is Adria?"

"She had to pee," Tyree said with a smirk and shake of his head. "You know how she is."

"Yeah, the girl is like a faucet," I murmured in amusement.

Tyree pointed out different areas of the room, where the cashiers would go, the makeup stations, even a red carpet running down the middle to an elevated three-way mirror. A Hollywood theme, he suggested, and though it sounded a bit much at first, I absolutely saw the vision coming to life.

"What do you think?" he asked when he was done.

"I just hate I couldn't have found you sooner," I said, impressed.

I could feel Tyree watching me, and though I tried my best to look engaged at my surroundings, I knew it was more than obvious I was distracted.

Without another word, Tyree walked over and hugged me, pulling back to leave his hands resting on my shoulders. "How you holding up, boo?"

The tenderness almost broke me. Almost. I blinked back tears and feigned a smile. "Not good," I admitted. "But taking it one day at a time."

"You know I'm here for you," he said. "With whatever you need."

"Thanks. But, Tye, you have your own life. Your own man. I'm not trying to—"

"Boo, if you don't shut up with that."

I laughed as he rolled his eyes. "I've been so wrapped up in my shit I haven't even asked about you and what you got going on."

Tyree waved his hand. "Same old drama. Men ain't shit. Nothing new."

The accuracy. I had to laugh. Immediately Jahmad flashed across my mind. According to Keon, he only had a week left before the big move. And according to Adria, his condo was already under contract. She said he had already stayed longer than he originally expected because of the funeral. But now, I guessed it was really happening.

I stepped from Tyree's grasp and turned my back to break this little emotional scene. "Let me go check on Adria," I said quickly. It was a good change of subject. An excuse, but it worked.

As if on cue, we heard a car engine turning into the parking lot. "I'll go get Mr. Quinn," Tyree said.

I glanced around and pushed Jamaal's stroller to a side wall out of the way. My baby was asleep again, which I was glad about. At least we would be able to talk business in peace. I passed several doors on the way to what I thought was the restroom. I didn't realize how big the place was. Four huge offices lined the hallway, with more windows. This was definitely the place for natural sunlight.

I was already picturing the grand opening. I didn't know how soon we would even pull everything off. My dad's death was still fresh, and I didn't think a party would be on anyone's mind. But I could absolutely hear my dad scolding me for putting my life on pause for him. "Baby girl, you got to live your life. You only get one. This isn't a dress rehearsal." I couldn't even remember the context in which he had uttered those words, but damn if they weren't relevant now.

I had just lifted my hand to knock on the restroom door when I heard the baby's cry rip through the air. He sounded distraught, and I was in a sheer panic as I ran back down the hall with all kind of images cluttering my head. My God, had he fallen out of his stroller? Hadn't I secured him? These floors suddenly didn't seem so beautiful as I pictured my son lying facedown with blood dribbling out of his little body.

Jamaal, baby—" I froze. My legs suddenly felt like lead and my breath caught in my throat with such force I felt like I was going to strangle on it. He wasn't on the floor. Nor was he in his stroller. Jamaal was now soothed with his pacifier back in his mouth. I felt a very slight reprieve to see he wasn't laid out on the floor in pain. But his danger had my fear rising. I couldn't even focus on the person whose arm he was cradled in. No, I was too much in a panic that for the second time in my life I was staring down the barrel of a gun. Slowly, so slowly my eyes lifted.

"Girl, your face is classic, right now." It was Tina's voice that snapped me out of my stunned silence. "I wish I could just take a picture." She appeared beside him with a smug look. I cringed when she dipped her head to brush a kiss across the baby's forehead.

Tears blurred my vision, but Tyree's blank expression remained etched in my brain. His arm was stiff as he held the weapon steady, pointing at me and daring me to move. Even if I could move, I wouldn't dare chance it. Not when he clutched Jamaal so tight in his other arm.

"Tye," I whispered in disbelief. I shook my head, not wanting to admit it to myself. "How? What—why—"

"Don't ask him shit," Tina snapped. "Because I told him to. You should know me better by now, Kimera."

I opened my mouth, confusion having me closing it again. Maybe it was better if I didn't say anything. They had my son. One wrong word . . .

"Girl, please." Tina waved her hand as if reading my thoughts. "Ain't nobody about to do nothing to this child."

I wanted to mention how I didn't trust that, considering she had tried to harm him before. But I kept quiet.

Tina took the gun from Tyree's hand while keeping it aimed on me. "Sit down. Let's wait a minute. We have a little time."

Tyree turned and carried Jamaal through the front door, and instinctively I took a step in that direction.

"Uh uh." The cock of the gun had me freezing again. "I wouldn't do that if I were you."

"Tina, please." I didn't give a damn what it looked like. Tyree had now disappeared with my baby. Where the hell was he going? What had she told him to do with Jamaal?

"Sit down," Tina instructed firmly, gesturing to the floor with the gun. "I'm not asking again."

I sank to the floor, my heart sinking just as fast.

Tina towered over me, a triumphant smile still touching her lips. "Déjà vu, huh? It was about this time, what, six or so months ago, we were in this same situation? Only this time, Leo won't be able to save you." She glanced at her watch. That made me uneasy. It was clear she was waiting for something. But what? How much time did I have left? And Jamaal? Where was Adria?

"Tina, why are you doing this?" I asked, nearly sobbing. "You have Leo. I don't want him. I'm trying to go on with my life."

"Yeah, well, it doesn't quite work like that," Tina said. "For some reason, Leo is in love with you. He broke every single vow to me to be with you. Ain't that some shit?"

"But I haven't been with Leo. I swear."

I screamed when a bullet shattered the wall behind me. It was so close that bits of the plaster sprinkled my back. My hesitant eyes lifted back to the gun where the after-smoke billowed up from the barrel.

"Stop the lies, Kimera," Tina said. "I know you've been with him. He swore he wasn't seeing you, but he was always with you."

"No, he wasn't."

"So you haven't been with him at all?"

I was crying now, torn between the truth and the lies. I thought back to our time in Punta Cana. Did she know? All this shit for that one time?

"I'm sorry." The words fell from my lips, because that seemed to be what she was waiting for. "I never meant for any of this to happen. I'll take my son and leave. You won't hear from me again."

"Your son?" she echoed with a frown. "Word on the street is that's Leo's son too." I didn't answer, and she nodded at my silence. "He's really adorable." A mischievous smile spread. "Looks just like Leo. You've given him the son I never could." Another look to her watch. I could almost hear the ticking, which only heightened my anxiety. Keep her talking, keep her talking.

"Leo Junior—"

"I know he told you about him, so don't even try that shit," she snapped.

"So it was all you this time?" I spoke the obvious. "The fire? The teddy bear? My daddy?"

Tina shrugged and glanced at her watch again. I could tell she was getting impatient.

"What is it that you want, Tina?" I couldn't keep calm anymore. This waiting, not knowing, was eating at me. Where was Jamaal?

"You," she said. "Just you."

The shot was so fast I didn't even have time to react. It tore through Tina's shoulder, blood and tissue spewing on me and causing a swell of nausea to bubble up in my throat.

Tina turned weakly, her eyes rounding at the sight of Tyree standing in the doorway, the smoke from his own gun billowing up from his hand.

"You son of a—"

Another shot ripped through her chest, causing Tina to stagger backward before collapsing to the floor in a pool of blood. Her head lolled to the side, and the gun went skidding across the slick hardwood.

I climbed to all fours as best as I could, half crawling, half dragging my body out of the way of the blood slithering toward me. I couldn't bring myself to look at Tina's corpse.

"It's okay." Tyree's voice was quiet with relief.

I couldn't stop the trembling as I buried my face into my hands. "Oh, thank God, Tyree. She—she . . ." I felt faint and didn't even have the energy to keep talking. I was just so glad this was over. "Jamaal." I mustered strength to climb to limp legs. "Where is he?"

"He's safe."

"I have to—"

"Kimera. I think you should calm down, boo."

"Oh, my God." My hand trembled as it flew to my mouth. All I could see in my mind was the bullet bursting through Tina's body. Now here she was lying dead at my feet. "She wanted revenge," I said. "All this because she wanted revenge."

Slowly, the gun that Tyree had still angled at Tina's corpse was now pointed at me. His face remained calm. "She wasn't the one that wanted revenge," he said. "It was me."

The shock paralyzed me, this time even stronger. "Tyree? What the hell is going on? Tina—"

"If I were you I would sit back down and let me explain," he said, mimicking Tina's earlier gestures with the gun. I was wrong. It wasn't over. Apparently we were just getting started.

Chapter 27

"Tyree." I spoke carefully, holding my hands up palms out as if in surrender. "What's going on? She's dead, but I won't tell. You did us both a favor."

His laugh was almost cynical. "Did I?"

"Please just put the gun down and let's talk," I pleaded, not removing my eyes from the weapon. "I'm not mad at you. I hate that she's pulled you into her lies, but it's over, Tye."

"Pulled me? No, no, no, boo, you've got it all wrong. She was in on my little plan. This shit was above her."

I was confused, and I'm sure it was written all over my face. Tyree walked closer and placed the barrel of the gun in my chest. "Call Leo," he said, snatching my cell phone from my back pocket. Damn, I hadn't even thought about it being there. How had he known?

My hands shook as I took the phone from him, staring blindly down at my screensaver. The picture of a sleeping Jahmad and Jamaal shone back at me, and I wanted to cry. "Where is—"

My question was cut short. The steel butt of the gun rammed into my temple with such force I saw stars. I stumbled in pain, the phone falling from my limp fingers.

"Now let's try this again," he said calmly. "I'll explain later, but you need to get Leo on the phone and get his ass here. Now."

My vision wavered, but I managed to pick up my cell phone. I briefly contemplated dialing the police but knew I would be dead on arrival.

"Put it on speaker," Tyree demanded, erasing all possibility of a sneak police call. Obediently, I dialed Leo's number. The ringing echoed in the empty room, and I silently prayed like hell he wouldn't answer. Of course he did. Almost too quickly. I could see a flash of anger darken Tyree's eyes.

"My love," Leo greeted as customary. "I'm so glad you called. I wanted to apologize."

My mind drew a blank. What the hell was he talking about? I struggled to ignore the feeling of the gun boring a hole into my chest and instead focus on something else. Anything else. Silent tears rolled down my cheeks. "Apologize? For what?" My voice cracked.

"For earlier. With what happened at the park. I know I was being a little evasive with you about Tina. I promise it's not what you think, my love."

I caught Tina's dead body in my peripheral vision, the bullet wounds in both her shoulder and chest continuing to pool blood underneath her limp body and stain her navy blouse a deep crimson.

"I just want to protect you, my love. You have to believe that," he went on. Funny. If my life hadn't been in danger I would have had to laugh at the irony.

"Okay," was my quiet response.

"What's wrong, my love?" His voice automatically filled with concern.

"I just . . ." I trailed off, looking to Tyree as I chose each word carefully. "Need you. Can you meet me?"

"Of course."

His answer was too eager. Why did I expect any kind of hesitancy? I tasted the disgust on my tongue as I led this man into a death trap.

"You sure it's not too late for you to come?" I asked before I even realized it. Tyree's jaw clenched, and he lifted the gun from my chest to my forehead. The metal felt like ice on my skin, but any minute, any second I knew he would warm it up by tearing a hole through my skull. Then, oh, God, what would he do to my baby?

"It's not too late," Leo said. "You know I'll come any time for you, my love. Is my son with you?"

I paused, unsure how to answer. Tyree nodded his head, coaching my response.

"Yes."

"Good. Where are you?"

I pulled the phone from my ear and rattled off the same address Tyree had texted me, luring me in.

"Why are you there?"

"I . . . was looking at the property."

"Okay, my love. See you soon."

Tyree didn't give me a chance to think. He snatched the phone from my hand and checked the screen to make sure the call had ended. Satisfied, he shoved it into the back pocket of his black skinny-leg jeans.

"Good girl," he said. "Now we wait for our man."

Our man? Slowly, confusion began to lend itself to clarity. "You and Leo." It was more of a statement than a question.

"You just had to fuck everything up," Tyree said with a shake of his head. "Pathetic. We had such a good thing going."

The realization left me staggered, and I wished for a table, wall, or something to lean on for support. "How long?" I whispered.

"Boo, I was there before you and Lena." Tyree's lips curved into a proud smile. "For the longest it was just me, Tina, and Leo.

Then he went and got Lena, and that was cool. She didn't give me any trouble. It was you that was the problem."

"Me? How?"

"Leo had to cut our time short because he was running after you. Trying to see what you were doing, who you were screwing. That man loves me, but all of a sudden, he was in love with you too. I've been living in the shadows for so long, content with him being in his little poly thing, because I knew it was for show. Knew that deep down I really had that man's heart. But he changed up on me. Said he loved you. Wanted to be with you. Especially after you had his son."

"But I don't want Leo!" I said, desperation causing my voice to elevate. I had thought Tina was the only one I had to worry about. Even when I was married to Leo, both Lena and I had assumed he was away so much because he was recruiting for wife number four. Little did I know how right and how wrong we were.

"You don't want him, huh?" Tyree's voice held the hint of doubt, evident he knew otherwise. "So you didn't go out of town with him?"

I pursed my lips. "It wasn't like that," I murmured. "I didn't even know he was going."

"So y'all aren't still having sex?" Again, more doubt in his voice.

I decided another tactic was better than digging myself further into the dirt. If I kept it up, the man was just crazy enough to put a bullet in me and leave me hanging outside the front door like a wind chime. Surprise, Leo. Here's your bitch.

My gaze fell and landed on Tina once more, her paled face frozen in a mix between shock and anger.

"This whole time," I said, chiding myself at my own stupidity. "This whole time I thought it was Tina. And it was you."

"I know. You really are a stupid one, boo," he said with a sympathetic chuckle. "You were so busy worried about her, you didn't even see me right under your nose. Keep your friends close, but your enemies closer, right?"

"So the fire? And Jamaal." I was silently begging none of this was true. That it was indeed Tina, and I wouldn't feel as bad because she was at least now rotting at my feet.

"Yeah, that teddy bear shit was genius," he said. "A little lock picking and I was in there. You know for a minute I just watched you sleep and wondered if it would be so much easier just to smother you right there."

So close to death. Right in my own circle. But not everyone had made it out alive. "You poisoned my daddy?"

My heart cracked and might as well have been bleeding on the floor like Tina's.

"I hated to have to do that too," Tyree went on. "I actually liked the pastor. But hell, he should have known some shit like this would come from having such a hoe for a daughter. Poor man. He was so trusting."

That stung. But not nearly as much as his admission about murdering my father. "But why?" I didn't even stop the sobs. "How could you? He didn't have shit to do with this."

"Collateral damage," he said with nonchalance. He gestured the gun in Tina's direction. "Kinda like that one. But I never really liked Tina anyway. That bitch had too much mouth. I know you wanted her dead too, so stop acting like you care."

I shook my head. "But she said you worked for her."

Tyree chuckled as if my statement was the most amusing thing at that moment. A chill worked its way down my spine. "Enough talking." He pointed to the back, not bothering to respond to my comment. "Get to the storage closet."

It was a risk, I knew. The dude probably wouldn't hesitate to shoot me in the leg or pistol whip me or some shit. But still, I didn't budge.

To my surprise, my stubbornness didn't appear to faze him. In fact, he seemed amused. "If I were you, I would get back there," he said with a smirk. "I think there is someone you need to see."

Now it was horror that had me turning and damn near running to the room at the end of the hall.

I swung open the door, squinting in the dark room. I felt Tyree reach above my head and pull a dangling string, clicking on a single light bulb that shone dimly, illuminating the room in a yellow hue.

My eyes were drawn down, and I gasped when I saw Adria unconscious on the cement floor. One of her wrists was handcuffed to an exposed pipe, and her face was peppered with black-and-blue bruises peeking out from underneath a blindfold and a gag stuffed in her mouth. If it hadn't been for the slight rise of her chest, I would've sworn she was dead.

"Oh, God, no," I cried, running to kneel beside her. I put a gentle hand to her pregnant belly, then her battered face. "Why did you do this?" I was nearly yelling as I stroked her discolored cheek. "What did she do? She's pregnant."

"You needed a little extra incentive," Tyree said, tossing a pair of handcuffs at me. They landed on the floor with a sickening clank. "Handcuff yourself to that pipe over there." He nodded to another exposed pipe directly across from Adria.

"Fuck you." I was near hysteria now. "Fuck you, fuck you, you sick bastard!"

"Boo, let's not go there." Tyree pointed the gun directly at Adria's stomach, and I sucked in a sharp breath.

"Okay, okay, please, I'm sorry." I slid my body into his line of fire, shielding my friend as best I could. "I'll do anything. Please just don't hurt anyone else."

Tyree gestured again to the cuffs, and I grabbed them and did as I was told, clamping the tight metal onto my wrist. "Please," I said again, looking on in fear as he still kept the gun angled toward Adria even after I was cuffed to the pipe. "I did what you said. Please just let her go."

"I think I'll keep her," he said. "And don't forget I have your precious Jamaal. Leo will be here soon. We'll see once and for all who really has his heart. I hope for your sake he has the right answer."

And with that, he slammed the door shut and clicked the lock into place.

Chapter 28

The longer I sat in the shadows of the closet with the rank smell of must and mothballs cloaking the thick air, the more I knew with everything in me that there was no right answer.

I looked at the situation from both sides, and the conclusion was the same no matter what happened. If Leo confessed he was in love with me, Tyree would probably be so pissed, I was dead. If Leo admitted to loving him, well, he wouldn't need me anymore. And I was dead. What the hell was the point?

I looked at Adria still lying motionless in the middle of the floor. She still hadn't stirred, and I prayed like hell she wasn't dying right there in front of me. And my baby. What had he done with Jamaal?

Thoughts continued to swirl in my head until the beginnings of a migraine carried such force I had to lay my head back on the wall and brace against the pain. Or maybe it was an aftershock from when Tyree had hit me with the gun earlier. I lifted my fingers to the tender area and felt the knot, hard and sore.

The whole confession was enough to make me sick. Leo was gay? No, bisexual, since he loved men and women? I couldn't even digest that news. How had I not seen it before?

Because I hadn't cared to. As I had said over and over, my relationship with Leo was a business arrangement. Sure, it had resulted in a child, my little oopsie, but a miracle nonetheless. And Punta Cana? That shit had been a mistake fueled by a broken heart if there ever was one. And now what? Tina was dead. Lena was dead. And it looked like I was next.

I heard a door open, and I knew Leo had come. Now what? Would he be mad at everything Tyree had done all in the name of love? Would he fight for me?

Holding my breath, I craned my ear to listen. An argument. Low and muffled, but it definitely sounded like they were arguing.

My arm's elevated angle had my wrist growing numb, and the handcuff rattled against the pipe as I repositioned myself. "Please, God, let us all make it out of here alive. Please."

A groan. I looked over as Adria struggled to sit up against the restraint of her handcuff.

"Adria, thank God," I whispered.

My voice obviously scared her, and she tried to scream, the sound muffled by the gag forcing the noise back down her throat.

"It's me, Kimmy," I said. "It's me, it's all right." But I lied. It sure as hell wasn't all right, and if I knew it would make a difference, I would scream myself. I remembered the isolation of the buildings and the empty parking lot when I had driven up. Shit was useless.

The blindfold blocked her view, but Adria angled her head in the direction of my voice. Even with the blindfold, I could see the fear etched on her face. Guilt raked my conscience.

"I'm sorry I got you in this mess," I said, feeling her pain. "It's all my fault. Tyree, it was Tyree this whole time, and I didn't even know."

She mumbled something and put her hand to her belly.

"What is it?" I asked in alarm. Damn, at this distance I couldn't even get to her to help. "Is it the baby?"

Adria nodded.

"Shit," I hissed. "Don't worry. I'm going to get you out of here."

My head whipped around for something, anything. A weapon, a stick, tools, anything. But with the exception of an overturned box in the far corner of the room and some shelving lining the walls, the closet was completely empty.

Without thinking, I climbed to my knees. "Leo!" I yelled at the top of my lungs. "Leo, help us, please! Leo!"

Silence. For a moment, I wondered if they had left. Then, single footsteps approaching. I held my breath as the lock clicked out of place and the door swung open.

Leo's face registered first shock, then sadness as he looked from me to Adria. I reached for him.

"Leo, please." I was in tears. "Help us. She needs a doctor. She's pregnant."

Leo's eyes slid to Adria, who lifted her head, the light deepening the coloration of the bruises against the skin on her face. He didn't move from the doorway. "My love, I'm sorry. This is not how I wanted you to find out."

What? My arm fell limply by my side. "Leo, please. Don't let him hurt us. Jamaal?"

"Is safe," he quickly assured me. "I saw him myself."

That was at least a good thing for now. But what about Adria? And me?

"I just need to sort out some things," Leo said as if speaking to himself.

"You said you loved me," I whispered the reminder. No telling where Tyree was. "You said you would protect me."

Leo lifted his hands to his head and massaged his temples. "I know." He tossed a quick look over his shoulder. Without another word, he closed the door and locked it again.

I looked to Adria. Her face was now crinkled in pain.

"Just hold on," I said. "I'll get us out of here."

I counted two days, at least I think it was two days that passed before Leo came back. I couldn't be sure. The only measure of time I had was the number of meals, and since we had been in the closet, I had counted two times Tyree brought a paper plate of biscuits, two times a paper plate of Pop Tarts, and two times a paper plate with a slice of bread and a string of cheese. All served with lukewarm tap water in a plastic cup. About twice, Tyree came, gun in hand, and escorted us one at a time to the restroom and stood watching while we handled our business. The third time, frustration had me blurting out, "Do you fucking mind?"

"Trust me. You're not my type, boo." And he continued making me pee and shit at gunpoint. It was degrading.

He had yet to remove the blindfold and gag from Adria. Why? I didn't know. But we continued the hostage situation in extreme silence. What else could I say anyway?

Finally, the door opened, and while I expected Tyree with some more stale food I couldn't bring myself to eat, it was Leo who entered with a bucket and a hand towel. He started with Adria, dipping the towel in the bucket of soapy water and using it to dab on her face and neck.

He then moved to me, and I kicked the bucket, spilling the water on the floor. "Don't fucking touch me," I yelled.

"Let me explain," Leo said wearily. "I know I owe you an explanation."

"Oh, Tyree already made it all perfectly clear," I snapped. "Told me all about y'all's little dirty secret. You're gay, Leo. I don't give a fuck. Why don't you let us go so you can go be with that boy?"

He winced. "It's not that easy," he said.

"What's not? Why the hell are you making this so complicated?"

Leo turned over the empty bucket and took a seat on the overturned bottom. "First off, I love you," he said, his eyes level with mine. "Ain't shit easy about that. Second . . ." He took a heavy sigh. "My father wouldn't approve. If he knew that I . . . he would completely disown me. I wouldn't have anything." He waited as if he expected my sympathy, and I could only look on in disgust.

"At least you still have a father," I said, narrowing my eyes. "Your boyfriend killed mine. And for what? All of this?" I gestured first toward Adria, then me. "Because you're trying to keep it on the down-low? Really, dude?" Leo remained quiet. "Now what, Leo?" I asked, anger icing my tone. "What's the end game? Tyree made it clear he's not giving you up. So ain't no loving me. I'm as good as dead."

Leo's eyes ballooned in horror. "No, don't say that. I won't let him."

"Then help us," I pleaded. I touched his arm, hoping to appeal to his soft side. "You love me, right? Show me, Leo."

He nodded. "I have an idea," he said, rising. "Just give me some time."

"No, Leo." I attempted to stand, pulled back to my knees by the cuffs. "We don't have any more time. Adria is pregnant. She needs a doctor. And Jamaal. Where is he? We haven't eaten. Leo, he killed Tina. Please just go get the police and bring them here. They'll arrest him and—"

"No, no, no." Leo shook his head vehemently. "No, I love him too. My love, you have to let me handle this. I know how to handle Tyree."

"Apparently not," I snapped. "Because my father is dead and we're here."

Leo didn't respond, only walked back to the door. "I'll take care of this," he said before trapping us again.

I had to think. Come up with some kind of plan. I knew we wouldn't last another day being held hostage.

Chapter 29

For the first time since we got here, I saw Adria's face, and I felt even sicker to my stomach.

Both of her eyes contained dark rings, evidence of the aging black eyes. The gag had created raw skin around her mouth that had rubbed to a bold red tint. Her face looked sunken from the obvious lack of edible food. I know I hadn't eaten, and because she had been gagged, I know she hadn't either. I don't even think Tyree had expected either one of us to eat. I don't think he gave a damn. Just biding his time until whatever master plan Leo had spoken about popped off.

Tyree cuffed Adria again, and she sat, legs outstretched in front of her, her hand on the underside of her belly. I don't even think pain was a factor anymore. After days, hell, I had lost count by now; I think we both had become numb.

"How are you feeling?" I asked once Tyree let us alone.

She didn't bother looking at me. "How the fuck do you think?" she said, not bothering to hide her anger. But it wasn't as strong as she probably meant it to be. Instead she sounded exhausted.

I watched her use her free hand to pick up a slice of bread from the nearby paper plate. She bit into it weakly. It was clear hunger overrode the taste. I had tried my own bread earlier, and the little bit of mold I had seen on the crust had me gagging and throwing it back down. It was obvious this shit had been sitting here for days, hell, maybe even weeks before Tyree brought us here.

"Don't eat that," I said as she continued to chew and force herself to swallow.

"What am I supposed to eat, Kimera?" Now her voice did have more strength behind the words. "They're not giving us shit, and I have my baby to think about. If she's even still alive." She cracked and dissolved under a fitful of tears. "Kimmy, they're going to just kill us."

"No, they're not," I stated, masking my own fear.

"Why not? We know too much. We know who they are. They're not going to let us get away." She lowered her head, her hair falling like a curtain around her face.

"Keon," I said, lowering my voice. "Does he know you went with Tyree?"

She shook her head. "No."

"Why didn't you tell him where you were going?"

"Well, shit, because I didn't know I was being kidnapped," she snapped. She took a breath. "Keon was out getting me something to eat. Tyree just showed up at the house. Said he was meeting up with you. I was confused and said I was going to call you to see what was up. I told him you wouldn't be making these kind of plans without calling me. I knew something was up when he kept being so pushy. So then I said I was going to call my husband to let him know I was running out for a little bit. That's when he stuck me with a needle and I blacked out. Woke up in this closet. I wasn't handcuffed at first, so when he came back here, I tried to beat his ass. Tried."

I didn't want to admit my hope was starting to diminish. My mom didn't know where I was either. Neither did Jahmad. Like my father, we had trusted too easily. And look where it got him. Look where it got us.

"What are we going to do?" Adria asked helplessly. She lifted black, tearstained eyes to me.

"They have guns," I said. "And Jamaal. We can't fight them. Tyree killed Tina."

Adria gasped at the news. "Damn, really?"

I nodded. "Right there in front of me. I can't risk that happening to you or my son. So we're going to have to cooperate." The thought left a bitter taste in my mouth, and Adria kept watching intently as I mulled on it a bit longer. "Leo said something about a plan. I don't know what he's talking about, but I'm going to insist he let you go. And you get the police here as soon as you can."

"He took my phone," she said.

"Mine too." I thought a bit more, bearing against my throbbing headache. "I was following my GPS on my phone, but there was a spa and a clothing store next door. And maybe some restaurants up the street. I know Keon and my mama have probably called the police by now, so I'm sure they're already searching for us. You get them back here as soon as you can."

"What if I can't remember how to get back?" she asked. "He had me blindfolded. Shit, Kimmy. I don't even know where we are."

I didn't either. I tried to remember the address Tyree had texted me and then the one I had repeated back to Leo to get here.

"Your car," Adria said suddenly. "Did you drive here?"

"Yeah."

"It has GPS tracking, right?"

I smiled for the first time in days. "Damn sure does."

"Okay, that will lead them back."

"And I'm going to ask that they let Jamaal go with you. Please, just take care of my baby, Adria."

She frowned. "What are you going to do?"

I sighed. Try to stay alive, though I didn't know how likely that was anymore. It was evident Tyree wanted me dead. And if that had to happen in order for my friend and my son to live . . .

We waited in silence a while longer. On the other side of that door, it was just as quiet. I wondered if they had left us here to die. My gaze landed on the scattered paper plates and cups at my feet, half-eaten food causing sprinkles of ants to crawl across the wet floor.

They hadn't been back in today. Neither one of them. I couldn't tell what time it was, as I could only catch snatches of sleep that had my body aching more. The cuffs had rubbed my wrist completely raw and now the flesh was red and burned to the touch. I felt like the death I knew I was coming.

"Tyree killed Daddy," I murmured, the fresh realization causing another bout of tears to cake around my eyes. "This is all my fault, Adria. If I hadn't—if we—"

The sound of a door slamming had us both jumping. All that could be heard was our shuddering breaths in unison as we waited. Footsteps approached the door, quicker than usual.

Instinctively, I climbed to my knees. I wished like hell I had a weapon or something. The locks clicked out of place, and the door opened.

Leo stepped in and, walking over, kneeled down in front of me. He cupped either side of my face and kissed me, hard and firm on the lips. I snatched back in shock.

"Leo, what the hell—"

"It's going to all be okay, my love. I promise." He was smiling, and his eyes seemed to twinkle with some hidden excitement.

I relaxed. A little. "Are you—Is he—"

"It's going to all be okay. I took care of it."

He kissed me again, this time more passionately. The needle

prick was so tiny, I didn't even know he had stuck me until my vision wavered, showing black around the edges. My body felt light and weak, and I crumpled to the floor. I couldn't even muster the strength to stop Leo as he turned toward Adria, and her eyes rounded in fear. Then everything went black.

Chapter 30

"*But what if she doesn't?*"
"*She will.*"
"*And if not?*"
"*Then we will do what we need to do.*"

I felt like I was floating in the sunken place. I heard talking, but it would fade in and out with so much ambiguity that I couldn't tell which part was a dream and which was reality.

I lifted my lids, struggled to bring my vision into focus. Immediately, I knew I wasn't in the storage closet anymore but a plush bed with soft cushions and pillows that smelled of ocean-fresh Gain.

A quick survey of the room revealed I was in a gorgeous huge master bedroom, empty except for the bed I was now lying across. Off to one side was a set of double doors that opened to an en suite bathroom.

I felt groggy and filthy as I rose to a sitting position, the days-old t-shirt and jeans I wore stiff with dirt, grime, and dried blood. I held my wrists into view, noticing I wasn't cuffed anymore. I lifted my body from the bed, trying my best to steady my weakened legs. Where was I? Where was Adria?

Judging by the look of the room I was alone. I stumbled toward the closed curtains and pulled them back, separating the blinds to peer out.

Nothing but acres of land sweeping out under the night sky. Not another house in sight. I groaned, dragging myself to the bedroom door. It was locked, and my fingers paused over the lock on the doorknob. Did I want to know what was on the other side of that door? Shit, what if it was Tyree? But what if it was someone else's house? Someone who could help?

I flipped the lock, vaguely surprised when the knob didn't budge. Then, without thinking, I hit my palm against the white wood. "Help," I screamed, continuing to bang the door. "Please help me!"

Someone came bounding up the stairs, and I stood back as they unlocked the door and swung it open.

"What's wrong, my love?" Leo entered the room, shutting it behind him.

"What's wrong?" I echoed angrily. "You keep me in a storage closet for I don't know how fucking long. Then you drug me and drag me here in the middle of nowhere. Everything is wrong." I looked around, wishing for something to throw, but he damn sure did good by putting me here, because there was nothing in sight other than the fucking pillows. Which angered me even more. "Where is Adria?" I snapped.

Leo raised his hands. "Sit down and let's talk," he said calmly. I sized him up. He didn't look armed. But I was weak from hunger and exhaustion. And mostly fear. I wasn't sure if I could take him in my fragile state.

I remained in place. "I don't want to sit," I retorted, crossing my arms over my chest. "So how about you tell me what the hell is going on."

"I thought you would be happy you're out of the closet," he said, gesturing to the massive bedroom. "And not in the hand-cuffs anymore. I saved you."

"Well, if I'm free, why am I here still locked up? Let me go home."

He sighed. "I can't do that."

"Why?"

"Because being with me is the only thing keeping you and your friend alive."

That iced my blood, and his attentive stare let me know he was completely serious. I waited for him to elaborate.

"Tye has done a lot to prove his love for me—"

"Is that what you call it? Killing my father and kidnapping me, my friend, and my son?"

Leo held up a steady hand. "Let me finish. It's his love for me that is keeping you alive. He wants you dead and gone, but he knows I love you and he knows it would hurt me if he did that. So he won't touch you anymore as long as I say so." He paused as if he were expecting some kind of ass-backwards gratitude for him loving me. As if his love for me wasn't what got me here in the first place.

"And Adria?"

"She's still in the storage closet back at the property."

"Let her go," I demanded, balling my fists. I would probably die trying to fight this dude. Leo had never been small, and I remembered how he used to slap me around before to let me know he wasn't about to let me get any kind of advantage. But still, I would sure as hell get some good licks in.

I took a step closer, and Leo didn't budge, instead keeping his hands up in mock surrender. "I will let her go," he said. "If, and only if, you agree to something."

My heart quickened. I didn't like this ultimatum. "What?"

"Marry me," he said casually. "For real this time."

"You're crazy as hell," I snapped, turning to the window. Shit, I would rather take my chances with the window and shimmying down the fire escape.

"My wife, my legal wife," he quickly corrected, "is dead. It would be official. The wedding you've always wanted."

"No, it wouldn't, because you're not the man I want."

My words hurt. It was all over his face, but I honestly didn't care. After everything that had happened, how could he believe I would actually want to be with him?

"I love you," Leo said. "And with time, you'll learn to love me like you used to."

I didn't dare say I never loved him. Now was not the time for that.

"You know I can spoil you like the queen you are," he said, coming up behind me. "Like you deserve." He placed his hands on my shoulders, and I tightened under his touch. Dare I say I wasn't the same woman, no, girl, I used to be? That money didn't matter anymore? I just wanted to be loved by the one I loved and do all that other happily ever after shit. Was that too much to ask?

"Why?" I said, sniffing back tears. I couldn't break down. I just couldn't. "Why do you want me? You said yourself Tyree has proven he loves you. And you love him. Can't you two just go be together?"

Leo's hands slipped from my shoulders. "I love you both," he said. "I need you both in my life. And you have my son. How could I live without him?" He took a breath and continued. "Besides, my dad would never allow it. If he ever found out that I was—I am . . ."

"Gay?" I spat. "Down low? In love with a man?"

Leo pursed his lips against my snide remarks. "He would completely disown me. I've lived in the luxury of my father's money all my life. What will I do on my own?"

"Get a job like the rest of us," I said, throwing up my hands in emphasis. "Be grown. Do like us normal adults do, Leo. At least you'll be happy."

"There is more," Leo said. "My dad is in with some very, very dangerous people. Like Ivory Coast cartel. I have been protected for so long just because of my family name. No one would harm an Owusu. But if he disowns me, I won't be protected anymore." He paused again, letting his words sink in. "So you see. It's not just my money at stake. It's also my life."

I felt like Alice, sinking deeper and deeper into this Wonderland that was more like a horror show. "So,"—I took a shaky breath—"what are you saying?"

"I'm saying marry me. Let me love you like you deserve. It will make me happy. And it will make my father happy. He always did like you over my other wives."

"And Jamaal?"

Leo smiled. "He's my son. I want him with me. With us."

"But people will be searching for me, Leo," I whined. Certainly he hadn't thought of everything. Would it really be this easy to just kidnap me?

"Already got all that taken care of," Leo assured me. "Different identities, different location for all of us. No one will ever know."

That was what I was afraid of. "And Adria?"

"I will send the police to where she is as soon as we board the plane. Otherwise . . ." He trailed off, and I nodded my understanding. Otherwise she'll stay trapped in that closet for God knows how long. Had they moved my truck? Maybe I could call in a tip to the police so they could track her down. Then how the hell would I get my son back?

"I want to see Jamaal," I demanded. "Now."

"He is already where we are headed," Leo said. "I promise you he is safe. And you'll see him soon enough. Just come with me to our forever."

"And Tyree?" I said. "Am I just to expect he's okay with all of this and just disappear?"

Leo shook his head. "No, he'll still be around. He loves me.

And I do love him at the end of the day. So it'll be the best of both worlds."

I turned up my nose in disgust. "So you'll have your cake and eat it too?"

Leo smirked. "What can I say? I'm used to getting everything I want." He lifted his hand to my face, and I slapped it away. Just the mere thought of his skin touching mine repulsed me.

"Just think about it," Leo said, heading to the door. "Take a bath, clean up, and think on everything I've said. Remember I'm keeping you, your friend, and your son alive. For the moment."

He closed the door on his words, and I buried my face in my hands. Because dammit if he wasn't right.

Leo's words swirled and swirled around in my head as I ran myself a bath. I filled the Jacuzzi tub to the brim and submerged my naked body until I was neck deep. The scalding water stung my sore flesh, and I wondered what would happen if I just slid down until the water was over my head. The thought was welcoming, the water filling my lungs until I drowned and my dead body floated back to the surface. Then where would Leo be? Hurt? Good. Pissed. Great. Depressed. I sure as hell hoped so. But then where would Adria be? And my son? Hell, I didn't even know how much time had passed since we had been trapped in the closet, and then again, how long had I been here? Adria needed medical attention. I just couldn't let him leave her there.

And not to mention my son flown away to some undisclosed location. Was he being mistreated? Leo insisted he was safe, but that lying bastard had assured me of a lot of things. His little vows were as useful as shit on the sidewalk. But still, I knew what I had to do.

I washed myself as best I could, but my joints ached and my bones were on fire. So when I felt like I was about to pass out from the pain, I rose from the water, now stained a deep red from my blood, and stepped from the tub.

I patted myself dry and crossed to the closet. A single ivory sundress was the only article of clothing hanging inside. How ironic. But I didn't want to put back on the dirty clothes I had just peeled off, so I yanked the dress from the hanger and put it on.

I looked at myself in the vanity mirror. I had lost weight, considering the size six hung big in certain areas. My face, though clean, was hollow, my cheekbones now prominent. The huge knot that had decorated my temple was still evident. I used my trembling fingers to brush my little bangs to the other side in a weak attempt to hide it. Well, most of it. I sighed and walked back to the bedroom door. Looked like I had another wedding to plan.

Leo opened the door before I had even knocked, as if he were waiting for me. His eyes scanned my figure in the ivory dress, and his lips turned up into a wide smile.

I didn't smile back. Inside I was crying. Inside I was dead, just like Lena. Just like Tina. I wanted to throw up every ounce of my insides right then and there. But instead, I took a breath, opened my mouth and said, "I'm ready."

It was a sacrifice, I knew. Even as I followed Leo down the winding staircase, my feet shuffling as if propelled forward by forces beyond my control, I knew I was giving up everything. I was out of options. And I wouldn't be able to live with myself if anyone else suffered for my foolish mistakes. I would just have to deal with my choices. And live with the consequences. For now.

THE VOWS WE BREAK

Briana Cole

ABOUT THIS GUIDE

The suggested questions are included to enhance your
group's reading of Briana Cole's *The Vows We Break*.

DISCUSSION QUESTIONS

1. What did you like best about this book? What did you like least?

2. Share your favorite pivotal moment in this book. Why did this scene stand out?

3. How did the title *The Vows We Break* relate to the book's content?

4. What underlying themes did you detect in the story? What were the main points you think the author was trying to make?

5. What were the dynamics of power between the characters? How did that play a factor in their interactions?

6. How did the characters change throughout the story? How did your opinion of them change?

7. How did you experience the book? Were you immediately drawn in, or did it take time?

8. In what ways were you able to identify with the characters?

9. Does the book remind you of any other novels you've read?

10. Were you satisfied or disappointed with how the story ended? Why or why not?

Meet Kimmy for the first time in *The Wives We Play*

Available wherever books are sold.

Chapter 1

Something told me tonight was going to be special.

I could hardly contain my excitement as I followed the host through the maze of linen-draped tables, each topped with a single candle and surrounded by overdressed patrons. The ambiance was certainly set for romance and luxury, and I blended right in with my Tom Ford copper-toned sequined dress, which hugged each and every petite curve of mine. A gift from my man, of course. Lord knows I couldn't afford a $6,000 dress like this if I had to make the money myself.

Another thing I couldn't help but notice was my brown face was one of only a few in the entire restaurant. A crowd of crystal blue eyes against porcelain-white skin turned curious gazes in my direction, no doubt wondering who the hell I had to screw to even be allowed in the building. I had become used to the questioning looks when alongside Leo. He was a man of power and great wealth, and me, well, I was just the arm candy. The trophy. And that was just fine with me. Especially considering my boyfriend already had a wife. Just let me look good and spend his money, and I was content with keeping my face made up, my body in the gym, and my legs spread in exchange.

The host showed me through a sheer curtain to a round booth.

It was dimly lit and entirely too large for a party of two, but I knew Leo didn't mind paying extra for privacy and comfort.

"My love." He rose to greet me and, as customary, I held out my hand. Leo turned it over and planted a gentle kiss on my palm. I loved when he did that. His eyes swiped over my body with an approving nod. "You look like a masterpiece."

I grinned at his words. The man could charm me clean out of my panties. "I know," I gushed, placing my hands on my hips. The gesture had the already mid-thigh hemline rising just a bit. "And, my oh my, don't you look completely edible." The cream linen suit seemed to radiate against the stark contrast of his black skin. His locs were fresh, and he had taken care to have them braided to the back. It had been a minute since I'd seen them down, so I didn't realize they reached past the middle of his back. Leo usually kept his locs piled high in a man bun on top of his head and out of his way. He smiled, his dimples creasing his cheeks and barely noticeable underneath the fine hairs of his well-trimmed goatee.

"So," I prompted as soon as I slid into the plump leather cushion of the booth. "You certainly went all out this evening."

"It's a special occasion."

My nose wrinkled in a curious frown. We usually didn't do the anniversary shit. That was for serious couples. Not us.

Before I could open my mouth and ask what he was referring to, our waiter appeared at the side of our table, a linen cloth slung over his arm, a bottle of wine in his hand. He greeted us and began to pour the rich red liquid into our glasses. No need to ask what kind of wine it was. Knowing Leo, it was delicious and expensive and that was all that mattered to me.

I hadn't even bothered to look at the menu. Leo ordered the same thing for both of us, some fancy dish I couldn't pronounce. We handed over our menus, and I waited until we were alone again before I spoke up.

"Special occasion?" I reiterated. "For us?"

"Just period." Leo reached across the table and grabbed my hand in his. He used his thumb to caress my knuckles. The excitement was all but twinkling in his chocolate irises and I felt my own anxiousness beginning to bubble up right along with this silky wine. My mind began to hum with possible scenarios of where this was going. But for some reason, my thoughts kept settling on him handing over the keys to either a house or a car. Hell, maybe both.

"How long have we been together, my love?"

"Few months."

"How many? Do you know?"

I didn't. I hoped that the question was rhetorical, but he waited patiently while I fumbled through the previous months and events we had shared. "Like around three or four, right?" I guessed.

"Eight," he corrected with a gentle smile. "Eight months, two weeks, and five days, to be exact."

I strained against the smile on my face, hopefully masking my apathy. What was he getting at? Was that too soon for him to buy me a house?

"It has been probably the best eight months of my life," Leo went on, almost to himself. "I hope you know just how special you are to me."

My smile widened. "Of course I know, sweetie."

"Well then, you should know me well enough to know I don't make rash decisions. I'm very strategic, calculated, and usually once I set my mind to something, I just go for it. No questions. No hesitations."

I nodded as my heart quickened. If it was a car, I hoped he had gotten it in red. Something sporty and flashy. I liked flashy. And I hoped he'd paid the insurance up. He knew damn well I couldn't afford insurance on any vehicle after a 1995.

Leo blew me a kiss before rising to his feet. He still held my hand in his and pulled me up out of the booth with him. His eyes slid past mine and nodded in greeting to someone behind me. Confused, I turned and eyed the woman who approached.

We had the same taste, apparently. She too wore Tom Ford, but her dress was black, ankle-length with a sheer side panel that revealed just the right amount of skin to be classy. A high weave ponytail cascaded down to touch the small of her back. She was taller than I am, a little more curvaceous, and had chocolate skin as rich and as smooth as a piece of black clay pottery like you could find on a vendor table at some art festival.

She held out her hand in my direction. "Kimera," she greeted with a huge smile. "I'm Tina Owusu."

Owusu? I glanced to Leo and back to Tina, my head reeling with the strange yet familiar visitor. I ignored her outstretched hand, instead turning my back on the woman to narrow my eyes at Leo.

"This is your *wife?*" I snapped, jutting the manicured nail of my thumb in her direction. "Did you really invite your wife to dinner?"

"My love, let me explain."

"Explain what?" I pulled on my hand to release it from his grasp, but he tightened his grip.

"It's not what you think."

"It's not? Well, what the hell is going on, Leo? Care to explain this shit to me? Because I'm not understanding."

Leo, still clutching my hand, dropped to one knee. And my heart dropped just as fast. I didn't even see him reach for the velvet box. Before I knew it, it was in his hand, the marquise-cut diamond glistening from the white cushion. I couldn't do anything but stand there speechless. Not because he was proposing. Hell, I had been proposed to a number of times, and usually I knew it was coming. But, no, I was shocked as hell because Leo's wife was still standing right there, waiting for my answer just as patiently as the man kneeling in front of me.

I took a step backward, bumping my hip against the nearby restaurant table. Somewhere, the jazz music had died down, and I felt as if all eyes were focused on me and Leo, still on one knee in his crisp linen slacks. I wanted to slap him. Slap him for putting me in this awkward situation. For making a mockery out of this whole thing.

Sure, I knew he had a wife. Well, let me correct that. I knew *now* he had a wife. When Leo first strolled up to my line at the bank where I worked, I didn't know he was married. I just saw a sexy-ass man with a complexion that looked like something fresh off an African culture oil canvas. His smile was slow and deliberate underneath the mustache as he made no move to hide his eyes wandering up and down my body. I felt the blush warm my cheeks and, smirking, I averted my eyes and busied myself with the Post-it notes on my counter.

"You shouldn't do that," he said, his accent seeming to caress each syllable.

"Do what?"

"Look away," he said. "Most pretty ladies like it when they see a man appreciating."

"Well, most men don't make it so obvious that they are appreciating," I said with a flirtatious grin.

"Well, I'm not most men." He held out his hand across the counter. "I'm Leo."

I paused before placing my hand in his. He took his time lifting it to his face. To my surprise, he turned it over and placed his lips gingerly against the tender flesh of my palm.

That had been all it took. The sexy Leo Owusu had plenty of charm and family money, and he hadn't been shy about lavishing both on me. I wouldn't say I was the kind of girl that would go weak at the knees over material shit. Well, let me stop lying. Yes, I was. The pot was damn lovely.

So when Leo finally revealed the truth, that he indeed had a wife, I had to say I really wasn't shocked. To tell you the truth, I knew my attitude was more of nonchalance. It didn't concern me. What he did in the confines of his own vows wasn't my business. He claimed they had an open marriage and that she knew about me. I'm not going to lie; that did seem awkward, but I quickly swallowed that pill too. The way I saw it, at least we didn't have to sneak around and shit. And after he assured me and reassured me I wouldn't have to worry about no bitch trying to catch me outside with fists and Vaseline, I was actually relieved.

"Kimmy." Leo pulled me back to the present and I again looked from him to the ring box he held in his outstretched hand. His wife, Tina, watched me closely, and it made me nervous as hell when she remained quiet and expressionless. She had drawn back the privacy curtain and now the entire ordeal was on public display like a Lifetime movie. I could feel a multitude of eyes from the restaurant patrons zeroed in on our little "romantic" scene. Anxious smiles and even a few phones were pointed in our direction to capture this moment. And here I was, frozen in embarrassment with a collection of curse words already gathered on my tongue. *What the hell did he think he was doing?*

"I want you to be in my life forever," Leo poured on the charm at my continued silence. "Marry me, Kimmy."

I knew my next move was about to be on some classic Cinderella shit, but I no longer cared about the audience. Or the appearance. Unable to do anything else, I turned on my heel and half ran toward the exit. I was slowed down by having to dart and weave through the maze of occupied tables and nearly stumbling in my six-inch stilettos. Anger propelled me forward, and I pushed through the glass door and inhaled the crisp night air.

The vibrant roar of downtown Atlanta traffic greeted me, and I welcomed the noisy relief. After the stunned silence, I needed the chaos to drown the confusion. What the hell was Leo thinking? First, he invites me and his wife to dinner tonight, only to propose with her standing right there? Looking on like this was completely normal. Who the hell proposes to the side chick?

"Kimmy."

Shocked, I turned back toward the building. I surely hadn't expected Tina to come after me. But there she was, seemingly gliding in my direction like she was in New York Fashion Week. I had noticed before that she was just average looking. The kind of Plain Jane face that didn't really give definition toward the pretty side or the ugly side but teeter-tottered somewhere in the middle, despite the makeup. Yet the diamonds that glittered from her fingers, ears, and neck had her moving with cocky arrogance like she was above any and everybody. I didn't like the bitch.

"Kimmy," she called again as if I weren't looking right at her.

I rolled my eyes. "Kimera," I corrected with a frown. "You don't know me like that."

She smirked, and her warm chocolate complexion appeared to glow with the attitude. "You have been sleeping with my husband for about eight months now. Trust me. I do know you like that." She took a step in my direction, apparently trying to see if I was going to storm off, but curiosity had me planted on the pavement. She closed the distance between us, and I could smell her Flower Bomb perfume permeating in the air. Well, to be honest, I couldn't tell if it was hers or mine, because Leo had bought me the exact same fragrance. *What were these people into?*

"What do you want?" I asked when she made no move to speak.

"I just want you to come back inside," she said. "Accept the proposal. Leo is serious."

"Did he send you out here to come get me? Seriously? His wife to come beg another woman to marry her husband? What kind of shit is that?"

Tina blew out a frustrated breath. "He was afraid that I may have been the reason you declined his offer."

"You think?"

"That's why I wanted you to hear it from me. You both have my blessing. I don't want to stand in your way."

I was so confused. I felt the beginnings of a headache throbbing at my temples. Shit was baffling me.

"So wait. Are you two divorcing or something? And why the hell are you so cool with this?"

"Divorcing? Who? Me and Leo?" Tina let out a snarky chuckle. "Girl, no. 'Til death do us part. I will always be Mrs. Owusu. But I am willing to share with you."

"Share? Your husband? Haven't you been doing that for the past few months?"

Now Tina's smile was genuinely humorous. "Touché. But now I'm offering you a chance to make it official. Because at the end of the day, what do you have to show for it? Some jewelry and some furniture in that raggedy-ass room in your parents' house?"

A fresh swell of anger had me tightening my fist; the urge to punch this smartass bitch in the jaw was overwhelming. Tina clearly sensed my intentions and held up her hands in mock surrender. "No offense," she said, though her tone was clearly one of an offensive nature. "I just mean that being the woman on the side only gets you so many benefits. You want to be the temp all your life, or you trying to actually get hired permanently?"

I was fed up. The bullshit she was spewing was absurd, not to mention unbelievable. How did they really expect to pull this off? And why? Where was Leo, and why had he sent his wife to handle this ridiculous sales pitch?

"Y'all idiots are crazy and deserve each other," I mumbled.

"Leave me the fuck alone." I was already turning and marching up the sidewalk.

"No, you're the idiot if you don't take him up on this offer," she called to my back. "I suggest you think about it and we'll be in touch with the details."

I kept walking. Since when did logic make me an idiot? And what the hell was there to think about? The certainty in her voice had me quickening my steps, even as her words continued to reverberate.

Connect with  **U**s

Visit us online at
KensingtonBooks.com
to read more from your favorite authors, see books
by series, view reading group guides, and more.

Join us on social media

for sneak peeks, chances to win books and prize packs,
and to share your thoughts with other readers.

facebook.com/kensingtonpublishing
twitter.com/kensingtonbooks

Tell us what you think!

To share your thoughts, submit a review,
or sign up for our eNewsletters, please visit:
KensingtonBooks.com/TellUs.